THE THIRD INFINITIVE

THE THIRD INFINITIVE

LAKSHMI GILL

TSAR
Toronto
1993

The publishers acknowledge generous assistance
from the Ontario Arts Council and the Canada Council.

Copyright © 1993 Lakshmi Gill

Except for purposes of review, no part of this book may be reproduced
in any form without prior permission of the publisher.

TSAR Publications
P.O. Box 6996, Station A
Toronto, Ontario
M5W 1X7 Canada

cover art: Laurie MacLean
cover design: Holly Fisher

Canadian Cataloguing in Publication Data

Gill, Lakshmi.
    The third infinitive

ISBN 0-920661-33-5

I. Title.

PS8563.I55T55 1993   C813'.54   C93-094972-2
PR9199.3.G55T55 1993

Printed and bound in Canada

To my sister Evelyn
and her daughter, Myra

Acknowlegement: Evelyn Gill Sulit, editorials in Chapter Sixteen from *The Knoll*, 1959, Maryknoll College, Quezon City, Philippines.

PART ONE

THE FIRST ORDER

Cavalry to take ground to left of second line of Redoubts occupied by Turks.

Chapter One

Red, white and blue
Stars over you
Mama said, Papa said,
I love you.
— a 1940s skipping rope verse

There on the bare cement floor, strong arms glistening in the water surrounding her, squatted the laundry woman, the full weight of her imperious self on her muscled legs, brown cigarillo stub in her mouth, as starchy as her bluing agents, raising a flat, polished bat to my sisters' sanitary napkins.

"Tina," I yelled, even though she was just a foot away, "where's Maria?"

She didn't deign to turn her head around, not for the youngest of her masters whom she could scare off with the most lurid of horror tales, and simply grunted what I construed to be "Go away." Not until I had yelled her name again, giving my voice a tone of "Now, look here, old woman," did she give a sign of acquiescence, this by the manner in which she let the ashes drop off onto the flowing water, discreetly away from the stained cotton squares, allowing me to assert my place.

"Well," I demanded.

"Gone."

"Gone where?"

"Don't ask these things." Her arm bolted down on my sisters' womanhood, shattering blood-debris all over, blasting everything clean.

I took my moment and moved out of the room as dignified as she would let me. Anyhow, I got an answer and the mystery of it was intriguing. She was a born storyteller.

So I ran around and up and down the servants' quarters, looking for Maria as though she were a gaily coloured Easter egg, a prize at the end of the hunt, except she hadn't been hidden by a generous mother who wanted me to find her.

"No, no," the cook said, as she turned her wild, malevolent eye from the machete in her gruff hand to the boiling cauldron on the stove. One entered the inner kitchens as into an inner sanctum and at one's peril, and as I was not stouthearted, I stepped backwards quickly.

"Don't know," from Mona, the girl who scrubbed the hardwood, a blank look on her round face, her eyes thoughtfully following the movement of the sole and toes of her right foot, like a claw over the brown coconut husk, back and forth, back and forth. Dustlight bathed her, giving her a disney glow, through the venetian-blind slats.

If all else failed, ask the chauffeur, the wizard who whisked us to enchanting places, waited in the car for hours and hours where he thought in grand philosophical isolation, or sometimes sat with other drivers in the kitchen where they exchanged all the gossip not worth spreading, choice tidbits that came from other houses, other besotted families rife with scandal. He would look at us all and *know* everything but he never told us anything. We just knew he was the Keeper of Knowledge best left unsaid, the All-Knowing Dread. He was no Judas betraying family honour to the enemy houses or to friendly houses which could turn enemy. You'd think, knowing so much, he would never smile, that he'd be taciturn, loins seething with hostility. Instead, he was benevolent. He treated our family well. Maybe we were less scandalous than the others; maybe he liked us. One never knew with the servants. They never complained.

So Bienvenido knew where Maria was but he wouldn't tell.

That was that, of course, so I gave up. I turned to my James Dean scrapbook, cut movie ads from the *Manila Times* and designed them onto the cheap brown page, thinking, wow, if only he hadn't died this year, I might have gone to the States and seen him walking down the street or coming out of Macy's or whizzing by in the fatal sportscar, wow, the stuff I missed in life. I was going to have to make a Dean Stockwell scrapbook soon, chosen because he shared a name and he wasn't bad-looking, and at least he was alive. James Dean had nothing more to add. Finito.

At lunchtime, twelve o'clock on the piano top, I made further inquiries about Maria's sudden disappearance, but Mama's scowl silenced me. This turn of events fascinated me more and more, as I thought of all kinds of possibilities while I pushed the shrimps underneath the mound of rice. When I looked up, everyone was done and Mama was lamenting once again, "You eat like a sparrow." She had to sit there and wait for me to finish, making sure I ate up every hidden shrimp, keeping me company since we couldn't eat alone. Finally, because I'd dawdled beyond her endurance, she got up and made Emiliana, fanning me from behind with a giant straw fan, sit and tell me stories.

Fortunately, Emiliana couldn't keep a thought in her head, so eventually,

as I dragged out shrimp after shrimp, she hinted about Maria.
Why couldn't she come to my room this morning to play with me?
She left in the middle of the night.
Why would she do that? Servants never left home at night. And she, being the cook's helper, only went to the market every day, at about eight a.m., when the sun wasn't so hot and there was a lull in the kitchen.
What strange call did she get that she had to leave the comfort of her bed?
She was sent away.
My eyes widened. Sent away? On a mission?
Mission schmission. Your mom booted her out.
Emiliana! I said, shocked. No one had ever been let go. As long as I remembered, all these people had been around. No one, not even in other families. Children's children stayed on for six or seven generations.
It's true. You ask your mom.
Little that would do. I had to milk this one if I were to know more.
Where to, I asked, coolly deflecting the interruption of emotion.
The man's house, maybe. I don't know. Bienvenido drove her.
Man? What man? A man was involved?
My eldest sister passed by. "What nonsense are you two talking about," she threw behind her receding back, "get off that dinner table, the maids have to eat." Her lion's black mane bounced about her stern imperial face, her black gaze fierce and uncompromising.

Emiliana leapt up and started collecting the remaining dishes; she had remembered that she was hungry and she wouldn't wait for me anymore. I gave up the last brave shrimp thankfully and followed her to the back kitchen where the cook, brandishing a huge gutted pig's thigh bone, growled at me, so I had to leave. They required their privacy.

Where men were involved, there was trouble, I sensed. I knew this because my sisters and their friends were constantly discussing relationships with men when they were sitting in the lanai, legs up on the white metal basket chairs, pitcher full of cold kalamansi juice, intense faces, punctuated sentences, staccato silences, run-ons and fragments, altogether very confused, as though they were solving a riddle. The language, which was oongga booongga, would become boongga booongga, word doubled for emphasis, for superlatives, crafted before primitive man discovered suffixes and declension. After two hours or so of these distressed signals, they gave up, danced and forgot about men for another couple of hours until the creep phoned and then they were back at it again. It made the head spin.

Conversely, where women were involved, there was trouble of a different sort. Women were mistresses and the wives didn't like it, but they all knelt together anyway, on Sundays, at the Communion rail, receiving Christ, people whispering *so and so is here, too, does she know? Oh well, why not, she lives just down the street from her, what's the difference.* It was welcomed trouble, accepted trouble, and it got nasty only occasionally, if one or the other felt like making a scene. Usually the drivers saved the day, making sure the offended party could leave first before the offensive one came out of church.

At any rate, my sisters and their friends were single, so women who were involved didn't matter to them. Yet again, some of their friends were getting to that age when they craved married men but, on the whole, they preferred their own age group, single and careless, like Gatsby characters.

Was this man married or single? What of it, he was trouble. He took Maria away from the shelter of our house in the stealth of the night.

Did any of my sisters know about this?

"Yeah, sure," the middle sister said. "She got pregnant and Mama sent her away."

Now how was it that she knew and I couldn't be told? Pregnant, wow, I thought to myself. My sister had dismissed me so I had to go to my room to think alone, lucky to get two sentences from her. So why was she not allowed to stay and have her baby with us?

I ran to my sister and asked.

She made a "tsk" and dropped words off the corner of her mouth: " 'cuz she wasn't married to him." I had to run back to my room and think some more because obviously my sister, who had been singing a cappella for an hour now, wanted to be left alone to her Joni Jones imitation, voice curled around the edges of the line, eyes turned lambent. *How important can it be?* Joni/Sis Two asked, the *it* being that *she had tasted other lips while hers was a young and foolish heart, seeking love at every turn,* a concept quite remote to Sis Two who hadn't known *the magic of a kiss.* Joni said, in her matter-of-fact voice, as though she were unfolding from an existentialist premise, *let the past just fade away, why get lost in yesterday, the important thing is here and now, and our love is here to stay,* the one eternal present truth based on multiple temporary past lies, hey! *even foolish hearts can learn.*

Not married to him. Why didn't he marry her first, then? Was she a mistress? Fourteen and a mistress, that must have been the all-time low.

I ran back to my sister, who threw down her songbook, a twenty-five centavo pamphlet one bought from the corner store made of cheap brown paper full of misprints and misheard lyrics written by some hack listening to a radio station for days, trying to earn a living off popular songs and people like sis who were too lazy to get the words off the records themselves. She was annoyed now, I betcha, she would be yelling any minute now and Mama would send Emiliana over to check out the trouble, or worse, she would come herself and scold me, "Why don't you leave your sister alone?"

"Was she a mistress?" I asked, risking the wrath of the gods.

"Whose mistress? Papa doesn't have any mistresses."

"Then what was she?"

"She was bad. So Mama couldn't let her stay or she'd have infected us all. Now go away." She turned back to her crooning, lost a bit of the curl, her muse interrupted. She would be in a sullen mood now for the rest of the day. Served her right for not singing like Sarah Vaughan. Sometimes she'd sing "Mean to Me" and "Little Girl Blue" but she'd remain soprano—she never hit that range to baritone. No vibrato, faulty glissando.

Having destroyed my sister, I went back to my room and thought some more. She was bad; being pregnant, not as a mistress but as a single fourteen year old servant, was bad. And if the man didn't want to marry her, it couldn't be covered up, like Joseph with Mary. So how was Mama to explain this to her friends? And who was the man? One of our servants? One of her friends' servants? Who would know? Bienvenido. I had something to use for leverage now—I knew a little bit. He'd think I was worthy to be so informed.

He wasn't to be found. This being Wednesday, Sis One must have gone to Baclaran for the hourly novena at the Redemptorist Church because she had a devotion to Our Lady of Perpetual Help. I sat on the Bermuda grass in the front lawn, the dew-drenched clumps prickly under my green toreadors. The house loomed behind me like a gigantic Baguio mountain face glimpsed from the front seat when one woke up suddenly as the car veered madly away from hitting it, the headlights illuminating for an instant its sombre expression. The house was a replica of a Tudor mansion, the dark brown crossbeams were like interlocking bars defending the frail occupants, reinforced by the twenty-foot stone fence which surrounded the property. After the house was burglarized, Papa added the iron grilles on the ground floor windows. The iron gates echoed them. I thought this was all an illusion because Letty's family was wiped out in the security of their grilled home by one servant, a Moro, who, one night, while everyone slept, went huramentado and chopped them all up. For months after we were told this news by the nuns, the gang and I felt guilty, because we had been mean to Letty just a few days before she died. We vowed we would be kind for the rest of our lives from that day on. Nevertheless, just in case, I slept with my hands and arms close to my body and my legs tucked up so that her ghost couldn't pull me off my bed.

For months, too, Mama kept assuring us that our servants came from her province so we were safe, though Letty's horrible way of going had made us rethink our way of life. After all, there were more of them than the five of us, and when the four went off to parties, I was left alone at home with all these provincial people who came in and out of our rooms as though they owned the place.

Just the other day, while I was playing with Mama's cosmetics and atomizers on her dressing table, lining up columns of armies ready for the battle, Rosa came in and out, ostensibly to change sheets, dust around, and all that. Mama claimed she'd never lost any jewellery but how would she remember every piece? I, of course, knew them all, because I knew which belonged to which army. And I especially knew the colonels and generals, the largest sapphires or the odd blue one directing the line of creeping barrage, pearl necklace skulking to Vimy Ridge.

Anyway, everytime I'd asked to accompany a sister, Mama would say I was too young. Buntut maya, Sis Two would add, a tag-along annoyance, last of the pack. Why do *I* have to bring her? she wailed in her Joni James high note. Coloratura, she was, every morning we would have to listen to her scales in the music room, un-soundproofed and self-indulgent. Musicians inflicted themselves on others.

So I was left alone, outnumbered and defenceless, like that white family in a film I shouldn't have been brought along to see, wiped out by Mau-Mau who swarmed in, in the cover of night, through their gracefully furnished home, rampaging and pillaging.

Maria was my only friend among the servants. She was brought from the province for me, two years older than me. She came just a few weeks after Papa had Beauty flown in from India, a purebred Alsatian, epitomized in her name, the most beautiful dog I had ever seen. That was also the month the packets of seeds came—marigold, zinnias, exotic names I'd never heard of—and Maria and I helped the gardener plant them all along the north wall dividing us from the convent. We'd climb up the atis tree, sit on a branch and watch the Carmelites at their vegetable garden, wide-hatted and heavily robed. I could never understand how they could endure the tropical heat wearing those heavy habits—was it the sackcloth mentality? From our angle, we could never see their faces. They had a Bugs Bunny style garden, well organized with rows and rows of carrots and stuff, neatly labelled on a stick, just like in the cartoons we'd see before the feature film in the movie theatre. I imagined little critters chomping at their neatly laid tops, pulling in the roots and scurrying off into their underground burrows. Of all the homes that have fascinated me the burrow would take the gold. I once read a book about a rabbit who, after a horrendous experience, learned this lesson: a good rabbit makes an exit hole. You've got to be able to get away, not through the entrance, but through a back door that the enemy doesn't realize you've got. It was published in New York.

Oftentimes, when we were out playing in the garden, I'd climbed walls and trees to see how quickly I could get away when the servants attacked us. It wasn't easy. The east wall was blocked by the servants' quarters above the garage, and the south wall which led to the street had broken bottles embedded on top. The west wall was unscalable. Grapevines on wooden structures were built close to it. I had no idea what was behind that wall, the only safe escape was over the north wall, onto the nuns' garden, ripping through their ordinary rows like Bugs Bunny being chased by Elmer Fudd, into their back door which they always left open, perhaps to let in air.

Would Maria have run with me? Well, obviously not. She proved to be useless, getting pregnant and all, no use to me or to herself, getting chucked out into the wild, having to fend for herself and baby. Who would take care of her now?

Poor girl.

At dinner time, seven o'clock on the piano top, I inquired why we couldn't have taken care of Maria when she needed to be cared for, and Mama, putting her tablespoon and fork down decidedly, lamented, "Not this again," so I had to keep my thoughts to myself.

The maids stood around watching us eat. The cook had graced us with her presence tonight. She got very resentful when we took only a corner off the bibingka, sipped at the pancit mami, put our noses up to dark bloody dinuguan, nibbled at the bland pale green soyote of the chicken tinola. She came out of her hallowed kitchen to tear the plate of reddish brown champorado off the dining table while muttering her contempt of our eating habits, so Mama had to pacify her by saying the children had had ensaymadas for merienda and you see, what could beat those lovely, round cheese-sprinkled buns for taste. Which didn't appease the betrayed cook since ensaymadas were bakery-bought. Mama, who was a terror unto herself, was brought to her knees only by the cook, who wielded the power of nutrition over our heads. Like a god, generous to overflowing, who slaved over the proverbial hot stove of creation for our existence, she expected our full cooperation for our own salvation. Like a god, in the evening, she whipped up the usual sumptuous, forgiving meals anyway, always hopeful we would come around and partake heartily, always betrayed in the end. I, of course, ate little on principle because I would not give in to her expectations.

The conversation drifted in and out of my mind, uninteresting bits of society-page chit-chat—Mama and sisters decked out again in imitation Balenciagas with the "400" in the fashion pages of the local papers—school news, world politics and local government, and at last, everyone was done and I was left with Papa who'd been designated to stay behind by some unseen code of rotation, until I finished. Our dialogue turned to moral issues very quickly, because I wanted this issue resolved. Maria was my friend.

Papa had no say, however; this was a woman's issue and Mama ran the household. He, himself, knew nothing about it until he was told that Maria was gone. However, it did seem to him that we were morally bound to keep her, since she had no other family in the city, or we should have sent her back to Samar. In disgrace? There was no disgrace for these people—this sort of thing happened to them all the time. On the whole, it was not an unusual phenomenon for them. It never happened to good convent girls. And that reminded me of Josie, who was expelled last year for posing in a bathing suit as a photographer's model—so she was cast out to do the potentially bad things she'd shown she was capable of doing. The nuns were right, of course, because we heard that she was now in a public school.

At any rate, Papa didn't know where Maria had gone to. One could ask Bienvenido and see if it was still possible to help her. But once sent out, the city swallowed one. Beyond these walls was chaos—so much getting and spending, a Wordsworthian congested world. Who would go out there to find her? Not even the servants liked to go out into the city. They had their own clubs, their own groups of friends they visited. Bienvenido whisked them around, too, into the safety of other homes. No one walked on the streets longer than to go into a shop, theatre, or restaurant.

It was too late for Maria. Nothing could realistically be done for her. I suppose, I muttered, she should have been more careful in the first place, but then, what could you expect of them? They wouldn't be servants if they were brighter. Victims fell into traps of their own making. Papa answered, perhaps it was her destiny. Sometimes we have no say in our fortune—all written in the stars. That was Maria's luck.

And that was that.

He let me leave my plate semi-full because he wanted to lie on the couch now, so we adjourned to the living room where we continued our discussion on Fate. Then he launched into his favourite theme, an extension perhaps of Maria's fall: the British Royalty. Brigands, all of them, built their fortunes by treachery and murder. He remembered Brighton Pavilion, how he had walked in and out of the opulent Oriental rooms sacked from some obscure Indian village I couldn't pronounce or stolen from some obscene-sounding Chinese town, and his voice rose because he had such healthy lungs. In the past, these kings and queens were cut-throats and adulterers, all their so-called subjects knew about their immoral lives. The British Crown was an invention of the government, right around the time of mad George to whom the politicians gave the title "His Sacred Majesty." Then every Tom, Dick and Harry down the power line got titles like "The Most Noble, The Governor-General," little despots in the colonies. And I reminded him that only William William Henry Stephen/Maud and Henry were brigands, but that Richard John Henry Edward Edward Edward Richard Henry Henry Henry Edward Richard Edward Henry Henry Edward Mary Elizabeth James Charles Charles James William and Mary Anne George George George George William Victoria Edward George Edward George Elizabeth were not.

Papa looked at me in disbelief as in, what had he spawned? And of these, I concluded, only four believed in the divine right to rule, three of whom were half-hearted. If the second James hadn't been so adamant, he wouldn't have been toppled. That was the seventeenth century, he said; by the nineteenth, people could no longer openly deride their royals. The British Crown had become a symbol of imperialism, expansion, destruction of cultures like the Tooth of Buddha in Ceylon in 1818. Papa really should have been a history professor; he missed his calling. I had sat through many after-dinner nights like this whenever he was home. I should have grown up hating the British government. Instead, I wished he would teach me his language rather than expend his energies in a past, in past experiences I didn't know. The destruction of Kandy, he continued, was like the destruction by the Spanish of the Incas, of indigenous Philippines. The British were here, too, you know, he sensed I needed to connect with my environment. Really? I said, when? 1762- 1764, just about the time of the conquest of Quebec, about the time of the Seven Years War. Since the Spanish were weakened by pockets of rebellion, the British invaded. Financed by the East India Company. Good for the Madras-Manila trade. Then the British Crown ordered General William Draper to let the civil government rule, but directed from London. He was back to the Crown. The Myth of the Crown: he said it like The Legend of King Arthur. All politics, this Imperial Patria. The English believed in either plundering or serving. But, he sighed, his voice waxing prophetic, all is impermanence. Things must be let go, would be let go, whether we would or not.

I couldn't believe him.

Papa was the overwhelming waft of an airplane's pressurized cabin contained in a luggage that hit your nostrils and sent a rush to your half-awake brain as you let the top fall onto the floor at 3 a.m., while rubbing the sleep off your eyes. And there at your knees, you discovered the bazaars of Hyderabad, still full-laden with gorgeous glowing silk, golden bangles, jewel-embroidered purses, silver-threaded shawls, ivory, and lo, tucked behind a sorcerer's bag of rubies the glint of sequined shoes, flat like two boats ending in pointed toes which turned upwards like a ship's figurehead, caught the eye, missed by your older sisters privileged to be awakened earlier than you, when they ransacked through these stalls, claiming the best by right of first seizure. And you gleefully tried to walk in them onto the next luggage and there was Papa again, amidst the aromatic treasures for Mama, their perfumes mingling with the airplane's interior, cool and heady, and you, in a state of half-sleep slowly awakening in a magical time bathed in the soft glow of turned-downed lamps, hushed voices of your parents and sisters around the dining table broken only by the clinking sounds of china and the shuffle of servants' slippers as they moved quietly in and out with pots of steaming delicacies, you woke to this exotica so often and always at 3 a.m. that you thought you would sail in your glorious babouche over Life's perils, unscathed, because Papa, the alchemist who turned dross into gold, would keep you rich forever.

Chapter Two

> Ti di di dum ti dum ti du
> I love you
> Ti di di dum ti dum ti di
> You love me
> I love you in the evening
> and I love you in the night
> I love you in the morning when the
> sun is shining bright
>
> —Tapdance song

In the following days the matter of Maria was expunged from our consciousness. No one spoke of her now; it was as though she had never existed. She'd been ejected from the ship like flotsam to pollute the ocean. And there was much flotsam out there, as disgusting as that time my aunt fell off the banca into the river filled with excrement and as she flailed about, shouting for help, my worst fear was not that she would drown but that she would swallow the yellow brown heap. I decided I would never swim again. Certainly not in the provinces, anyway, where people were so primitive, returning the fruits back to nature via a hole in a closet that shot into the river underneath the house where they bounced there for days before finally floating into the open sea.

Maria lingered in my mind longest but to talk about her was pointless. Life went on. Tina, the laundry woman, continued to harass me with her horror stories as she walked me home from Sunday Mass whenever I slept in and missed going with the family. Emiliana and I continued to fight over who got to read the *Hiwaga* comics first after I sent her to the gate to buy the latest issue as soon as we heard the hawker's yell. She'd dawdle coming back to me, skimming over the glossy pages even after I'd explicitly said that she wasn't allowed to do that because I wanted to know what happened first. By the glint in her eye, I'd know she had disobeyed me and I'd feel so angry I could've plucked her phosphorescent eye out like Mama did the fish eye, delicately and with grace, putting it gently into her mouth, saying it's the healthiest part of the fish, you should try it, as I watched her in disgust, ready to puke. I swore everyone around me lived to taunt me, to goad me into violence.

Instead, I pretended I didn't care if I didn't get to read this particular issue first (because there have been days when Emiliana didn't skim and scan). I had, after all, Papa's whole library at my disposal and she didn't, so I could generously allow her to peek and I said, ok, I would read it later. I was going to sit in the library for a while. This took the joy out of her but she, too, was defiant, and she shrugged then ran off with her trophy. Meanwhile, I had to go to the library to keep my word, and I sat there, staring at the rows and rows of books and the giant oil paintings of Gandhi, Nehru and Chandra Bose looking back at me and the leather chairs of imitation British Raj, and Mama's corner with the ivory and ebony chess set elegantly displayed where she would play for hours and hours with houseguests, and I'd end up playing with the knickknacks on Papa's desk, lining up the paper clips as the Germans in North Africa, the enemy staples lurking behind the paper dunes, all of them menaced by the steel seal that looked like Hannibal's elephant.

I sat in the library for a respectable time, just enough to seem to have read a hundred pages so Emiliana would be appeased, then I emerged looking thoughtful, heavily laden with the Meaning of Life. Emiliana looked at me, I thought with a little envy, then I dashed after I turned the corner, up to my room, where she'd laid the comics on my bed. There I spent the rest of the morning lost in the magic of the stories about poor people who aspired to be rich, about Narda, the squalid child who, when she yelled, "DARNA!" was transformed into Wonder Woman who did wondrous adventuresome things, fighting, among her many enemies, my favourite monster, the woman with the kerchief around her head who, at the moment of the battle, would fling it off, uncovering her hair of snakes, and all night I'd have nightmares of crawling snakes on my bed and Emiliana yelling "DARNA!" and I'd wake up suddenly and check to see if my hair had metamorphosed. Even though my hands touched my usual coarse black hair I never felt reassured. I'd pray the Rosary on my fingers, call on my guardian angel, promise not to fight with Emiliana ever again, and if none of these worked after an hour, I'd run to Mama's room, untuck her mosquito net and push her to give me space, then tuck the net back to make sure the monsters couldn't follow in. Mama, three-quarters asleep, would mumble and sleep on. I had so many nightmares that some evenings Mama would let me sleep in their bed automatically so she wouldn't have to be awakened in the middle of the night. Depending on the events of the day and the ferocity of Tina's stories, I could normally predict it would be a nightmare night, so she'd sigh and just move over.

Whenever Papa left for his business trips abroad, I got to sleep on his side of the bed. The monsters never visited me when I was with others—being alone is hell. Sis Two beat the monsters by making her maid sit behind the pillow, the mosquito net tucked around her legs dangling from the bed; her maid combed with her fingers through my sister's hair for tics which were never there, but the motion and the massage on her head made her feel sleepy, so the maid would do this for an hour or longer until my sister fell asleep, and then when she was snoring, her maid would carefully extricate herself from her uncomfortable position and go to bed herself. Sis One prayed on her knees beside her bed before going to sleep, like children do in the movies except she prayed for an hour or longer, going through the Rosary and a barrage of Novenas with their required set of rosaries, so that by the time she was done she was either plain tired out or fully armed against a mass of devils. Not having her religious stamina nor my other sister's authoritarian ways, I contented myself to protection under my mother's wing.

It was there that I often plotted my escape from any attack, by servants or monsters, since I would wake up early before the household arose and had to lie in bed waiting for movements downstairs. Through the convent back door, waking up the nuns (it was always night when they attacked), past their front door, and then I'd stop short—where to go after that? Outside was the vile city. I'd backtrack and stay with the nuns who were all married to God and therefore in His favour. And God, like Arjuna fierce in battle, would slay all my tormentors.

Sometimes I'd think of all our houseguests and choose from among them the best champions on their mighty steeds. There were two men who'd win out; one, the Indian general who stayed with us briefly and left his autographed photograph and sent me letters saying I was his favourite nine-year-old. My parents said he was brilliant and distinguished and helped oust the British from India. Second was an American colonel who stayed with us for months, maybe a year. He had a sawed-off haircut, blonde, very close to his head, his pink skin taut on his cheekbones and his eyes twinkled. Although he was generic American, a good ol' GI Joe, I, like an Auschwitz survivor would be able to identify him years later. Colonel Richards taught me how to cheat at cards, how to turn the card just so in the palm of my hand and pretend to feel with the other and guess at its suit and number while the eye very quickly saw everything through the corner of the palm, how to rig four piles so that the four kings would invariably come up when I turned over the top cards—all these magic tricks he taught me as he ate our food and drank our liquor. He played the piano with me while my sister sang, danced to Patti Page on our record player, played chess with Mama, all the time smiling profusely. He taught me "Don't Fence Me In" and other cowboy songs and for a long time my dreams consisted of open prairies and coyotes in wide-brimmed hats. He taught me American history like we wouldn't have learned in school—the expanse of it, the smell and tastes of it. I think I got my American accent from him and the attitude that everything was possible. By the time he left I learned to swagger, too, be expansive, smile a lot, and call people "honey." These didn't last long because when he disappeared one morning from the breakfast table, Papa announced in grave and bitter tones that Colonel Richards was a CIA man, planted in our home to investigate Papa's activities—this was in 1952— The whole family felt betrayed. We had liked him.

Once again, an enemy in our midst. He could have been a champion.

"But don't you remember how we met him?" Sis One said. "We were playing at the airport waiting for Papa's plane and he approached us."

"Yes, he was very friendly." Sis Two said.

"Then he introduced himself to Mama and said he had no food, that he was very poor and could he eat in our home once in a while."

"And Mama said, yes, of course. She always says yes to people who are hungry."

"I don't remember. It must have been years ago."

"Hmm," Sis One murmured. "He came to visit a few times, at dinnertime, and slowly he became a fixture—it must have taken almost a year to infiltrate us."

"Then one day he moved in. You know how parents are always letting in people to live with us."

"Yes," I said. "It's fun but scary. All I remember clearly is when he was already living with us. But what was he investigating?"

My sisters, who knew everything, exchanged glances. Was I old enough to know these things? I was always the last to know.

"He had a bad temper whenever Mama beat him at chess or ping-pong," I said to fill in the silence while Sis One considered my maturity. I had to show that I knew him best because he spent a lot of time entertaining me, the youngest patsy.

It didn't faze my sisters. It just meant I had more idle time at home. But Sis One relented. "Well, you know Papa was going to sell US war surplus to India."

"The radar, especially," from Sis Two.

"From the depot."

"Where's the depot?" I asked.

"That's irrelevant. It's somewhere down the pier. I don't know. That's not the point. It's some big US depot where they keep parts, trucks, and so on because they couldn't ship them back to the States after the war."

My sisters forgave me my stupidity and continued.

"The question to ask is, why was Papa selling radar to India?"

I didn't know.

"Because India is at war with Pakistan." My sisters looked at me waiting for my face to brighten. It didn't.

"Colonel Richards first pretended to be poor to get into our house, then once here he pretended to want to be Papa's business associate. He started going to the office to get to know the business."

"Do you remember those two army men from India, a lieutenant and a major who were sent to look at the stuff in the depot? Mama and Papa put them up in an expensive hotel and dined them for two months."

"Yes, and you two got to go to the nightclubs with parents."

"Hmmm, well, you're too young."

"I'm always too young."

"You were scraped off the barrel," Sis Two said, echoing my mother.

"They must have spent 25,000 pesos. Anyway, Richards used to go to the office and that's where he met these two representatives of the Indian government one day and found out about this big deal. He set up a meeting with the US Consulate-General in the American Embassy for Mama and Papa. He claimed that the Consul-General wanted in on this."

"Why bother to join up with them?" I asked. "We were doing ok on our own." I thought my sisters would be pleased with my insightful comment; instead, they smirked.

"Well for one thing, they were going to put some money in."

"For another," Sis One added, "Papa needed Embassy approval for shipping the radar out—it was, after all, their stuff."

"Ok, so everybody's in on the deal."

"When they got to the Embassy, the whole conversation was taped. Richards waited until everything was placed on board. As the ship left the Philippine waters, it was intercepted and everything was confiscated."

"We were wiped out."

"It was a letter of credit," Sis One turned on Two. I was overjoyed. "We weren't wiped out."

"We could have made millions," she saved herself. "Do you know how much money is made on arms deals?

Back to me. "Why was the shipment confiscated? What's so wrong with selling to India?"

"What's radar used for?" From Sis Two.

"War?" I asked timidly.

"Yes! India's at war with Pakistan."

Now they thought my face would brighten up. It didn't.

"I don't understand," I said meekly.

Sis Two despaired of me and turned to her songbook. Sis One, bred in the Catechetics, tried again.

"Do you know which country the US is in favour of?"

Ahhh! I smiled brightly. "But what's Papa's business to do with the CIA? Or more correctly, what does the CIA have to do with Papa's business?"

"The CIA is in everything."

"Richards deceived Papa," I said, astounded by the obvious. Pierced, at our heart.

"That's how it's done. From Inside."

"Trust no one,"Sis Two said, dramatically.

"Well, anyhow, Papa gave him a good send-off." As the words came out, my sister almost bit them off. She didn't want me to know about this event. I didn't press my luck—I had come out not too badly and so I left the room in search of Bienvenido who knew the juicy violent scenes.

"So," I began, "you drove Colonel Richards to a hotel?"

"Are you kidding?" Bienvenido snorted. "Your Papa confronted him in the library and they'd both been drinking and your Papa was going, you son-of-a-bitch, goddam you and he hit the colonel, down the colonel went to the floor, I had to drag him out and put him and his things on a taxi. Shit, he was a piece of shit. You know how strong your Papa is. He might have killed that bastard."

I left Bienvenido very quickly because his swearing and Papa's swearing embarrassed me and now I could see why my sister couldn't tell me this part of the story—it couldn't be told without using bad words. They bothered me so much I had to go to Confession to tell the priest I had this concupiscence of the ears, there was just so much sin around me. But secretly I was happy to know Papa was strong and could deck a man and that the servants knew because as long as Papa was around we were safe, for he was our true champion.

Later on, Mama said, she'd shared an elevator by accident with Richards and since she was a forgiving person, she greeted him with, "Hello, are you still around?" fully expecting him to have gone back to the States after his mission was accomplished, and he, surprised to be publicly recognized, garbled a mutter and quickly got off on the next floor. Of course, Mama thought, he had other missions, he was probably the man based in Manila from this year to that year, was likely promoted for doing the job so well. My sister said, I bet he hangs around the USIS gathering and dispensing information. *USIS?*

To keep up with my sisters, I had to read the newspapers every night, starting with the editorial page. Otherwise, I couldn't make all the connections they made so easily. USIS? Pakistan? Tashkent? Communists? Everything's connected, Sis One said.

"Your father's not a communist," Mama said. "Because he was the president of the Indian Independence League here before and during the war, the Americans threw him in jail."

"When they came to 'liberate' us," Sis Two hissed.

"To appease the British, their allies."

"Papa loves India so," Sis One said in great admiration. "He would die for her." She had a martyr complex.

That didn't make sense, I thought. A dead patriot is a dead man. What good was he to his country?

Anything but that dreaded word.

"The communists are Godless," Sr Rose said in a hushed tone, her grey eyes piercingly clear with the Truth. The whole class shivered collectively with one chill.

Nationalist yes, communist no, according to my sisters. But to the nuns, anyone who wasn't pro-American was a communist—it was an all-encompassing word that spread out its eagle wings to swoop down on any monkey it could devour.

The communists were also poor. Every so often we had to give to the poor in China. If we ate in excess, we felt guilty that we were taking from the mouths of the little Chinese babies. If we complained about the food in the great dining hall, we were reminded that Chinese children only ate noodles. Day after day and some days, not even that.

The Poor loomed large in my dreams: masses of them, covering the entire surrealist frame and beyond so I would sometimes just glimpse the profile or the beginning of a face, half-eaten into the undrawn corner, dark-haired, white-faced, one-stroked eye. No fate worse than theirs. We were obliged to pray for the poor communists, the communist poor. It had been a request from the Blessed Mother of God, as told to Sr Lucia in Fatima.

At night Mama would round us up and set us in front of the altar in her bedroom and we'd pray one rosary for the family. "The family that prays together, stays together." Because it was such a protracted rosary, with much meditation in between decades, and litanies at the end, we were to include the communist poor, our relations and friends, the Sisters, the priests, Papa's business, our school work, and I'd include Maria while I suspected my sisters included their latest boyfriends, and sometimes my mind would go blank in the middle of meditating and my bottom would fall on the comfort of my upturned soles and a vigilant sister would turn around to catch me off my knees and glower, so I'd have to re-focus and pull myself up again. One such night I was so rushed to get down on my knees because they threatened to start without me (there must have been a party they had to go to) that in my ardour one shoe went flying off my foot straight at the statue of Christ, knocked it down to the carpeted floor where it didn't break, thank God, and I felt doomed; I had desecrated a holy place, God Himself, and from that night forward, I knelt in front and stayed on my knees until sweat trailed down my spine and my thighs burned in pain.

That's what Grandfather Apolonio did—on his knees for hours and hours, Mama said—as she encouraged me with a shining example. The harder the penance, the stronger the soul. He would put his arms out on his sides sometimes, to punish himself even more. He did this every night, for hours, for many years, till his old age. What was my one hour compared to that?

Feeling even more despicable for being so weak, I'd leave Mama's bedroom to look for my cats and I'd sit with them to watch them play or stroke their fur hoping my old asthma would act up. When I was five my asthma was so bad I had to drop out of kindergarten. Mama used to sit up all night with me until I fell asleep at dawn. Our doctor advised us to move out of the congested city, to live in the suburbs where there were less people. Somehow cleaner air was equated with less people, like going up to the mountains—the higher up, zero people, zero air. Papa bought the house in Quezon city. In the 1940s, Quezon city was a jungle, selling for five centavos a square foot. Doña Magdalena said to Papa, I'll give you so much and so much hectares, you clear the land and in a few years you can make estates. Papa said, but that's just a jungle, who'd build out there? Now here he was, ten years later, having to buy a house on a whole development he could have owned for nothing. Still there weren't too many people yet and the air was clearer. The high wall kept people out. We could bathe naked in the rain until I was seven, then I had to put on a chemise and now I could only do it fully dressed. But it was still fun.

I think it was the time when the gang and I went about comparing each other's breasts. Lita had the largest, but that's because her father was a doctor and we think he used to exercise her with a machine. Pilita's mom got in on the act when she checked Pilita and me and she happily announced that Pilita was larger and for days I went around with my arms across my chest, my shoulders humped, my back concave. That was 1956. Pilita's mom was related to the President and a year after he came into office they had this enormous house built on their old lot, so huge there was no grass between the gate and the front door, just concrete, it was so tasteless, we had to party in the front verandah with people watching over the low walls, the loud music blasting from the living room, the latest Rock and Roll records her father brought from the States when he came back from attending Union bosses' conferences. They were the new rich, my sisters said, so our gangmates were civil to them but Pilita never really made it into our circle. I liked her, nevertheless, because she let me play on her roof, a marvellous concrete slab that went all around the house like a flat sombrero. Aside from that, her uncle was Papa's friend who set up some business deals with him. When he died mysteriously in the "Mt Pinatubo" crash in 1957 (was it CIA, was it his enemies), we mourned.

We mourned, too, the passing of an era. 1957. Carlos P Garcia Filipino First. The Austerity Program. In school, I won the class debate: pro-austerity. I had worked on the speech for days.

"Do you think this is a good thing?" I asked Sis One.

"I hear there are many poor among us now."

I shuddered. The Chinese receded; the Poor were at our gates. Were we communists, too?

"It's important that those of us who can should tighten our belts."

I looked at her blankly.

"So we wouldn't want too much."

"Oh, I see." I didn't see. I thought the phrase meant people were getting thinner. "But what's wrong? Have the Chinese invaded us, have we been infected by their poverty?"

She frowned at me. "The Chinese have nothing to do with it. Where did you get that idea?"

"But Sr Rose . . . "

"It's the Bell Trade Act, the free trade, the military bases agreement, JUSMAG—the Americans have impoverished us. They control our politics, our elections, our sugar, our barrios. Magsaysay gave us to the Americans. Garcia is trying to rectify that."

"I thought Papa said Magsaysay was a good man—he solved the Huks problem, he was developing the rural economy,'land for the landless'." I loved slogans. They rolled trippingly on the tongue. I had never seen the landless, except in the *Pilipino Comics,* very crudely drawn, with pants rolled up to the knees, legs deep in the rice fields, bolo on one taut hand, kerchief tied around a bull neck or the forehead, browned in the scorching sun, the noble Magsasaka.

"He was a good man, albeit somewhat simple. But he was too pro-American. Garcia is a nationalist." And her eyes shone. Nationalists were heroes, like Papa, who would die for their country.

"It's good to go hungry once in a while," Mama said at dinner. "Like at Lent or on Fridays."

I looked at our meagre meal, down to three dishes, and wondered. Were we being prepared for something terrible?

"Today Sr Judy said that we are living beyond our means," Sis One announced.

"Esther's Uncle Lorenzo said that there's a lot of graft and corruption in the government—that's where the trouble lies," I countered. I didn't like the tightening-the-belt idea.

"He is correct," Papa declared. I felt vindicated. I ate all my shrimps. Still, there was something ominous in his voice. He was oddly quiet. When Emiliana brought the fried bananas in a cracked dish, he hit his plate on top of it, shattering both. "There," he said, "the bad luck will go away."

Afterwards, sitting in the living room, he said that from day one after the war ended, graft and corruption were synonymous with the word Philippines. He couldn't decide which president was more corrupt. Each one seemed to outdo his predecessor. Manila was open like a sore, he said when he was sober, like a whore he'd repeat later when he was drunk. Either way, parasites dug in.

He thought Quirino could have been the worst because murders were open. Open, too was government looting—the presidency itself a form of looting by this "Malacañang squatter." But then Papa was biased. He and Jose Laurel denounced the man in after-dinner conversations, denounced colonialism, denounced American domination of Philippine affairs. They both hated the up-for-grabs atmosphere between 1945 and 1955, the ten years when, if any millions were to be made, they were made. After that time, one simply consolidated or expanded. And if you were, like Papa, morally intact, you watched your wealth sucked underneath the bog of frenzied feeding.

Chapter Three

> Shoo, fly don't bother me,
> Shoo, fly, don't bother me,
> Shoo, fly, don't bother me,
> 'Cause I belong to Comp'ny C.

The Holy Ghost orchids were the first sign of change. Their roots dangled from the tree trunk, a loose mass flapping in the wind. The whitemoth looked as though it were ready to fly away, the brown-speckled yellow star grew dim. The purple Christmas drooped, like ornaments that should be thrown out after the season, the hybrid ones looked like mongrels. I would sit on the wooden two-seater swing and wonder why the orchids were dying. Pepito, the gardener who used to live with us, only came on Saturdays now from his own house. It didn't seem unusual when he left, because Papa loved gardening. I thought Papa kept the gardens thriving. He planted the grapevines, the vegetables, the kalamansi bushes, the yellow bells near the gate, the bougainvillaea around the lanai. But I see now that Pepito maintained all the plants and flowers because, of course, Papa was always away on a business trip abroad. As he was now, for two months, and Pepito had neglected the orchids, he had only so many hours on a Saturday to tend some part of the estate.

Another portent was the swimming pool that was left to collect leaves and debris. Bienvenido used to dredge them out, expertly moving the long pole so that leaves would slide into the net. It didn't take him long and we'd spend afternoons in the water with our friends.

Then the piano lessons stopped, which was fine with me because my teacher used to slap my hands. Sis Two's voice lessons stopped too, which was a pity because her la la la la la la la was my alarm clock on Saturday mornings. Also, she genuinely loved to sing. Her "Danny Boy" ripped one's heart out and when she sang "Ave Maria" I could hear the symphony orchestra in the background in a majestic cathedral. She sometimes sang in a radio program, I think because the announcer was so handsome. He and his colleague were invited for dinner and drinks one night by my parents and I nearly died when I saw him—I went with Sis Two from then on to the station to cheer her on and drool over him. That was short-lived, too, because Papa didn't think much of the entertainment world in terms of his children. When Sis One was waiting at a movie house lobby for her friends, she was approached by a movie director with a star offer because she was so beautiful. When she recounted this at home, Papa hit the ceiling. We were banned from going to the movies for a month.

Which was a true punishment. We loved the movies. We'd go in at one in the afternoon and come out at five, sitting there for four hours straight watching the same movie twice in a row. Our bums would ache but we loved it. We never saw a movie just once, we always saw it twice. Sometimes we'd be late and come in halfway, so we had to stay one more round. We sat in the loge and our maids were in orchestra. They said people there were dangerous. They went home after one showing because there would invariably be a man sitting beside them whose hands wandered onto their laps and did unspeakable things, not the things under the bed but on the bed.

The bed had never been a haven for me. I hated to go to bed. A redeeming grace of being in bed, my Sis Two said, was that your guardian angel who stood at the left-hand side, top, by your head, stayed awake all night and watched over you. This assurance got me through the night. She never needed an alarm clock—she merely told her guardian angel to wake her up a certain time, and every morning she did. It was incredible. But I reserved my angel for serious things, like defense against demons for which, I believed, angels were created.

And these were hard times. A subtle change in school was my math teacher. She was a Filipina nun. Slowly, the American nuns were being duplicated by natives. Filipino First.

This was a good thing. Everyone loved Sr Carmen. She gave me a C in geometry but that was my fault—I couldn't understand her or the subject. And I used to spend an inordinate time in the school library reading irrelevant books instead of studying. I was reading Plutarch's *Lives* underneath the oil portrait of St Francis Xavier, beached, slumped on some rocks, when Sr Rose peeped around the corner of low shelves, hovered, then sat across from me, staring at St FX. I turned around, worried that the Saint had come down from his frame and was standing behind me.

"He was a missionary to India, Jazz. He never made it to China."

My ethnic origin may have inspired her to say the first statement. She was relating with me. I put the heavy book down; this may take long.

"Communist children testify against their parents," she continued, looking like a demented Torquemada. "Willingly."

My heart froze. There was no one else in this corner of the library, that was why I chose it, for some quiet reading over the noon hour.

"But it's not their fault," she sighed. "They're taken away at a young age and indoctrinated."

I glanced at the pathway through the shelves. But she could grab me. She sat near the exit.

"Someday," her voice rang staccato," you may be asked to testify against God. Do not deny Him."

I shook my head.

Her vigorous nod shook her entire body. She gave me yet another estampita of Pope Pius XII. She glanced at St FX once more, sighed, then said as she pushed herself off the table, "We are surrounded by communists. Hold the fort." Then she was gone, but the scent of her, heavy combination of sweat in her linens, remained.

When the whoosh of her habit was out of hearing range, I leapt up and joined the gang, chatting outside in the bright sun. I recounted the event and Esther said, "You should read under the Gainsborough "Blue Boy"—it's the poetry section." While I couldn't get the connection, it must have been reasonable advice so I sat there ever since and ended up reading Byron and the Romantics all term under the prat-stare of the Boy.

My enforced reading at home was changing, too. Mama used to let me memorize whatever I wanted so I'd spend hours in my room chanting Shakespeare's soliloquies for the mellifluous language of them, but now she'd given me a poem I had to learn by heart: "Man with the Hoe." It was about noble peasants and the illustration above the poem was a drawing like "The Reaper" or "The Sower" or "The Miller." I had to recite this poem to her and she taught me the gestures that went with a line or a word and as I was fourteen now, I began to feel silly about these declamations. She had been making me do these for school contests since Grade 2 and because I was successful, I had to do this year after year. They used to be great poems I could naturally gesticulate to, like "Charge of the Light Brigade" but this man, bowed down by the centuries, was depressing. He wasn't me. But I role played him, anyway, to please Mama, because she enjoyed these moments when she coached me, but in the end I persuaded her not to enter my name that year. I was in the school play anyhow—that was good enough.

It was not a big role. Everyone thought I'd get the lead, and so did I, because I had had the lead since Grade 4 when I gave a brilliant Tekakwitha performance. So on the audition day, I took the reading for granted but, of course, the gang was crushed when it was given to a brilliante Filipina, instead. Who was, on top of it, Esther said, poor—she was practically a ward of the nuns. We were now inundated by the new rich and some questionables, because the nuns were opening up the school to anyone. There were so many new faces, the gang got closer together and tighter. Divisions were so clear now that even the nuns had to acknowledge them. The gang made things clearer by using put-downs and name-calling—they particularly hated a girl who looked like a servant and had an unfortunate long face—they called her "Peanut." At volleyball, they'd yell "Throw it at Peanut!" and I'd feel a twinge each time it happened. After Letty's death at the avenging Moro's hand, I had vowed to be kind to classmates, so I befriended her and called her often by her true name. She didn't last the year. She just wasn't there one day and nobody asked about her. She was good in math, too.

I couldn't really see the point of my own gang's harassment of this intelligent wretch. They were all natives. But then there were degrees of nativeness. Esther's ancestors were peninsulares, the first class, the Spanish who came directly from Spain. Her high cheekbones would have made her a world beauty queen. Lyn, who looked like Elizabeth Taylor in *Little Women*, was a mestiza. Nilda, too. She was so white skinned, she ended up as a model in Australia before she graduated from high school, passing for white. Lita, the doctor's daughter, was true insulare, the Spanish born in this country, not just a mestiza. So was Fina, who was brilliant and whose architect father owned a yacht where we partied a lot. I fitted in because I was a foreigner whose entire household, including servants, spoke English, because Papa and Mama couldn't communicate in each other's languages. In any case, Mama's father was an insulare, his father a peninsulare who managed to secure several small Visayan islands where he built up successful copra plantations. Our pedigrees were impeccable.

Then there were others: the Chinese mestizos and the Indios. The Indios, these days, were now being called the Tao, or Man, which the nuns transformed to Common Tao. The Common Tao were rising all around us, invading our school preserve, getting the leads in annual plays. They were the "Man with the Hoe," refusing to till the land for foreign landlords but taking the land for themselves, asserting their sovereignty.

"This is a good thing," Sis One would say to me over and over. She was now editor of the College literary journal and for her first issue she broke tradition by printing poems and short stories in Tagalog along with the usual English contributions. With Sr Judy's approval! It shocked some of the other nuns and Sis One was called into the Principal's Office. But the tide could not be stemmed, the floodgates had been opened, and all such other clichés.

"Why is this good?" I asked her.

"A people have to be free," she answered. "The first step to freedom is to take your language back, to speak in your own voice."

And, in fact, the Philippine language was now a subject in school, along with Spanish. The medium of instruction was still English but rumours came to us that in other schools the nationalization had reached them—they were being taught in Tagalog. Sis Two became so proficient in this subject that she would regale us with deep Tagalog during dinner and the servants loved her when she sang "Ang Dalita." She sang "Ako'y anak nang dalita"—I am a child of woe. Gone were "Danny Boy" and "Ave Maria." I didn't get high marks in the subject but my sisters flourished. I had that unfortunate Alabama accent that the majority of Americans here seemed to have, the Woorsh Woorsh we called it, because I had been such a good mimic, and then there was that Colonel Richard episode that implanted it on my tongue for life. As well, I disliked the bastardized Spanish, and Tagalog seemed to be misheard and mispronounced Spanish that became apritada, unibersidad, abante, eksibisyon, agosto.

Our filipinization stopped at the dinner table, however. Sis One broached the subject of changing our diet from the Western-style to a more peasant like one. Mama, God bless her soul, put her foot down to the tinapa, a fish so dry and salty we were all choking. The tuyo didn't fare so well either, in spite of the fact that Rizal had eaten it every morning.

Thinking of Rizal, Esther too was getting nostalgic these days. She was now researching the really ancient past, past beyond the Spanish conquistador, way back to Lapu Lapu and Mactan and the death of Magellan, to datus and Rajah Sulayman, and all those Muslim names, and she was championing Jolo and Sulu and the Muslim cause, their independence. She would play "Granada" on her nose flute—*Granada, I'm falling under your spell*—Granada of 1492, last bastion of Islam, her flute notes skipping two octaves after solemn notes so that the silence could pierce one to the heart. She would draw the vinta, the Muslim boat, against a stark sky. She decried the destruction of their culture, the wanton desecration of their beliefs by the Spanish zealots, and I used to think, this must be her rebellion against her own blood, we were now at that age when we rebelled against anything. And as people were rebelling all over the place for real reasons, we just went along with the flux. Esther had forgotten that the servant who killed Letty's family was Muslim, or if she remembered, it was all right now, he had probably just cause. As we recalled, Letty was annoying; her family was peninsulare of the worst sort, they were probably very mean to the servants. They may have deserved to die, a prelude to a coming national bloodbath. But the man was insane, I said to Fina, who still remembered and was sensibly not caught up in this hysteria of Blood Compacts, as we sipped Coke in her yacht.

She adjusted her glasses against the glinting sun. It was morning, and mornings didn't have shadows, no affected chiaroscuros, just plain light, straight from the sky, bathing everything with equal glow, it was the only democratic sign in the country, clear, transparent mornings, without guilt or excuses. As my eccentric godmother Conchita would say in her vibrant voice, "Jazz, the sun shines on us all, rich and poor alike."

Fina caught the sun in her eyes and she squinted. "It's the insane who see clearest of all." She was given to twisted metaphysical sayings, and when she was in this life-is-a-paradox mood, there was no getting sense from her. There were days she'd wear flowers in her hair like the drowned Ophelia. As she did today, wreaths of white sampaguita around her neck, their sweet pungency attacking my nostrils, and bouquets of sampaguita on top of her head, the white blossoms a strong contrast to the blackness of her long, fine hair. I didn't like the way she'd look longingly at the water, clear and clean as the sun, glinting slyly back at us like the flirting Catholic boys before they came to get us for a dance, we in our chiffon and Thai silk party dresses, flirting back on wicker chairs set out on the lawn and the back lanai, our Spanish fans flicking back and forth. They'd come, the bold ones, and make small talk, first hanging around, above us, looking taller than they normally were, then finally the carefully-worded question, with the deferential bow, the gently insistent smile, don't say no, it said, please, or my friends back there will kill me, and it gave one such power, that one's yes could mean life and death, as one rose gracefully, chiffon swaying, fan folding neatly in one motion, falling like a dying swan onto the palm of one's hand, for a lady always carried something in her hand, and the giving of the other hand onto his, and his grateful receiving of it, the walk towards the dance floor, his cocky, hers on winged feet, and the final semi-embrace to a slow drag beat from the latest American band. A ballet of manners.

When the boy was in love, there was no end to gifts. Gifts at each visit, gifts sent through his driver when he couldn't visit, gifts from his mother who'd just come from a pilgrimage to Fatima. Gifts. They made one sick. "The more you have, the more you're given," Papa said, as we would wake up to gifts everyday. Everybody gave them. From food to worthless items. And they had to be displayed, tasteless as they may have been. Mama had curio cabinets, nooks and crannies and surfaces for these things in indiscriminate tastelessness. Some rooms looked like gift shops, they were so full of art objects. The living room she kept sacrosanct, decorated with Papa's brass lamps from India, ivory elephant and inlaid statues and exquisite sweet-smelling wooden Philippine carvings. The leather sofas and glass-topped tables on Indian carpets reminded me of a British club, British Only, no

Natives please, and I didn't like sitting in the living room, it was just far too big and uninviting but it fitted the purpose of cocktail parties and large dinners parents had to give. Give, giving. That's the word, in all its forms, that epitomized these people. "The poor," Sis One said, who had only salt for their meals, "would give you the shirt off their back (if they still had that) if you came to visit." They would somehow find a way to get a piece of dried fish for your supper, then they'd return to their salt as soon as you left.

It was a nation of gift-givers.

They had no sense of money—they didn't keep it, they spent it for others, in restaurants and nightclubs, in things, in movies, in parties, in costumes for festivals, flow, flow, flow, sometimes it just flowed right out and it took a while for the flow to come back in. Meanwhile, they waited. Patiently. Strong in the hope that it would flow back, And so the cycle went.

"But how do you know so much about the Wretches?" I asked her. I had read *Les Miserables* and I glorified the poor into the Wretches.

"Sr Jean has been talking about them lately. We're going to be carolling to the poorer districts at Christmas, handing out presents afterwards. We've started the Social Justice Club."

Of course, I thought. This was an extension of her peasants -in-the stories and her second literary journal issue. More and more, the nuns were becoming aware, no, more than that, were actively engaged with the problems of the Wretches. Sis Two had joined, as well, putting her singing talent for the glory of God. I was too young to join; they were both in college. But this year, instead of my usual birthday party, my sister got me to celebrate it at the St Anthony's orphanage, so that I could give presents to the children, instead of receiving the usual tonnage at home. My gangmates didn't appreciate this but the times were changing, so they accepted it. We had a quiet exchange at noon hour at school on Monday, and I got my jewellery and perfume which I just added to Mama's collection because I didn't like wearing any of these anyway.

If people weren't giving, they were arranging, bartering. The movie star Leopoldo Salcedo who lived down the road with the barbed wire on top of his stone fences as his answer to burglars, came to visit one day (bringing the customary basket of fruits) with his prize dog. He wanted to cross his dog with our Alsatian, and Papa listened politely, said he'd think about it, and sent him off on his way.

Beauty died before all this breeding came to pass, virginal and pure, and went straight to Heaven.

Papa was abroad when Beauty died. She had to be put to sleep because she had been infected by a stray spaniel Sis Two let in through the gates, caught up as she was in her sympathies for the Wretches. When Mama sent him a telegram about what should be done about Beauty, he called his approval of the vet's decision. She telegramed again after the deed and later when Papa came home, he said that he cried when he found out that she was truly dead. He loved that dog so. She used to know whenever Papa came back from his travels. She would climb up the stairs, straight to his bedroom, nudge open the mosquito net and greet him with her wet nose and a strong paw.

Papa was just as bad as everyone else in the giving department. He came home with gifts for everyone in the family, including the servants, friends and business associates. In fact we only got half of his loot; half would be thrown away even before he got home. He gave away 10,000 pesos to start a school in his village without consulting with Mama.

He left behind a bag of rubies in his airplane seat. Money—the actual physical feel of money, the numbers on them, the faces gracing them, didn't mean anything to him. He had a foreigner's carelessness and not quite distinct knowledge of the value of the money in his hand. Peso, dollars, yen, kyat, rupiah, rupees—these interchanged in his palm, flowed in and out, flow, flow, flow, like soapflakes down the drain. He expected to be given and he gave as much in return. When someone complimented him on his Rolex, he took it off and gave it to the man. He could afford generosity. This was all natural, simple behaviour, like people sharing bread, coffee. Nobody counted how much the other ate, drank. It was only the Wretches who counted, who had bookkeepers and ledgers, who had budgets and savings, reserves and expenditures, obsessively writing and rewriting figures in notebooks, adding and subtracting, totally given to computations and permutations, to possibilities and probabilities, to an abstract world of if I had this amount, I could do that, illusions of power, universes undivined and unconquered, then the sad awakening to the reality of the empty June yet to be traversed, yawning like a chasm before one, wide as the desert July still to follow and the unscalable peaks of August even more beyond them and then the year gasped at one like an emaciated prisoner, chained at the neck, wrists and ankles. Money. Given meaning, it became a spectre that sucked life juices from the petty king in his ludicrous counting-house. There was never enough. It never balanced. Something always missing. Had to check again.

Papa could be rich or poor; it made no difference to him. He was untouched by greed. He was innocent.

So innocent, Mama said, that people took advantage of him. She wanted some check on the spending, a say on where the flow was to go. But why, Papa said, what's the point. It's only money, it comes and goes. God provides.

And God did seem to provide—His providence was bountiful.

"And what about the others?" Sis One said. "Does God provide for them?"

"They're alive, are they not?" I said.

"For how long? Their children have bloated bellies." She was bringing pictures, not of children in China, but of those right here, outside our gates. She described houses that were not, but shanties, corrugated iron roofs on cardboard walls, open lavatories—descriptions not taken from Pearl S Buck but from right here, outside our gates.

"Jazz," she said. "It's now immoral to be rich."

Her statement devastated me. It conjured up visions of Siddhartha, who had walked among the poor and gave up his riches to live with them in search of enlightenment. It frightened me that my beautiful and brilliant sister, with her fair skin and limpid eyes, like a doe in a field of cattle would be trampled, dragged in the mud and buried in manure with this new-found altruism.

This had all gone too far. I thought it was immoral to be poor. That was the American attitude. Rags to riches. The American Dream. You had to climb out of the hole because being in the hole was bad. It was the Spanish attitude. The Indios were low class, low breed. It was the Indian attitude. The Untouchables were despised. The princess got the prince. If she came from the peasantry, being made into a princess was the happy ending of the tale. Then she went back and made her family rich, too; the entire village must have prospered because everyone sang and danced and had plenty to eat.

What did this new concept mean? It was far too spiritual, ascetic, Christ-like, hermetic, wisdom-of-the-Desert-Fathers. Did she expect us all to open our gates, all 400 families, just slide the metal bolt and open the gates?

"Yes, why not?" she answered.

"But that's communist," I exclaimed. "You've gone and become a communist!"

"It's social justice. It's very Catholic."

It's those Dominicans and Jesuits, I thought. They'd indoctrinated my sisters. Gone were yelling for Emiliana to bring them a glass of water. They actually went to the kitchen and asked in a low voice. Gone was the sitting up all night for Gracing to put Sis Two to sleep with her gentle head-massage. They had gone beyond Christian—they were Christ. Still, I noted, not everybody belonged to the Social Justice Club. It was very chic. The liberal students were leading the pack, trekking to the shanties instead of to Antipolo. It was called Christ-in-Action. My sisters were so fervent, along with their Jesuit-taught young male companions, off to these excursions for the poor, the holiest among the crusaders, the most popular. Now in the chit-chat around the basket chairs in the lanai on Sunday afternoons, it was not the handsomest, the richest, the brightest, the funniest, or the young man with the fastest car who figured most but the holiest, the one closest to becoming a priest that one of them could ensnare before he actually became formally consecrated. What a coup that was—to get a *good* man who wasn't actually a priest, someone blessed by God but not married to God. I suspect half the fun of helping the poor was the quest for the holy husband. Of course, the men went for holy women, as well, because my sisters never had a dull week. God provides.

Providential God was helped along by providential presidents. From Manuel Roxas to Carlos P Garcia, presidents of the Third Republic, in the years of my childhood, helped the people who belonged to their families, to their clans. If you were from Manila, Roxas was your man; from Ilocos, Quirino; from Zambales, Magsaysay; from Bohol, Garcia. It helped, if you had a favour to ask, a business to finance. And fortunes were made and lost with the coming and going of presidents. So often elections didn't just mean a democratic exercise; it meant one's life and death.

Death it was in the towns, in the provinces, people shot because they were Ilocanos and not Pampanguenos, doubly whammied not just for class but for birthplace. I would shudder whenever someone proudly stated his or her origins. Foolish, foolish, I thought, watch where the wind blows your words. But they wore their beginnings on their shirts like medals, it was infused in their beings through their accents, intonations, in their mannerisms, they could be spotted a kilometre away, targets, and proud of it. Look at me, look at my roots. Shoot me. In contrast, I collected eclectically—Palawan baskets, jewellery from the Cordilleras, Maranao sculpture, Tagbanua wooden carvings—mixing regional crafts, blurring, erasing, reconstructing, hiding. No one was going to point me out. My goal was to blend with the wall.

Not so my eccentric Godmother, the one whose sun shone on everyone. She was a first cousin to President Manuel A Roxas, on the side of the initial A, and reminded us at each visit. She was more Spanish than the Spanish and spoke only Spanish even if she knew the national language. She refused to speak English, not having conceded her defeat in the Spanish-American War of 1898. Most summers she went on pilgrimages to Spain, Portugal and France and brought home exquisite large rosaries with glittering beads, so heavy on the fingers they were diabolically punitive. I had to use them for a few Sundays to show my appreciation, then when she had forgotten about them, they went into the jewellery box where they gleamed brighter than the real gems. Some were good enough to wear as necklaces, but that would have been a sin.

Her entry into the home was announced by a loud and steady stream of

Spanish words which sent the servants scurrying. She'd yell Mama's name fortissimo. Mama would greet her and off they'd go all afternoon at their Castilian merienda. She wore outrageous clothes, the finest silks in the 1930s style fit for dancing in the poshest nightclubs, but at teatime they were out of synchronization. They were most probably, her 1930s clothes, still wearable, still fitted to her unchanged tall slim body. She deliberately cultivated an age that had died long before any of us were born. She must have been just in her forties, but to me she was older than old, a spinster past her prime, passed over by modernity, frozen in dead years. But whenever she visited, she brought the sunshine in. Mama would be in a good mood all week, speaking Spanish jauntily to uncomprehending servants, asserting her own roots.

I just couldn't understand all this display. It was bad enough that one day as we waited in the theatre lobby, someone hissed "Bumbay" at us, and my sisters grimaced at him but he wouldn't go away. They were more integrated with the natives than I was, more in sympathy with their causes, and yet they were being hissed at, being pointed out as outsiders. How it must have hurt them.

I was used to it. I had always felt like an outsider, never fitted in. Ironically, this was all part of the nationalism process, the nationalism that Sis One approved of, and it was being thrown at her face, whispered against her by some sleazy, slick oily-haired Common Tao.

Down to name-calling. Give enemies a name before you destroy them. First it was the Chinese—Intsik Beho; now it was us—Bumbay, a corruption of one city's name to dehumanize the whole race. But then were they not Indios, our brown brothers, little monkeys? It goes on. I attempted to blend more and more into the wall, become a chameleon, wear fatigues, grease my face with mud, be a guerrilla, go underground.

Guerrillas are dangerous, my uncle, back from building a bridge in Vietnam, said. It was a very hushed evening when he came to visit. We all sat in the smaller, more intimate music room, Sis One at the piano doling out a mournful tune, adagio, larghetto, largo, Sis Two and Mama and I around my uncle, listening to stories of mutilation and hardship. They made Mama melancholy, reminded her of the Japanese occupation.

My uncle Manuel looked like Errol Flynn with the adventurous spirit of Rimbaud. He didn't just look adventurous, Hollywood-style, he truly went out and did devilish things. He was an engineer, not a soldier, but consulted by the military. I wasn't quite sure whose side he was on, he may have even been neutral, but that he cared for the suffering lent him a noble brow. Here was another holy man, I thought, another hero.

Sis One ignored him, all the while. *Soon the lonely nights will be ended,* the piano tinkled. When Uncle Manuel left for bed (he was so tired), I lingered, sitting behind Sis One on a lilac Queen Anne chair, and waited. Something gnawed at her.

"Before Vietnam, there was us," she began. "1898. The American rationale was to help us get rid of the Spanish, but the people had already got rid of the Spanish by 1898. There were only outposts of Spanish rule left when Spain ceded us to the Americans at the Treaty of Paris. President McKinley's 'Benevolent Assimilation' was assimilation by force. He sent US troops to put down our guerrillas."

"We had guerrillas?" I asked. The Huks didn't count; they were communists, the nuns said.

"Oh yes! The Americans say we all collaborated with them, but there were many pockets of resistance. US infantry would go around killing people, burning houses, animals, the fields. They tortured us to get confessions or information—atrocities like the water cure, quartering—looted, massacred indiscriminately. It was bloodier than World War II."

Uncle Manuel lost his lustre.

"They turned Batangas, the garden of Luzon, into a jungle. Let him talk about Vietnam. The oppressed are here, right here. We've been oppressed for centuries. Let him build bridges here, where we need him. He goes to Vietnam because of the money. The Americans pay well. They should. They're using him, native against native. The idiot." She slid off the bench, her face twisted in contempt of my hero, her body tired with the burden of life. She closed the door behind her softly, like a balloon let go unwillingly but finally. I lingered longer in the music room, the sad song echoing in my head.

And it was a balloon let go into ineluctable space, taken by the wind higher and higher into the clear sky, the sun blazing down upon us. We were helpless in the changes of direction, in the march of governments, in the drum roll of our past in which we had no control, not having been born in it but fatally influenced anyway. History. I hated it. It was all written, all done with, interpreted as necessary by the country, by the government involved, it was all truth and facts and lies, selective information, propaganda. Real lives receded into the venerability of history. Real lives became statistics. When Sis One retold it, it became flesh, became fiction, a story to mull over in my mind as I lay in bed, past breakfast, because I wanted to finish the story or whatever story I was writing in my head that morning and Mama would give up trying to get me up and would send Maria to put on my socks even as I still lay in bed, and my uniform, hanging neatly pressed on a hook, would be wound around me to signal my return into the real world of school, and I would be driven there, late but accepted, anyway, the nuns being so open hearted and forgiving. Better late than never. They formed my sisters' moral awakening and political consciousness. And they were Americans.

Some of my consciousness was formed in the library of a Supreme Court judge's home. He was the father of Sis One's gangmate. Whenever we visited their home, Sis One would go off swimming with the gang, while I waited in his library. There I read Alan Paton and learned about apartheid. But it was very very far away, Negroes and whites of which I was neither, and still, though I sympathized, it didn't seem to be my cause. I didn't truly know what it was like to be black-skinned in Johannesburg in 1949. If anything, because I was a foreigner in this country, I felt closer to the white family attacked by the Mau Mau, felt their fears, suffered their wounds. Yet, I knew the sting of colonialism, because I heard my father and sisters speak of it all the time and, in fact, was born and raised in its grip, as had my father before me. But on Mama's side, her ancestors were the imperialists. Pickaninny. The closest I got to the colour black was when Mama called me that. And "My African Daisy." Because I was scraped from the bottom of the barrel, I was darker than my sisters; they had aquiline noses, mine was short; they had pale pink lips, mine was beige. Even their nipples were pink while mine were brown. What a confusion. These ten years of my awakening I looked back upon as a maelstrom.

Chapter Four

I feel, I feel,
I feel like a morning star.
Shoo fly, don't bother me,
'Cause I belong to somebody.

Churning away, stirring and mixing, my aunt's muscular arm attacked the bowl. Doughnuts. Our cook had disappeared, been sent away. My aunt, a better cook, had taken her place for the past few weeks. She let me into the kitchen to watch her, to keep her company. She let me have the doughnut holes. Mama couldn't cook. When my aunt went home and on week-ends, Papa showed us a talent we didn't know he had. He cooked the most succulent curry chicken dish we had ever tasted, crushing potatoes to enrich the liquid, filling the whole kitchen with that cloying smell that entered into your whole being. He made chapatti his own way, not bitter or crusty. We had begun to enjoy meals, now that we saw the preparation, now that we were involved.

A procession of aunts and cousins, sostenuto, had all taken the place of our cook, and it had been great fun. They did washing-up as well, and then they stayed on as our houseguests. Some of them came from the provinces. They lived with us while they made their way in the big city and once they had found work they moved out into their own apartments. Meanwhile, they helped out at home. One of my aunts, my favourite, taught me piano, so my lessons were on again. In return, I introduced her to Lita's father who placed her at the Veterans' Hospital he was connected with, and she went to work happily. And so the churning, round and round.

As the wheel turned, people flew off. Emiliana returned to the province to get married. Mama was very sad to send her away, but she had to live, Mama said, we couldn't keep her like a possession. I grew up with her, it was so strange to wake up next morning without her. She had kept the household running andante, it seemed to me that now things would really fall apart. I was surprised that she had become a woman, an adult, and when people became that, they had to go out and make a life. I didn't want to grow up then, because out there was the Unsafe.

There were just as many people in the house, even if the servants were being depleted. My aunts kept the count up. Mama had more relations than angels in heaven. They came out of the woodwork, ate more than they cooked, then went off. Papa was becoming annoyed. These were the same relations who had rejected him when he proposed to Mama. He was a foreigner, they said, you should marry one of us. But then he became wealthy and suddenly they were all visiting from Samar and admiring his acumen. They always felt awkward in his presence, though he treated them generously. But these days, it seemed there were more of them, a steady stream of them.

"They're all coming out to find work in Manila," Papa explained. "Emptying out of the distressed provinces."

"Times are hard," Mama said. "They think there's work here."

"Is there?" I asked.

"Somewhat more than back home. More chances here. I have to provide for them in the meantime."

"Some of them come out to study," Sis Two said. "Better schools out here. Others are already highly educated."

"Some of them go back if they fail here," Sis One said.

We were all sitting or lying down on our parents' bed, languorous, indulgent, indolent. It had been a spelled-out day, slow and hot, and the night did not cool it down. Air conditioners were coming into vogue now and our parents had one in their bedroom, so we all gathered around there to cool off. It felt like being in the movie theatre without the flickering darkness. I didn't particularly like the artificial coolness, it had a cold touch and a smell like death. It did away with all the mosquitos, at least, which was the main blessing. We still used Katol outside when we sat in the terrace in the evenings, the incense smoke choking our lungs as much as it did the bugs'.

The family sat around more often these nights this year, Papa was often with us now. The business trips abroad had tapered off, rallentendo, I hadn't noticed the gradual contouring but now saw that Papa was at home when he should have been out there making money. We had all grown closer together, Mama and my sisters turning down invitations to spend more time with Papa and me, the five families, I called us, and they laughed, one family, Mama corrected, but I saw us all as individuals larger than one, with potential lives ready to explode outwards, a centrifugal pull, rather than an implosion or the centripetal dissolution Mama thought we were experiencing. No, the flow was outwards, we were all growing up, my sisters were going to be adults and they would have to go out there. Even as we grew tighter, and our nights longer, we grew away from each other to make our lives.

Those tableaux nights filled with words and song, with love and safety, like nights of travellers around the fire, with histories and stories exchanged late into the dawn in warm camaraderie, those nights died away like the embers and ashes crushed under one's foot, as one prepared to journey on. Those nights were like the eclipse when the sun was suddenly covered and the cicadas were fooled into chirping and the breeze thought to blow and we looked through our film negatives at the black circle with its corolla, awed at the magic of life, at the greatness of God, and all this profundity only for a few seconds, then back light came, the fierce midday sun. We had witnessed something that we might not again in our lifetimes, like that comet that came once in hundreds of years, come and gone, making our togetherness even more ephemeral and tragic. But the more beautiful butterflies evaded Gide, as well, and he wouldn't have had it otherwise. Thus I viewed the family's nights, talking away, away, away.

The eddies widened. Mama gave away her share of the plantations; she said she would never return to the province now, her sisters had more claim to her land because they tilled it.

An Indian bishop stayed with us for a few days and when he went back to India he arranged scholarships for my sisters and me to British universities. We were now being sent away, too.

Papa was talking about moving his business to Hong Kong. He had a number of Chinese friends who were willing to set him up. In times like these, foreigners banded together.

It was now our midafternoon, when the sky was a mother-of-pearl and the greyness was a prelude, the stillness a bated breath. The transparency of morning was transformed into a black and white photograph, with much grey shadows, a monochrome of long, sultry, sticky hours that one waited out. Wait, the soft grey day says, the night will be quick and beautiful.

I spent some of this time listening to records. Be Bop. Charlie Parker just died and I heard him expel his breath into muted tones. Rock and roll. Elvis Presley was new and Papa brought me his latest long-playing records, imported from Hong Kong. I had gone beyond the classicals of my piano days.

I sat beside the record player, ear to the massive cabinet. The marvellous wooden chest was carved for Mama and deep in its caverns lay the apparatus that performed this magic of sound; so to enjoy the music, without turning up the volume at full blast, I had to curl up near the speakers hidden within. If I were a mechanic, I would rip the insides off this great coffin and let the raw metal free. I wanted to crack open this veneer, this surface craft and let the true rich art wash the room with its musical waves, bouncing from wall to wall, forte, maestoso.

But I had to wait. I had to wait out this long afternoon, as the trumpet wailed its long note, as the rhythm flowed indistinguishably beat after beat, finger snapping, one, one, one. I was now reading Jack Kerouac.

Sis One had turned from Dostoyevsky, T S Eliot, Graham Greene, Evelyn Waugh, Francois Mauriac, and the list went on and on of all great literature, to reading Nick Joaquin, N V M Gonzalez, and other writers here whom I didn't know. She was reviewing their works in her literary journal. She went to local artists' exhibitions, saw local movies, most of them long shots of men riding horses on a hill. Sis Two was talking more and more in the national language and learning dialects. The two of them were going more native than the natives.

I alone kept up with American literature, with Hollywood. This was not my cause. I had no quarrel with anyone. I wanted to be a firefly which glowed in the night, but once caught, the light would go out and the enemy would cup his palm and be tricked and then open it in dismay, then off I'd fly away free to glow once more.

One, one, one. Our midafternoon, our merienda time, time after siesta, was the doldrums. My godmother still came to cheer us up and her adage was becoming more meaningful to me. There were no more bevy of servants to scurry from the barrage. Only Gracing and Mona stayed for the marketing. Only Bienvenido and Tina, the faithfuls: the first, because no one knew how to drive, and the second, because everyone refused stoutly, understandably, to wash and iron. Papa could cook, Mama could sew clothes, my aunts could clean the house, but no one wanted to go on the wet cement floor and wield that bat. Tina ruled triumphant. Her stories became more and more horrible and hit closer to home. Gone were the strangers crawling on my bed, or that awful woman whose hair turned white when she raised the mosquito net curtain and saw a decapitated head on her bed.

This time it was about a step-aunt (since my grandfather remarried) who wasn't allowed to join us, who had to stay behind in the province, at home, locked up, one might say. She tantalized me with this missing relation. At last one night when everyone was away and the house felt like a mausoleum, and I was wandering up and down the hallways, looking for an aunt who may have been in one of the rooms, Tina found me and dragged me to the ironing room.

Her coarse frizzy black hair, white streaks flaring at the temples, and her wild eyes brought shivers down my spine. Hot steam billowed from the iron as she waved it in the air, and hot steam rose from the sheet pressed against the board. She exuded the dark Satanic mills of Blake's London, this one-woman industrial infernal machine. Her voice was gravelly, made grating by the putrid brown cigarillo she smoked endlessly.

"Your aunt," she began fixing me with a look that would not deny me a genetic heritage, even as I corrected her in my head, "would spend the entire morning beautifying herself and cleaning the living room. She would dust and dust, arrange and rearrange the knick knacks, fluff and refluff the cushions on the sofa. She would run to the window and peer out and return to her cleaning, all the time exciting herself more and more." She turned to the sulphuric mass underneath her steel arms and pressed vigorously, leaving me to my imagination. I waited.

"She would sing a plaintive song," and Tina's voice rose, as a gravelly voice can hope to rise, pulling out of her depths a most horrific sound like cats caterwauling in the dead of night, the sound of aborted babies, choking their last wail.

"Then her face would light up because she would hear tap tap tap at the door. She'd fling it open joyously and let him in, her lover, handsome as the soldier from the war that he was, with that clean shaven face and that clean officer's uniform, he was Danny Boy come back. You could hear her sweet voice, talking, talking, talking, gaily, coyly, telling him to sit, drink, what was it like, tell me about it, how did you feel, do you still love me, did you think of me." Tina's voice turned magical, her eyes became misty, did she have such a lover, I thought, once, far away, before she came to us.

"Then she would bid him goodbye tearfully and she'd close the door and go to bed. The next day, she went through it all again."

We were now surrounded by this evil steam that hissed and snarled at my head.

"Had there been a lover?"

"Yes. He was killed by the Japanese in WW II."

I rose to go.

"Watch out, Jazz," her doomed voice followed me. "It runs in the family."

Step-aunt ! Step-aunt!

Just don't come to visit. It was the dead lover who touched me. How worthy he must have been to have deranged her so. What was this man like whose death, in whose dying, a woman could discover a new world more real than the one that saddened her, a creative created joyful world that sustained her. This dead lover filled my nightmares like Dracula floating in through the open casements, pushing aside my filmy curtain and then . . . Then I'd wake up because I was not allowed to see those kinds of movies and should a scene like that happen to appear suddenly on the screen, I averted my eyes in embarrassment.

The dead lover haunted me in the doldrum days, loomed large across my mind. The flash of his sabre, the red coat, the sturdy steed that bore him—all loomed large across my vermilion field of vision. Until one merienda, when Godmother didn't show up, I asked Mama what happened and she said that Godmother's sister was sick.

"The flu?" I asked.

Mama looked abstracted. "Yes, I suppose so."

"Why doesn't her husband take care of her?" Many nights Papa sat up with Mama, nursing her through asthma attacks.

"She doesn't have one. She lives alone in this great big house, the old family home."

"Alone? How can anyone live alone? Isn't she scared?"

"She's crazy. The man she loved died and she swore she'd never marry anyone else."

My heart went sforzando. Another woman demented over a dead lover. There was a pattern here. The focus changed from the men to the women. There was nothing extraordinary about the men; the women just made them so. The women *were* crazy, love *was* a disease as the Greeks said. Love was dangerous, like monsters, servants, houseguests, Americans, communists, guerillas, and the Wretches outside our gates. There was no end to the Unsafe, life was a perilous journey as the writers claimed.

And so that day, I lowered my step-aunt's ghost back into the grave, his bayonetted glorious body, scented with tiny sampaguita petals, laid to oblivious rest. I stayed close to Mama all day praying that none of the craziness would rub off on me. She sat by her Singer sewing machine whirring away , her right foot at the pedal, and her left hand on the wheel. My role was to thread the needle because my vision was perfect.

As long as I could remember, visits to the modista were a whole big affair. We had to go on separate days because it took so long to get fitted, to choose the cloths, agree to the designs and the embroidery, wait for changes in drape. I would sit in my undergarments in the private fitting room while Mama and the modista argued over fineries, bolts of cloth passing through fingers and scissors, beads and gems flung like fur here and there. I was never consulted and I never bothered to give my preferences. They were experts; they knew the latest fashions and what suited me at the several ages all these fittings took in the past ten years. The same modista, the same discussions, the only difference was my stages of nudity, from just panties, to chemise, to bra and panties. Even our bras were made by her, she was so consummate an artist. As the years went on, I had begun to call her aunt, Tita Lupe, and when we finally had to stop going to her shop, we all cried as though there had been a death in the family. We exchanged gifts and never saw her again.

We were reduced to bi-weekly visits from a seamstress who came to our home to accept Mama's designs and fit us. The seamstress, with smudges of black on her face which I felt like scrubbing clean, would regale us with her sad story (as she discussed the design Mama wanted her to copy). She and her family of four had just moved in to a place without running water (the taps were there but no water came out) and the "comfort room" (her words) was outside of the house —all at 800 pesos a month. Where she used to shower every night, now she hadn't washed herself in days, this as her fingers went through the fabrics Papa brought from Ceylon spread on the coffeetable. She had to transfer to this place because she had given her word (to whom?) and she never went back on her word. Instead, she suffered.

Mama had learned a lot from Tita Lupe so we continued to be stylish. No one would have suspected the change in our fortune. And there were the movie actresses we could always emulate—the Sabrina neckline—acceptable for now. The magazine illustrations paled beside Mama's creations.

The seamstress lasted a year, got us through 1958, but now in the beginning of 1959, Mama sewed our clothes. Mostly she altered the modista's line, transforming my sister's rainbow-coloured chiffon into a dinner gown for me. Reused clothes were a common trick among all fine families. Hand-me-downs were not frowned upon. Nothing was thrown out.

"Left-over idea, from the war," Mama said, as the treadle machine whirred. "We had to reuse everything, from party dress to kitchen rag."

She would then plunge into recollections of the War, the brutality of the Japanese soldiers, the near-death episodes, the usual piles of corpses, babies thrown up in the air and bayonetted as they came screaming down. I'd seen it all in movies; in fact her stories were projected in my mind like a film. Although I was impressed with the atrocities and sympathized with her sense of horror, still it all seemed far away and alien.

I liked one story about the last days of the Japanese. When I was baptized in the Manila Cathedral, I was brought there in our do-car, an ingenious concoction where the back half of a car, decorated sumptuously, was attached to a strong horse. Only the wealthy had this, but better yet by the end of the Occupation we had a real car. A Japanese officer came to our house to bring us with them to Tokyo as the bombs fell all around us—we lived in Pasay, the heart of the city, where American bombs fell most—and Papa said no, something like bugger off, and the officer took off in our car. I bet losing that car really riled Mama.

Esther's father died in that war, which explained why her mother's hatred of the Japanese was colossal. I thought he was killed with other members of the family in their living room, while the women were herded in the kitchen. I wasn't clear on this. I think not even Esther knew for sure since her mother wouldn't talk about it. He was probably in the resistance movement, along with my Justice-mentor, the Free Philippines movement. Although the majority of the wealthy elite collaborated, there were the few urban elite who managed to resist and still live. I wondered if after her father's death, they thought twice. I wondered if opinions then vacillated. The character was too conciliatory, too apt to compromise. It went where the wind blew.

Esther, who was her own man, gave me a Japanese doll in a glass case when she came back from Japan. This was during her rebellious stage when she was buying Japanese inspite of her mother. I put away this doll in the closet with the other dolls from around the world the houseguests invariably gave me, thinking that this was what a little girl wanted.

There were so many in there now that I was dismayed to have to open the door yet again to put another one away, because it scared me to see the whole lot of them stare back from the darkness. In some nightmares, the dolls would come walking out of the closet, gasping for breath, and attack me in bed for keeping them locked up. I hated dolls. I thought doll manufacturers were sick people like horror-story writers whose ghouls and zombies tormented innocent, normal girls. And what about voodoo dolls—were they possibly the origin of this evil?

Marionettes were not as scary. We gave marionette shows in school, the nuns letting us make up the stories and build puppets ourselves. Marionettes had strings we could control—they moved and spoke to our bidding. It was when Pinocchio broke off his strings and his wooden figure began to move on its own that I resisted liking him. That he became a real boy in the end redeemed him in my eyes. There had to be a meaning to independence; it had to go beyond the wooden, brittle stage.

Paper dolls were not frightening, either. We fashioned those, cut them out, played, crushed them and made new ones. If they were already made in those cardboard versions, which came with clothes having tiny squares on each shoulder that were utterly useless, they never lasted beyond playing twice anyway, they ripped so easily. The most fascinating indoor playthings, of course, were the chess pieces made of white ivory and black ebony. I would set up the dominoes as a fort or castle and the enemies surged up the battlements. The hero was a flawed ivory rook which had fallen off the table one day and chipped its tower, like an amputee Lord Raglan. Its imperfection distinguished it from the perfect others, made it unique, enhanced its Greek-tragic character, its hubris. Outdoors, nothing beat the dried papaya stems for swordplay. Sis Two and I had seen all the pirate movies ever made; we knew all the possible jabs Tony Curtis and Errol Flynn jabbed. Not to mention the royal sabres.

Fell like a cannon shot,
Burst like a thunderbolt,
Crash'd like a hurricane,
Broke thro' the mass from below,
Drove thro, the midst of the foe,
Plunged up and down, to and fro,
Rode flashing blow upon blow,
Brave Inniskillens and Greys
Whirling their sabres in circles of light!
Glory to all the three hundred, and all the Brigade!

Those wild-adventure-days were over, now that we were in our teens. Now there were boys to joust with. My sisters spent their hours matching clothes to shoes—a feat unto itself since we had to make at least three dress changes per day, because of the heat and the requirements of the events—and hanging on to the telephone so that one of us was in agony for hours waiting for the call from our chosen boyfriend of the month.

Mine for the moment was a gentle soul with a Karmann Ghia he raced on Sundays. He walked and spoke softly but when he was in that strip, he was Marlon Brando-James Dean on a motorcycle. His uncle raced, too, and between the two of them, they won most prizes. His uncle was the more daring devil—he drove his Ferrari underneath a truck just for the drag of it. I was keeping this boyfriend because it was the only way I got to see his uncle, who, like him, was in college, and devastatingly handsome.

In America, we heard about couple-dating at our age, but here we still went out in groups. We saw each other in parties and everything we did was watched by authorities: the nuns and priests who supervised our school dances, our parents who were in the living rooms when we were dancing in the terrace. Priests were with us in yacht parties and trips to Antipolo, more dashing than our boyfriends.

My chosen one's uncle was changing all these. Rumour was he and his girlfriend ("a fast girl," Mama said) went out alone and we all predicted, once the nuns found out, she'd go the way of Josie of the bathing-suit fame, thrown out to the wolves of commerce. I could hardly wait. She was so sexy and lovely, he wouldn't look at anyone else.

Wait, wait, wait. Our midafternoon wait. Mama said grandfather had constructed his coffin and had put it in the livingroom, set up for his wake. It gave him a sense of security to know that everything was organized after his death. Now, he just waited.

We waited for the letter-of-credit at the end of the month. It didn't come. We waited another month. Papa half sat, half lay in bed, waiting.

Mama outbid others at NAMARCO and won the contract. She waited for Papa who was in India arranging the delivery of the cattle.

Americans we saw at church stood waiting for the interminable homily at gospel to end. They stood by the door where there was a breeze but their shirts were still stained and you could see where the perspiration trail went from the neck to the waist. They were very handsome and I was in love with all of them. Sis One disapproved. She told me that they were bums in their own country and when they came out here, they were glorified. They dated movie starlets and frequented brothels. My aunt who worked in Olongapo told lurid tales about sailors from Subic Bay. Still you saw these American men gracing society pages. They were invited to parties because the colonial mentality was all-pervasive.

Our own boyfriends ended up in American graduate schools, mostly Fordham, Harvard, Princeton, Notre Dame. For all the nationalism talk, their parents still sent them abroad for further education before they returned to take over the firms. Some came back before their time because they discovered that they had to wash their own clothes, make their own meals. Senoritos that they were, the world outside was a shock. Once again, I was reminded of the Unsafe beyond. But my boyfriend's uncle, who had gone to San Francisco and survived, told us that there was hardly anyone out in the streets where he lived except for the occasional teenagers playing catch on their lawn, and downtown, one could park the car and walk around to look at shops without dishonour or disturbance. He once walked all around Market Street just to enjoy the scenery and the variety of people. People, he said, were clean and well-dressed, and walked with purpose, as though they were coming from somewhere and going somewhere. Office people, on their lunch hour, with things to do. It was quite exhilarating, he said. Action. Movement. Life.

Of course, that it was cold made things go briskly—none of the shuffling about one did in our Escolta. How admirable, I thought: he'd gone walking in our downtown. We were not encouraged to do this. Once his girlfriend did it in her shorts. A great offense. Shorts, the nuns said, are for the beach. Our clothes must be Mary-like; hemline two inches below the knee, high collar, long sleeves. (what did it matter if the temperature was 98 degrees Fahrenheit? Were they not wearing yards of linen?) Each occasion called for appropriate attire. But his girlfriend committed every sin in the book. She smoked, used lipstick at school, wore two-piece bathing suits, pencil-cut skirts, low necklines or strapless, dated, went on a trip to his country home alone with him for a weekend, read books from the Index or without Imprimatur and Nihil Obstat—the list went on and on. Her days were numbered. Her father being a sugar baron wouldn't faze the nuns.

Nevertheless, I rubbed my skin as hard as I could with cream, whitening agents, because his girlfriend was Spanish white. I heard some girls actually had their skin bleached, probably in Japan. My boyfriend insisted that my skin was kayumanggi, "Kayumangging Kaligatan" when he got excited, but I couldn't erase Mama's epithets that easily.

Another thing that a few girls were doing differently was that they were carrying lady guns. These were small pistols that fitted in your hand, red and silver design, very pretty. A friend had one by her bedside. To my question, "What for?" she replied, "You have to be ready all the time." She didin't mean burglars; she meant murderers. That sense of fear had doubled after the mayor was gunned down in a nightclub. Bodyguards were common now and when one day I saw an odd-looking man reading the *Daily Bulletin* in the sitting room, I was quite surprised to know that he had been Papa's bodyguard for quite a while now. I had no idea. Two more men went around with him in his car.

Romy, this bodyguard in the sitting room, was short and wiry and very gentle. He spent the afternoon watching me read a book, conversed in a low, quiet tone, sotto voce, played cards with me. I couldn't envision him with a gun. As the weeks went by he hung around the house a lot and became our friend. Later on, I found out he had a law degree from a public university.

People with PhDs were sweeping the streets. This was probably the Southeast Asian country with the highest literacy rate. Everyone, it seemed, read and spoke English. Nationalism was changing all that.

Esther had got so nationalistic that she was dragging out ancestral corpses. She'd discovered that she was related to Jose Rizal, martyr of the La Liga Filipina, author of the *Noli Me Tangere,* which she made us all read, and *Mi Ultima Adios,* which she made us all recite, and the original of the statue gracing Luneta Park. People accepted him as a symbol of Free Filipinas. The Common Tao who couldn't speak Spanish went around gesticulating "Adios, patria adorada." Some scholars had translated his poems into Tagalog but it was taking a while for those verses to bite into the national consciousness. He had, after all, been dead for only sixty-three years, he was still fresh, some of his relatives were still alive.

Rizal was not encouraged reading at school. He did go after the friars and that bordered on being communist. Even though Recto's Rizal Bill passed, the nuns would let us read just the bowdlerized version, citing that only 25 pages were patriotic while 120 were against the faith. Or was that 170. Numbers flew around. Sis One had to read a pamphlet in religion class called "Statement of Catholic Hierarchy of the Philippines in the novels of Dr Jose Rizal, *Noli me tangere* and *El Filibusterismo,*" which very studiously noted for us the exact pages where one could find the attacks on Mother Church: in the *Noli,* 1950 Nueva edition: against confession, pages 26, 183, 191, 231, 232, 233, 277; baptism pages 263 . . . and so on through each dogma stained. I was convinced this man was executed not because he was a "traitor" to Spain but because he was an heretic. He was, after all, an ilustrado, a Europhile, and an assimilationist. The day he was arrested he was on his way to Cuba to serve as a doctor for Spain.

Esther persisted. Maybe it was again a part of her rebellion, but she bathed in that new glow. She had a root claim to the land. We'd stand underneath his stone top-coated statue in Luneta, feeling Filipino, while we ate balut, crushing the embryo duck egg between our teeth, picking out the odd feather. It would still be hot, just purchased from the night hawker who would call around the park, yelling rhythmically, "Baaa-luut! Baaa-luut!" Her ancestor, his eyes regally gazing out at some vision, had done his duty and ignored us.

Or perhaps he was thinking, looking over at Intramuros, "Is that the Ateneo? I spent many happy years there." His back to Manila Bay now, no traitor he to the sculptor. Then, when it was Bagumbayan, he acquiesced to the Spanish captain and faced the bay, but after the first shots were fired, he had turned himself around so that he could lie in death facing the sky. Just wouldn't play by the rules. Never trust an Asian poet in an overcoat. Legend said he had never worn a see-through Barong Tagalog. Pockets, like Papa said. It was all in the pockets.

We went to Luneta often to watch the sunset in Manila Bay. We had to go at night because there were few people there then, which made it a private party. The sunset over the water was an arpeggio of colours—orange, purple, rose. The sky was orange, the water was orange, and everything else—the ships, the little hill—was black silhouette, but before you were lulled into delusion by these warm hues, the sun set prestissimo, and suddenly it was all dark.

Very quickly colourful then dark.

I was having my usual nightmares. The house was so quiet. My aunts were in their rooms, each an imagined Mrs Rochester. Tina and Bienvenido were in the servants' quarters above the garage, across the back terrace. At least, I thought so. That was the usual order of things. Each member of the family was in the regular bedroom. There was a certain comfort in knowing all these trivial details, knowing the clock moved clockwise, knowing that tomorrow Romy would be in the sitting room, the nuns would greet us in the school's circular driveway, past the all-white Mary statue on the knoll in her garden guiding us all. It was like reviewing the troops before battle, riding up and down the thin red line, checking the gold-laced pelisse, the cherry-coloured pants, the royal blue, everything in its place.

I guessed it was because the house was so quiet that I stirred. I was lying in that half-awake state when the dream can be analyzed, when a part of one's self stands aside saying, *Wait a minute, isn't this character dead, why is he talking to you?* And then this disinterested Self, this detached Buddha begins to philosophize, saying things like Life is just one big solid monolithic memory bank and everyone is dead, each living moment sliding into death each moment, life only one moment even as it dies, until I, detached Buddha, unravel each memory-moment so that I am living in each memory-moment when in reality , in the real moment, everyone is dead. Something like that. The dream Self was not as articulate as the Romantic poets claimed it was, because they couldn't remember every philosophical word when they woke up.

Then an explosion of colours. By the time I had reached the hallway, the top floor was on fire. I couldn't get into my parents' bedroom and the smoke prevented me from peering into my sisters' rooms. I didn't know where anybody was. The sounds of shouts, curses, and general bedlam funnelled out of the smoke. I ran automatically towards my escape route. The grass was wet with dew. The breeze blew through my cotton nightgown chilling me to the bone. I lunged into the valley of death. In the blur, I saw bodies sprawled on the ground. I didn't know who they were but Mama's stories of war came to mind. She was walking fast through the rubble, past heaps of bodies, piled one on top of the other, and she was thinking, I must get to the other side, across the bridge, to safety. She lost a shoe, she took off the other, barefoot she struggled on, her whole attention focused on making it to safety.

I got to the tree at the north wall that we shared with the convent. I hadn't looked back or around, I was just running to this spot, charging as to a battery. At the top overhanging branch, I turned now, before I made my leap to the convent's tree, and saw the orange-purple-rose flames making a dawn of the night sky. It was dazzling—a glorious radial of colours, just bursting in frantic, inexorable abandon.

There was gunfire. I swung down onto the nuns' garden. I saw the brown habits swirl by the back door. They had come out to watch the blaze above the wall. They had probably wondered if the fire would reach them. Everything was connected, energy leaping past transitions, flowing one on to the other.

They rushed to me as I rushed to them. As they scooped me into their fold, I looked up at their anxious faces. My body grew limp in unalterable fatality. They were whites. They were next.

PART TWO

THE SECOND ORDER

Eight squadrons of Heavy Dragoons to be detached towards Balaclava to support the Turks, who are wavering.

Chapter Five

. . . trying to find a way of becoming what I would so much like to be and what I could be, if there weren't any other people living in the world.
—Anne Frank

Jennaryn, toritai, hana ichibomi,
Jennaryn, toritai, hana ichibomi.
Something like that. Probably was an obscene chant. We didn't know what it meant. Sis One was eight years old, 1945. The Japanese children would taunt her, call her name mispronounced, then chant, toritai hana ichibomi. It sounded like that.

Mama was walking home. She had to cross the bridge at Pasig. Somewhere in the rubble she lost her shoe. Bodies were piled all around her. The stench was unbearable. Why was she out there? I couldn't remember. The story has been told to us over and over. It melted within the other stories.

They were rounded up in a field, she, Papa, we children, two other families, a young woman. The soldiers were going to kill us, there was just some momentary hesitation and discussion. Probably waiting for orders. Why did the captain hesitate? Had not everyone here seen them herd people into a church and machine-gun them down? The young woman talked to the captors in Japanese. The soldiers were surprised, pleased, released us. Language saved us. What did she say?

Whenever the air raid sirens sounded, Sis Two would wet herself. Whenever the bombings started, I'd run under the table and mumble, "As I said, we should have gone to Azcarraga." Why there? I must have seen that street one day and thought it safe. Two years old and I spoke in a correct sentence structure. Two years old and already I was hiding, looking for an escape route. From the day we children were toilet-trained to a couple of years ago, a maid sat at the bathroom door to keep us company.

Ten years later, we'd incorporated the chant into our family repertoire, still without a clue to its meaning. Parts of that war, like shrapnel, were embedded in our psyche. Mama's nerves were shattered. Occasionally, she had a nervous breakdown. When she relived it for us, her whole body trembled.

Sometimes we didn't want to hear anymore, no more onomatopoeic associations, but I think she needed to tell us these stories because the images piled up inside her and they had to explode. They didn't make me hate the Japanese, although she ended with "Never turn your back on a Japanese." She told them so vividly that they were well-narrated tales of horror. I got mythic nightmares. My mind retold them in my head, refashioned into even more horrible configurations. But I grew up facing the Enemy over and over. I got to know him, his every move, his every thought. I was vigilant. I slept with one eye open.

After each nightmare, sweating, I ran to my parents' bedroom, dislodged the mosquito net on Mama's side and pushed her over. Some nightmares were played out for a whole week, so I automatically started out in my parents' bed and then I was carried to mine when I was fast asleep. The solution this year was to put my bed in their room. In other years, my bed was brought in to Sis Two's room where I discovered that she couldn't fall asleep without her US Army woollen blanket; and I thought I was disturbed. Other times, a maid slept on my floor. I rarely slept alone in fifteen years.

Papa's stories were less frightening. He was working as a journalist with a major local newspaper run by an American. He brought incriminating papers down to the basement and incinerated them over an empty gasoline barrel even while he heard the boots thumping upstairs. In this way, he saved the American. Because he was fighting the British then, the Japanese liked him. They brought in sacks of rice, which he promptly redistributed to Filipino friends. He kept many families alive with all the food he got, feeding off the enemy. Later on, in his trial, those families, some of them American, came out to testify on his behalf.

His bail was set at the same price as Laurel's, who had the misfortune of being President during the Occupation, but had it not been him, it would have been another one in the exclusive political hierarchy. They shared a cell. Recto and Madrigal were not too far away. Patriots and nationalists were terrorists and commies to the other. But in the world of Philippine moneyarchy, labels really didn't mean anything. Soriano and Zobel, Papa's business associates, were MacArthur's friends. So they were Franco supporters, the Manila Falange incarnate, but so was Fr Silvestre Sancho. And then there were the Religious sympathizers: the Dominicans, Fathers of St Francis, of St Agustin, the Ateneo, San Beda, and why not, Tabacalera! No Filipino collaborated with the Japanese or the Americans; each collaborated with the other. Osmeña was out; Roxas was in, so the Americans believed. Was there a line of MacArthur here? He was a blip in the radar of the metropolitan elite. We knew who our real friends were.

It was during those years of the Occupation that our tradition of having houseguests began. Filipinos and Americans, Indians and other Asians came and went for different numbers of months, quietly, secretly, bedded here and there in the house.

The hidden houseguests. Hiding was bred into us.

Maryknoll education was a "hidden life"—the life in Nazareth when Christ was being educated at home. Maryknoll education was Mary's life with Christ. Thus the nuns taught us. What did this mean? Selflessness, restoring the world to Christ and Christ to the world, and Mary learning from Christ, from Truth itself. We were being trained for leadership and right living.

October 9, 1955, Mother Mary Joseph, the foundress, died. The whole student body had been reciting the holy rosary continuously in the chapel, taking turns in groups, when we were first told that her sickness had turned critical. On the 10th when the nuns received the cablegram, everyone went into the Marian auditorium to recite the rosary led by the principal. A requiem mass was incorporated into the three-day retreat that followed for the college girls. Sis One went but because Sis Two was a senior and I was a freshman in high school, we stayed home. That was about the time Maria disappeared.

How simple life would have been if these hidden rules of behaviour had been made manifest, if the Bible left us clues, but then all was to be revealed later, in the Revelation. Meanwhile, we trusted the nuns who were showing our parents how to educate us by teaching us, the children, leadership and right living.

The next month, November 21, Fr Honorio Muñoz, O P, professor of ascetic and mystical theology at the University of Sto Tomas Central Seminary, gave us a talk on Mary-like standards in dress. We were all again in the auditorium, a splendid place where we spent half of our school hours, here this afternoon as part of the sodality reception day celebration. It was a pep talk, a prep talk, before the mammoth rally of December 8 at the Luneta Park for the Purity Crusade. Objective: modesty in dress. The Mary-like Modesty Dress Crusade made these four conditions: modest, stylish, selective, attractive. The school paper, *The Chi Rho*, featured students posed in Mary-like dresses. Esther and her cousin had their share: Esther's was a green, silk dress with tight-fitting puff sleeves, pearl collar and shirred bodice with a wide belt. Her cousin's was a printed nylon dress with a modest, round neckline and puffed sleeves, tulle sash ending in flowers.

I was twelve years old and loved veils. I might have been a Muslim just because they wore veils. The Crusade worked for me because I liked to be hidden.

Whenever I had a chance I would lose myself in Mama's collection of veils. She had one in every colour to match her clothes for Sunday mass. Some came from India in the purest silk with gold threads. Others were made here in this country from the finest European lace. Still others came from Godmother, after her annual pilgrimages, blessed from Lourdes, Rome, and Fatima. They were all neatly folded in a special drawer, all delicate and scented. Mama would put one carefully on her head, set in place by a special pearl-handled pin, as she sat in the car, just before disembarking at the church lot. It was the finishing touch.

While I liked playing with her veils, for church I wore only one, given to me by Sis One, a plain black lace triangle which covered my face at the sides, so I could concentrate on my prayers and not have to see anyone peripherally. I clipped it to my hair with a plain black hairpin, perpetually stuck onto it that it left a permanent rip on the veil. It seemed to me that the point of a veil was to hide one—not to attract attention to it and thus to one's person. I wanted very much to be an Arabian woman with her long black veil over her long black dress. *That* was Mary-like.

I pasted their photographs in my scrapbook, along with pictures of the Sahara. The desert, the bedouins on their camels, this Arabia, uncolonized—this was where I wanted to be. But Sis Two said it was very hot there and even dustier than Manila; so I returned to my first love, the frozen North, where I could wear overcoats and furry headcovers.

The following year in November once again, Saturday morning, the 24th, we were in our usual rows in the auditorium, rows and rows of uniformed girls in green skirts and tan blouses, listening to the principal explain the Divine Office. We were now to pray Prime instead of the decade of the rosary in the morning. The college seniors and juniors were to start on December 3, the sophomores and freshmen to join them by December 10. We high school students would have our day. Booklets were handed out.

"The Divine Office," the nun said, "is everyone's petitions brought together in one prayer, and thus eliminating individualism."

It was an interesting choice of words. I thought she meant communion, communal celebration, because individualism was an American virtue. Or thus we argued, Fina, Esther and I, afterwards.

"She didn't mean *eliminating* individualism, did she? Was that just imprecise diction?" I asked Fina.

"Did she say that? I wasn't listening."

"Don't Americans prize 'rugged individualism'?"

"Yeah, I think you're right."

"And each of us is unique," said Esther, who was indeed a unique girl.

The next month Colonel Nicanor Jimenez of the Armed Forces of the Philippines gave us a talk on the nature and dimension of communist threat in the Philippines. We were all back in the auditorium staring at huge posters and listening to a recording of communist speeches. Colonel Jimenez urged us to participate in events that would offset this aggression. He said that our Catholic Faith was the unifying force that would keep the nation together. It was December, 1956, the Huks were in the hills and Magsaysay was settling that communist problem.

"But I thought the Hukbalahap are rebelling because they want land, not that they're communists?"

"Where did you get that idea?" Esther said.

"From Papa. We talk about these things at the dinner table."

"They're dangerous. They're evil," Nilda said, her ponytail flicking.

I touched my cropped hair involuntarily. I had cried the whole hour the hairdresser sheared me and under the Martian hairdryer this weekend during my annual rape of the lock. "Suppose they're just poor and want land so they can farm for themselves?"

"Taruc? Have you seen pictures of that bandit?" Lita asked.

Fina joined us. "This school is so clean that the janitor wiped off my shoe scuffs even before I got out of the washroom."

"Next to Godliness," Esther chimed. "Anyway," she concluded, "anyone who's going about killing people and hiding in the hills can't be very good."

"What if he has no choice? What if he's the hunted?"

Nilda and Lita looked at me with disapproval. That Papa of yours, dangerous ideas. Everyone saw gargoyles melded on cathedral walls.

The Dean's Assembly every Tuesday of the month called us to the auditorium again. Here we heard her talk for thirty minutes on various topics, such as the importance of a Catholic education, and on this date, at 3:30 p.m., on the "Importance of You" as children of God where the individual is important, and everybody counted so participate in all school activities.

Back again to renew our annual consecration to the Sacred Heart of Jesus, a thirty-minute ceremony, Holy Benediction and Act of Consecration, followed by a short talk by a Jesuit priest, exposition of the Blessed Sacrament and singing of hymns.

Lita nudged me as my voice rose because I was out of tune and jarred her nerves. So I shrugged and mouthed the words instead, just in case one of the lay faculty members turned around and wondered why I wasn't singing. At home, though, I sang these hymns aloud to my heart's content, alone in my room.

This priest said, "Jesus is the greatest lover anyone can have." I discussed

57

this with the gang afterwards.

We were so constantly looking up at the stage that life was a drama to us. Life revolved around a stage, we en masse as captive audience, or we on the stage playing out yet another role. But of course we were in the Marian Auditorium to watch and listen to the visiting guests that we wanted to watch and listen to: the Ateneo Glee Club, prime example.

The Jesuits and Dominicans so badly wanted us to be good, they could just taste it. The force of their faith brought us all up to their rules of behaviour, their way of thinking. Praying was now inbred, we automatically prayed for anything and everything, anytime and everytime. If we missed daily mass and communion, we felt guilty. We were all little missionaries, their mirror images. We looked up to them, literally on stage, we all wanted to be priests and nuns too. I am certain that ninety-nine percent of Ateneans and Maryknollers had at one time during their school years fervently wished for a vocation. Both my sisters wanted it and the boys told me that they thought I was very religious and wanted to be a nun. But, so were they religious. On a Sunday outing, we had to wait in the car while Dave and Tony went to Sto Domingo Church because they hadn't gone to mass in the morning. We all said that one more extra prayer to the Blessed Mother just before going to sleep. Sis Two said this was what would save our souls as a last chance. As Baudelaire lamented, we automatically made the sign of the cross before going to bed.

The Blessed Mother, aside from being the country's patroness, presided over our daily lives. All through the work of the untiring missionaries. It was really quite a remarkable effort. They'd certainly saved their own souls and a great number of ours, as well. They demanded heavy penances and drive from us, just as they did of themselves. They wanted martyrdom for themselves and bred that thought in us: thus, Thomas More for the men, Joan of Arc for the women, Maria Goretti for the girls. We all came out of lectures, speeches, private talks, dinner conversations, parent-teacher nights, party exchanges, wanting to die for God if called upon to do so, by our noble standards.

There are times I cannot help but see them in the light of Kali. God seems to be a machine that devours sons and daughters. Why must there be heroes, why must my child die?

Sis Two came home very tired twice a week from having taught for half an hour in the slums, Kuliat, Old Balara, Quirino Projects 2 and 4, she taught during lunch hour or after school, taken there in the school bus on dusty roads, confronted by putrid and rancid rooms, and children who were fed with missionary words.

But it was an overwhelming situation. I supposed the Religious knew this; they were not stupid. Perhaps the plan was to nurture us into action for our people in the future—they spoke all the time of planting, a seed that grows. Certainly their schools were successful because the students were cooperative. While the student body came from wealthy homes, were creative and intelligent, full of idealism and energy, the schools would run smoothly.

And they did. My sisters and their gangmates were presidents of their classes, in the SAC, the newspapers and literary journals, in plays, in paper and bottle drives, leading everyone else in active participation, all done cheerfully and to the glory of God, and with fun besides, we were all very happy under the skillful guidance of the nuns and priests. As long as the money held out. Without the financial backing, our schools would deteriorate, become second-class, and the flow of resources would be curtailed, and even if new nuns were brought in from the States to replenish us with the latest, if we, the students, could not keep the base going, we would see a decline. Even now, many of us were leaving for studies abroad. The tendency was to send children for further education outside the country and oftentimes they stayed out. They might come back for a year but once they'd tasted the freedom of American universities, of French streets, then there was no more holding them back. If we continued to leave, the schools would not retain its old flavour. The new breed would be different—it would be money, not land. At the American Embassy I overheard a Filipino protest, "But my parents own lands in the province!" to which the haughty clerk said, "Well, that's not money, is it?"

But a Jesuit turned to me at the dinner table: "We have formed you. Wherever you go you will take that formation. Give me a child before the age of seven and I will show you the man."

"Ah, so we are doomed," I answered. "We will have to die for God as you so wish for yourself."

"It is what God asked of His Son."

"But He was saving the world."

"And so are you."

Never argue with a Jesuit.

I tried my theory out instead with Sis One.

"If Christ had already saved the world, why does it need saving again? And again?"

"He was our example. He said follow me. Do as I do."

"Yes, but my question is, was the world not already saved?"

It's a cycle, needs repeating. Man's nature. Constant vigilance. War of good and evil. Such were her key words.

These constant battles and war images troubled me.

Onward, Christian soldiers!
Marching as to war
With the Cross of Jesus
Going on before.
Christ the royal Master
Leads against the foe
Forward into battle
See His banners go!

Somehow I cannot see Christ doing this aggressive act; but then, what do I know of men?

"Why don't we just share the wealth, that way we wouldn't have these conflicts?"

"Well, I'm willing to," Sis One said solemnly.

"That's very naive," Esther said, in school. "It's more complicated than that."

What could be more complicated than the war of good and evil?

"Those are simple abstracts," Sis Two said, at home. "Nothing complicated in them."

Easy for her to say; her faith made everything simple. And she didn't even leap for it.

I watched Sis One write her cosmology report on Aquinas's *Summa Theologiae*. I had read all her books in the past four years of her college, so I could keep up with her writing. I read St Thomas as well, mindful that Pope Leo XIII in *Aeterni Patris* had made his work required reading for theological students and that his teaching was the official Church. But the owl of Minerva had to unfold for me at dusk, so I ended up singing "Adore te devote" instead. What to him was an affirmation after understanding, to me hymns filled the void.

Chapter Six

"Oh God of loveliness . . . "

I was back in Papa's library writing my tract on Christ, among the heavily scented brown leather furniture, and the three blind mice looking down on me. I was sitting, legs curled up under my buttocks, small in the ugly brown armchair.

Christ's dilemma. Had his mother been more aggressive, less silent, less compliant, she may have healed him. She saw how he suffered, she, Mater Dolorosa, Our Lady of Sorrows. She suffered watching him suffer. What a life. To have borne a child into the world, just to see it suffer. And be unable to do anything about it. There were other Biblical women who were strong—Judith, Ruth. Could she have done something? Gone out with him on his search? Maybe she had other smaller children, Joseph's, she had to stay home, another cause of separation, Jesus being the only son from that other father. Was there a stigma?

Did Jesus feel he had to leave home? Why would anyone go away from domestic comforts, live under the onslaughts of nature, unless he felt he had to go (a) because he felt unwanted or was like an extra thumb, and (b) he was looking for something or someone. Theology aside, which was that he had to go about his father's business, i.e., to do God's Will (or did he mean: I have to do something about this father business which has been disturbing me for so long?) he did leave home, not to get married which was the usual route out. When did he go? Did he hang around after the age of twelve until he was thirty? That sounded unlikely. If he did, it must have been hell at home, being the odd one. And if it wasn't hell, he didn't have to go out in such a self-discovery way if his mother had been able to heal him during the eighteen years she had a chance to do something for him.

No, he must have left a year after he was found in the Temple, which was his first break, his first attempt to find himself/his father, at age thirteen, fourteen, or fifteen. Say fifteen. He must have left then, a child wandering among the people, on his own. What he must have learned. What he must have done. Fifteen years later, he emerged as a man, seasoned by life. His hair was long and matted, his body was thin, clothed in one long gown, presumably dirty, his feet were grimy and needed to be cleaned periodically by Magdalene's tears or hair and scented by Mary's bowl of oils. His speech pattern lacked transitions. He had boiled words down to their essences. He had reduced them to symbols. Signs and symbols.

If I were his mother, I would have cried to see him so physically unhealthy. I would have worried about the low-lifes he associated with, I, the housewife who stayed at home to raise these healthy normal children. I would have worried about the hours he kept, the food and drink he took, the parties with drunks, fishermen who had abandoned their jobs, i.e., the unemployed, the bums, the prostitutes. Theology aside, this was going too far. He had done everything socially unacceptable. But then again, was this not what happened to abandoned, wounded, neglected children? Do they not go out and hurt themselves, lead unhealthy, lost lives from fifteen (or earlier) to thirty?

He no longer read. He drew lines on the sand. He carried no books or writing tools with him. He may have brought them with him when he first started out, but as with all his things, he had lost them along the way. He, too, was neglectful. He had not appreciated things and now they didn't mean anything anymore since he was focused on only one thing. In fact he told people to give away their things because they were encumbrances. A man who was constantly on the move would travel light. And since he had learned to reduce everything to the bare bones, things were inessential. Why carry a chair on your back in the summer heat? Sit on the ground. This from the carpenter's son who must have seen a lot of chairs around. Probably was happy not to have to make anymore, let alone carry one. So what did he have? Not even a bowl for food and washing. Just himself in his robe and sandals. I would worry about this son. There's some psychological damage here.

He didn't work. He expected to be fed and cleaned by others or to share whatever in his community. He was now a holy man. He interpreted the signs and symbols for us. Thankfully, he wasn't just a bum. He had found his destiny. He had had his confrontation with his father in the Garden and he had to accept the dying of a horrific death if he wished to have his father's love. Pitiful but a logical outcome of an abandoned child's desire to be reinstated in his father's favour.

Dad, look at me. I've been so wretched looking for you and still I'm willing to suffer even more, if you will only love me. I have been loved. Women and men have loved me. People listen to my words. They follow me everywhere, I have to run away from them to get some privacy. I have a faithful band of men who go with me everywhere—my gang, my body-guards, my friends. I have friends. I have lots of friends. I am on stage. I am a poet, a speechmaker, a lyricist, a songwriter, a figurative language maker. I am loved. I am controversial—those who hate me are wrong, misguided, pharisees, rich people who should know better, fundamentalists, readers of the letter of the law, conservatives, tyrants, authority figures. I am the eternal rebel against social mores, the radical thinker and upsetter of old traditions, the anarchist, James Dean.

James Dean?

I extricated myself from the clinging leather chair to go to the kitchen for a snack.

Let's go back to the Garden. Having rounded up support for his demands, by going about the country on speaking engagements, lecturing and teaching people the Our Father, getting people to repeat after him, remembering the words and believing in their rightness, Christ then presented his case to God the Father. Here, you see, these are reasonable and reasoned out. The people are backing me up, they're behind me one hundred percent. You have to listen to the people's voice. It's democratic. Listen. They're singing my song. It's a popular, catchy tune.

OK. Since this is a negotiation, if I were to accept your terms, you'll have to do something for me.

Sounds fair. You scratch my back, I'll scratch yours. What are your terms?

Only one. You have to die for them. You love those people so much, let's see you give up your life for them.

I can do that. You want me to take poison?

You're not getting off that easy, son. You have to die a slow, horrible death.

Oh, great. What's the point? Dead is dead.

I want to see you suffer. The fun is in the torture. Seriously, a polished stone becomes a gem. Dead is dead. It's all in the art of dying.

Gee, Dad.

I knew you'd back down. Not man enough, eh?

Oh no, I'm not saying no. But is there any other way?

Oh sure, there are all sorts of ways. But this is mine. If you want me, you'll have to pay for it and dearly. I don't come cheap. I'm worth it, too. You've got some pretty heavy demands there, son. If you want me to save you, you have to save others too. I expect you to work for your benefits, not just for your wages. Talking about work, you chose not to work for your living the normal way. I gave you a foster father with a good steady job but you thumbed your nose to the carpenter—OK, you chose to do my work on earth as you've bummed off others all these years, you'll have to pay back your debt to society by making them acceptable to me.

What happens if I don't accept your terms?

Then it's no go. I'll keep on rejecting you. You want me to love you, then prove to me that you can love back all those people who you say love you.

I guess I've compromised myself.

Yeah, you have to finish what you started.

OK, I accept this cup, bitter though the taste may be.

Yeah, you based your premise on LOVE, and love is bitter. The Greeks say it's a disease, you know. Or, I suppose, you don't know, because you haven't been reading much lately.

I wanted to tell Christ something. I didn't know what it was like to have a father-son relationship, since I was a woman and I had no brother whom I could observe, but, if I were God, I wouldn't be so hard. I thought I'd see how much this poor son wanted me to love him, and ragged, dirty and smelly though he was, I'd embrace him and say, I see the deep desire you have, I see your love for me, I see what you want, I see what you lack, let me take you in, let me fill you with my love, you don't have to prove anything to me, I'll take you as you are. As for that other thing, restoring humanity to me, I'll think up another solution. I'm master of alternative thinking.

I wished I could understand how men thought and acted towards each other, particularly in this very basic father-son business, so I could understand the God-Christ situation. I won first place in the national catechism contest during Marian Year because I memorized the catechism word for word. To know Him, to love Him, and to serve Him. I hadn't gone past the first infinitive. Ad finitum.

Reading over what I wrote a few days ago, I saw how easy it was to be irreverent. Let's look at this JC thing reverently. Begin again. Let us look at the question of Christ's humanity with reverence.

Suppose Mary was effective in healing her son because she *was* so patient, gentle and obedient to God, her "husband" and Lord. In cases of abandoned children, maybe silence worked. Don't talk to me about him, you don't want to know, the things I could tell you. Oy vey.

I saw I was slipping into irreverence again. I was no Kierkegaard with obtuse heart-rending dark words nor a St Theresa with clear heart-wrenching light words. I was a product of American cinema scriptwriters, movie language, mediocre film dialogue. Rebel without a cause.

In contrast to Rebel Jesus who had a cause.

So Mary healed him and at thirty, he took up the Cause. He *was* different, as she said, and he accepted that. Of royal birth, since God's kingdom towered above any that man might conceive. Was he not from the line of David and was David not a king? What he had to do was proclaim his royal lineage. So, Father was a king. But better than earthly kings, he was king of all worlds. As a king, He was too busy to attend to this son. He left him to a good woman who cared for him until it was time for him to go and do what he was born to do. What was that Cause? To die for all men.

It took some time for Christ to find out how this would come about. Prophets became his role model because they seemed to know signs and symbols best. So he expressed the prophet in him and discovered he had to die on the cross. It was the best way to fulfil God's will, to fulfill his birthright, his reason for being. And so he took up his cross and died.

It helped to know the sign that he would rise again three days later and in greater glory.

As for being in a bad physical state, looking once again from the point of view of a mother, that may have been acceptable since that's how prophets dressed and smelled. It came with the territory. In any case, that wasn't the point of being a prophet. It was the Cause. The First Cause, the Uncaused Cause. What was this flesh? We must concentrate on the spirit, on God. Everything else meant nothing. If I could see that my son was focused on this highest state of creativity, on the Creator Itself, I too would want him to die if this was the covenant. We are of noble birth. The higher the rank, the greater the responsibility to the people. The royal sacrifice. Aside from the question of love, there was the question of noble obligation.

Chapter Seven

> ". . . how worthy to possess
> your heart's devoted love."
> —A Catholic hymn

While I wrestled to know God, Sis Two loved Him without question. Blindly, as in blind faith. She acted like the peasants who swarmed Quiapo Church, moving towards the altar on their knees, white handkerchief on the floor, rosary in hand. They knelt there, praying loudly, then lifted one knee to peel the handkerchief off, lay it on the next square in front of them, then thrust their knee forward back onto the cloth, propelling the rest of their body on. Thus, inch by inch, they moved closer to God.

Sis Two never thought of theology. She got an A in Schola Cantorum because she sang God's praises eloquently. She didn't win in the Marian Year catechism contest because she never opened the tiny blue book. She didn't have to. She knew God already; she just loved Him. That was that.

Sis One served Him. She, too, got first prize in the famous contest, university students' category. She knew her Catechism by mind, heart, and soul. Each day she proved her mettle by going out to the poor and in helping them, served God. She went to daily Mass, received daily Holy Communion, went to weekly confession, observed all the rites for all the liturgical seasons, prayed on her knees even when no one was watching, was a member of the Sodality, and wore the blue and white outfit regularly, took off her brown scapular only when she showered, and kept the gold cross necklace on each moment of her life. She wrote a poem called, "I Am a Christian."

Her room was decorated with pictures of the Holy Family, Christ alone, Mary alone, the saints, the current pope, and sculptures of the same emerged from nooks and surfaces. She had a collection of rosaries from Italy, France, Spain, because friends couldn't think of anything better to give her. The beads sparkled in coloured glass, emeralds and rubies from chains made of silver or gold. The linking squares or triangles (the Our Father or Glory Be) were sculptured silver pictures of the Holy Family in various permutations or inlaid precious stones. Some rosaries were so distractingly magnificent that the eye lingered on their design and God was dispelled from the mind. Some were scented, the smell of which was not only alluring but enough to knock one out senseless. To avoid all these, Sis One used her old wooden black rosary from Lourdes, brought back by my bizarre Godmother Conchita, who by some odd chance picked up a basic black to throw in among her usual glittering cache. Ah, fashion.

Sis One also had a collection of estampitas, holy cards which were exchanged among her friends, like baseball cards were among American boys; were handed out as prizes for say, an A in a religion quiz; were used as a bookmark, particularly in religious books, bought for their art value, for sheer beauty of composition; were given as the saint of the day or the month; were received in lieu of a proper gift or as an extra, a bonus, a one other thing on top of the usual; and as a general all-purpose thing to do, were automatically spread around school by the nuns and the what-have-yous, as amulets and charms to ward off the devils. Very popular, estampitas were owned by more schoolchildren than comics were.

A variation on them were the holy words instead of holy pictures. Sis One's favourites were St Ignatius Loyola's, St Francis of Assisi's, and St Margaret of Alacoque's. The holy-words cards pierced her missal at nearly every fifteenth page forming mini-spines from which the thin onionskin pages drooped, and when she opened it they all sprung up like a pop-up book or spectres from the graves, soldiers of God ready for the battle. She took one out, read it fervently, then slipped it back into its original position without a dent on any of the others, as though each soldier stood on guard while the other performed its duty. Of course, she knew these prayers or wise thoughts by heart but she read then off the cards, anyway.

And then there were the holy cards with indulgences. These were most unpoetic and had to be read because they were most unmemorable. Their prosaic measures had no rhythm, their diction was imprecise. It was as if they were written by some Italian secretary to the Pope's assistant secretary, the two having had 1000 English words between them. They had a Nihil Obstat and an Imprimatur and a guarantee of several years off one's stay in Purgatory. One used these cards as often as one could, just in case. For the hell of it, as Americans would say.

Duly armed, Sis One would go to Heaven. She did everything right. Sis Two would join her because God is Love. And I? I struggled with the first infinitive.

Chapter Eight

> This life a theatre we well may call,
> Where every actor must perform
> with art;
> Or laugh it through and make
> a farce of all,
> Or learn to bear with grace
> his tragic part.
>
> —Palladas

Because Bienvenido was just learning English with Papa, he mixed up his verb tenses. I never knew whether he was in the present or the past. Time flowed for him in a tidal manner and only he knew where he was at the moment. It was very confusing. He was both order and disorder. Keeping up with him was a Holmesian challenge. So, Watson, what the devil was Bienvenido saying?

We were in the car now to pick up Mama who had been playing mahjong for three days now. Papa had finally sent the car to get her once and for all. We were on our way to Mrs Wu's house, which was the Tong for this round. It was said that Mrs Wu could play mahjong for a week at a stretch, getting up from her seat only to go to the washroom. People said that she had to be carried off at the end of the week because her back was so painful she couldn't get up on her own.

She lived in Parañaque when she could have lived in Forbes Park. It had something to do with her philosophy of life. People said that when she withdrew money from the bank she put the hundreds and hundreds of bills into a straw bag so that it looked like she'd just been out shopping for fish.

Her house was not at all ostentatious from the outside. The fence was barely high; one could sit on top of it and eat peanuts. The grass was fairly high; one could swing at the tops of dandelions and see them fly. There were no trees. If we had sped past, we wouldn't have looked twice. It was dark for one thing, roof made of corrugated iron, the facade uninviting, a grey concrete with unobtrusive squares for windows.

Bienvenido parked the car on the street, beside a narrow canal with stagnant water. The gate was big enough for a person, not a car. There must have been an alley somewhere, to let the cars get through to the garage. The new rich always owned more than one car. Behind the house, however, was the sea. Journey across the length of the city and then: "The sea, the sea!"

I went in with Bienvenido. The gate squealed for lack of oiling. We were greeted by a young uniformed servant, another sign of the new rich, very tacky, Mama thought. The square concrete facade opened into a courtyard. When the doors closed behind us we seemed to have left the Philippines and entered China. Huge stone animals, their mouths open, glowered at us. Street sounds vanished.

The next door led us to a long hall. There were little streams, fountains and bridges here and there. It felt like an aquarium, we the fish sailing by. There were ponds, in fact, with fish, and Bienvenido said, they looked like they were cultured.

Past the hall was another yard, this one open to the sky and made of earth. It was as though we had stepped outside again, to a mini-farm. I heard the sounds of chickens. But this was ridiculous, I thought. Just two doors away was the city.

That door surely must lead to her living room. But no, we entered another square room that was empty and semi-dark. It was smaller than the other passages, giving us the illusion of box within box. There were stunning carvings of Buddha and other Dharmas, made of bronze and iron, some life-size, all life threatening, guarding our actions.

The servant opened the fourth door. From this room we could hear the muffled sounds of tiles banging on each other, and clinks of china. Seven half-moon archways teased us like Fun House mirrors. Where were they? Which was the true entrance?

As if sensing our question, the young man turned around and smiled at us. He looked positively diabolical—as though he had lured us to his trap. Stepping into and waving aside his web in one motion of bravado, I lunged through one archway. It *was* a living room but they weren't there. What were there were a thousand green plants, hanging from the ceiling, draping from the floor, darting from the panelling—little plants from ceramic pots, huge plants from clay planters, splendiferous plants whose foliage concealed their containers—plants, all of them artificial.

"This way," the young devil murmured gleefully.

True enough, there was Mrs Wu, fat and inscrutable, and her warring allies deployed in six gaming tables, Mama in one of them, looking half-dead in battle-fatigue. There was little chatter, just all intensity and strategy. We were greeted with temporary cheer at Mrs Wu's table where Mama sat and I had to kiss all the damp women around as I was introduced. It was not appreciated that Mama had to go but they may have secretly been jealous that she *could* go. They blamed it all, of course, on Papa, her foreign husband. In any case, her replacement had not yet arrived so we were dismissed to sit and watch, which was no fun, or wait in another room. We were fed.

The scent of myriad perfumes hung in the air. No windows were visible so we must have been breathing trapped air. A large oscillating fan distributed the mixture of odours so one could not attribute individual smells to their owners. When Bienvenido moved to light a cigarette, he was asked to wait in the car.

Click, click, click. The rhythm of the game was making me sleepy. I couldn't comprehend how they kept up their concentration. The tiles were beautiful, ivory on one side, deep green on the other. The dragons, winds, flowers, characters, bamboo sticks, balls cut into the tiles, were works of art in bright red and black. I wanted a set for my military games. The women were not playing Mandarin but Filipino style—sixteen tiles, simplified flowers, different scoring system.

My eyes fixed on Mrs Wu's hair. It was dyed blue black, bunched heavily on top of her head, every wisp tucked in and lacquered. It didn't look slept in. A geisha would have envied it. Everything about her was plastic and unreal.

"Chinese?" Mama replied sleepily in the car. "Mrs Wu is a Filipina married to a Chinese businessman."

That explained it.

Later on, Papa forbade Mama to cultivate that friendship.

Chess was our game. Susan, Sis One's gangmate, and I were playing chess when Rick phoned, so Sis Two talked with him for a while, then Susan took over because it was my turn at the board. When I finally got to him he said it had been three weeks since we last talked, and that had been a particularly nasty quarrel. I calculated nine days. He said he didn't want to call me too often because I might say it's him again. Holy smokes! He didn't know the third of it. In spite of the fact that he lied a lot. He said he was in Laguna then phoned, forgetting he said he'd be away. He said he had to hang up because his mother was there, and I thought, how does his mother know he's talking to a girl? Sis Two told me he was using techniques on me, that this was what boys did. I didn't understand these things—why bother to use these techniques? I had already chosen him. Sis Two explained it kept the flames going.

"You know all those Filipino businessmen who go to Japan? The wives here worry about how their husbands fall for the geishas."

"So that's why wives pamper themselves so?"

"Yes, they have to maintain the interest. Lots of competition out there. You have to be resourceful."

Conquered by Japanese soldiers then, by Japanese women now.

But is not love struck once and forever? So what did that Jesuit priest mean when he said Jesus was the greatest lover anyone could have?

"Charity," Fina answered. "Love here means charity."

"Not ecstasy? As in the cases of Margaret of Cortona, Teresa of Avila, John of the Cross?"

Esther said, "You read too much into things. You mustn't listen too hard when these lectures are given."

"Stop interpreting and just accept what they say," Nilda added.

"But they have to be clear," I insisted. "Otherwise their words will have to fall into interpretation. They can't just throw out a sentence here and there. What do they mean, what do they mean?"

"She's in a state," Esther said calmly. "She drives herself into ecstasies over casual words—"

"That's it, they mustn't be casual."

"—and we all already know what these words mean. Now look, you're going to give yourself a headache. Why do you do this to yourself? Let's go to Melico Fountain after school."

We did and to "Maracaibo" afterwards. These weekly and weekend outings made me tired, too tired to go to school. I was constantly tired.

Casual words surrounded us, too, at parties. It was as though everyone was determined to live casually by casual words. Boys said I love you, don't make me jealous, wow, can you dance; they flattered, cajoled, and pleaded their needs and wants. The girls' heads were turned, right around, or at Watteau's 135° angle. We were compositions for admiring.

"It's great fun," Esther said, passing the jar of Horlick's around. "Don't be a killjoy, go along with the fun."

"You want to be left out?" Nilda said. "Everyone says sweet things to everybody."

At home, Sis Two said I was too abrasive. I should be sweeter to the boys at parties. I should powder myself, change my clothes for the visitors, comb my hair. Rick was annoyed everytime he visited because I met him with my hair uncombed. He wanted me to prepare myself for him. I said that he had to accept me as I was, that people had to accept me as I was. They may, he answered, but how many will be courting? I strove to be sweet for a few days but my true self resurfaced. I knew that eventually being myself would be the ruin of me. I would be left out. I would be a spinster.

"Yes," Esther agreed. "You'll end up without a lover, without a husband."

No fate worse than this. Marriage was the goal.

"You have to get married or be a nun," Nilda said. The two choices left to us.

"Jesus is the greatest lover of them all," Esther mocked my interpretation.

"She will stand in grand solitude," Fina intoned while piercing her fine hair with sharp stems of wild roses. "Ever at the crossroads, with the orange sun behind her, fixed in time."

Fixed in time? Horrors. Pinned to the wall.

"I think the nunnery flourished during the plague," I said.

Married to Christ.

To be Christ's wife, what greater accomplishment? Better than the bank director's wife or the president's wife. But how polygamous. The very idea of this perverse harem, billions of women throughout the ages of Christianity giving themselves to Christ was demeaning to him and degrading to a woman: though she had committed herself to him alone, he had not. Who wanted a husband who shared himself all over the place? The Holy Phallos. Who wanted to be a mere vessel, waiting a turn in line, waiting to be called at his whim, drawing yellow lines on one's face for adornment, for fantasy, to entice him. Take me! Take me! Jesus never asked for this kind of woman; if anything, as with Mary of Magdala, he took her away from the line-up.

I watched my aunt profess, prostrate on the cold cement floor of the altar, her arms outstretched like Jesus on the cross, consecrated virgin, a spiritual coupling, a mystic illusion, Christ's bride in this holiest of marriages, and she proudly showed us her gold ring afterwards at the reception, then she left in a shroud of robes, and we never saw her again.

"In heaven," I told my sweet gangmates, "there are no marriages."

"So what?" Esther retorted. "This is the earth."

"I mean, if heaven is the perfect state, the perfect state is singlehood."

"Well, that makes sense, doesn't it?" From Fina. "You can't have any babies in heaven."

"We must perpetuate the species," Esther said.

"For this imperfect earth, the perfect state is marriage."

For once, the two girls were in agreement against me.

"You have one half nuns, one half mothers. Balance of nature." Yet again from Nilda, who was one-track minded.

"Absolutely nothing in between? Just one or the other?" I asked.

"Yes," they said in unison.

"Then I'd go for the one closest to heaven's perfection. Wouldn't you?"

"Are you crazy? Be like Sr St Anthony?" Esther's voice rose.
"I'm going to have five kids," Nilda said.
There went her model figure.

Chapter Nine

For the degradation of being a slave is only equalled by the degradation of being a master.   —Virginia Woolf

Half-day.

The white walls of Maryknoll receded in the distance as we drove towards Katipunan road, the white walls a shield bouncing off the pellets of the noonday sun. There, within, were the hands that shaped our lives, the minds that directed us.

I had just had an encounter with one of these spines under the armour, just a few ten minutes before I hopped into the car. I was on my way to the circular driveway, my head up in the air as was my posture, when Sr St Anthony brought me up to attention.

"Young lady, you do not pass by a piece of paper without picking it up." Her thin finger pointed down to a candy wrapper behind me.

I had to turn around and look down to see it. If she had seen it, why didn't she pick it up?

I stopped, puzzled.

She took this for disobedience or rebellion. Pulling herself up taller than she already was, she continued to point down like an angel of death telling me where to go. Her face got redder and the seconds ticked. There was obviously no point in saying I hadn't seen it, had I seen it I would have picked it up, why not?—and if she had seen it before I did, what stopped her from picking it up herself? Were we not all Americans, egalitarians, democratic citizens, children of God? I stooped down to pick it up, my fingernails digging into my palm. The act seemed like an obeisance to her upright figure, a dead idol, an image which may have quelled her temper, because she gave me a triumphant smile as I discarded the garbage into the bin.

What had she taught me?

There within the white walls lie the bones, wise as runic stones.

We had to pass by Ateneo first before going home because Sis Two had to see Fr A. Instead of waiting in the hot car, I walked around the grade school grounds. Since it was lunch time, the boys were eating at the long, low tables, their nannies sitting outside waiting for them to finish so they could be wiped, cleaned and powdered. I looked at bulletin boards full of children's drawings, paintings, printings, what nots. Mindful of the Sacred Heart, one board had hearts pinned on it—hearts cut out from white paper crayoned red in bold, uneven strokes, some dark blobs evidently pushed down so hard that the crayon broke and stuck to the paper. It reminded me of my elementary days when Sr Mary Jean described sin in the image of the heart: venial sin meant little red dots, mortal sin was one red stroke making the entire heart red. Grace wiped everything white again, after a good confession. No, the heart was not LOVE for me; it was the region of sin. When I returned to the car, it was so hot inside I felt like rushing to the washroom, when my bottom touched the seat.

After lunch we decided to go to Hollywood Theatre to see *King Creole* and *A Certain Smile*. As we were about to leave, Rick called to see if I wanted to go with him to see *Gigi*.

I asked Sis Two if we could go, but she said she was seeing *Gigi* tomorrow. "Sorry, but if you want to come with us, you're welcome."

"Have pity," Rick said.

"What does that mean?"

"KJ. You're a KJ."

That burned me up. "Well, you don't want to come with me, so you're a killjoy too." I banged the receiver down.

Sis Two and I left. When we arrived home at half past four, Mama and Papa who were sitting in the front garden said Rick and his friend had just left after asking for me. The maid had told them I had gone to the movies. I thought that he probably realized I was angry. In the evening he phoned to say that he and Ben were not on speaking terms because he had gone to the theatre looking for me, couldn't find me, missed softball practice, and so Ben got angry.

"Why did you look for me?"

"Don't you want me to do that?"

"Oh well, and I *was* in Hollywood Theatre."

"May I call you again tomorrow?"

"Of course. Why not?"

"Some girls don't want to be called more than twice a week."

"That's nonsense."

He laughed. "I'd like to give you a gift, but I don't know if you'll like it or not."

What circuitous ways. This young man puzzled me.

Just before supper Mama made me rewrite the essay I had written for

English class. It was too sketchy, she said, my thoughts were undeveloped.
"Expand it. It's too brief. Too many ideas not fully explained. Go sit in your room until you've got a sizeable number of pages."

To my back she added, "Drop by drop fills a tub." Close to tears, I plodded towards my bedroom. It was bad enough the first time around. English essays were devised to extinguish love of language.

She then turned around to Sis Two and told her to do her homework which she hadn't even begun. "Discipline," she said. "This entire household lacks discipline." She went out the kitchen to find more helpless souls to discipline.

Sis Two followed me up the steps, into my room with her books and we worked together in agony and silence. After half an hour, the essay still thin and insubstantial, her essay still unwritten, we stopped to talk. Long writing is for people who like solitude at elongated, protracted stretches.

She was breaking up with her boyfriend, much to Mama's relief because she didn't like his family, peninsulare though it was. Sis Two was going to return his love letters to him through another friend.

"Why are you breaking up? You look so nice together."

She was playing with the gold chain of the necklace he had given her, at the end of which hung a golden heart. "I don't know. I can't understand it. The feelings have gone away, from him, and I think, from me, too. Though I still like him. I feel very lonely. More than that, I think, I'm feeling . . . destroyed."

We talked on about feelings until Emiliana came in to call us at seven. Our homework lay unsullied. Suddenly worried Mama would want to see what we had accomplished, I asked the maid if Mama was home.

"No. She went to a despedida."

"Who's leaving?"

"Mrs Siy. Going to Europe," Sis Two answered.

"Again? I swear that woman only goes for a trip so she can regale us with stories. 'When I was in Rome . . .' she'll somehow get that phrase in when she comes to visit."

"Of course. Trips are for boasting."

"Not for education."

"Can you see Mrs Siy learning something new?"

While we were incarcerated, our friends had called and we had missed them all. Later, someone called and Sis One said I was busy. We were all in the TV room watching Boris Karloff. In a few minutes, Papa was passing by the phone when it rang and he said, she's outside bidding her friends goodbye. When the phone rang again, I answered it. It was an old friend of

Sis One's whose love she didn't reciprocate. We talked for a few minutes before I handed it to her. He said he was getting married in April. I was happy for him. He once told me that he was lonely and wanted a wife. At last, he had found someone.

In the early morning, Sis Two was very sick. She screamed in pain and said her arms and legs felt numb. Mama stayed up, rubbing her down with the holy water that Godmother had brought back from Lourdes. She finally fell asleep, but Mama sat beside her bed, because when we woke up we saw her in her soiled Mandarin housecoat, asleep on a chair, holding Sis Two's hand. When she woke up, she said Sis Two was cured by the holy water. Sis Two *did* seem perfectly fine.

While Sis Two rested at home, I had to attend the funeral of two of our classmates' father. They were Americans, twins, very tall and pretty, who distinguished themselves in baseball and tap dancing. At a drop of the hat, they'd get up on stage and go tap tap tap, *ti di di dum ti dum ti di, you love me. I love you in the morning and I love you in the night.* Their movements were smooth, coordinated, light; their voices harmonized.

Esther, Nilda, and I arrived at the funeral parlour, signed our names in a guest book, and condoled with the twins. Their mother was very brave, walking around the room as at a state reception. She had no veil on, and the black dress she wore was astonishingly smart. No stricken widow, she. She even smiled at us as we were introduced. She looked to me as if a great burden had been lifted off her. Are you all going back to the States? we asked. No, the twins replied. We're staying permanently in the Philippines. I wondered why people wouldn't want to go home when tragedy struck. Or was this home?

One of the twins, Gretchen, brought us over to where her father lay for viewing. I hesitated but Esther whispered we had to—custom, courtesy, that sort of thing. I expected something horrible, like a grey face, ashen skin, long fingernails; instead, he was pink, immaculately suited and looked like he had just gone to sleep. At first I was grateful for this but after a while, as we stood there for a few minutes over his open casket, ostensibly for private prayers, and as I glanced at Esther (indeed she seemed to be intoning the Hail Mary) I realized how awfully grotesque this display was. He wasn't asleep. He was dead and we were invading his privacy, two schoolgirls whom he had never met, gawking at him and he couldn't even wake up to say, go away, what are you looking at? And that makeup, that suit he probably hated wearing in his life—all false, what did they hide? Underneath all these embalming magic tricks was a rotting corpse. Life slid into bathos. I was bound to have nightmares tonight.

I nudged Esther to move along but she was deep in helping his spirit on to heaven. And I remembered those words etched on the glass window overlooking Runnymede, something about God being in Heaven and in Hell, and in the morning as their wings flew across the sky, God would always be with them, holding their hand. It was the finest memorial I had ever seen in my life, in Englefield Green, tucked away in some manor estate. We had a hard time getting out there but Papa refused to stand around the Buckingham Palace gates with the commoners and insisted that we find the RAF memorial so his friend drove us all the way to Surrey. Papa wept at the 20, 000 names, the Indians whose graves were unknown, bodies blown to hell (but God was there, too) all over some French countryside. Just a few more years, he said, and these fine young men would have had an independent country and they wouldn't have flown with the British. Just a few of them, I thought, look at the Canadians—over 3,000! The white stone walls were warm with care. The memorial had just been built, four years ago on the day we saw it, I was 13 then, just turned teen and thinking I could now die for a country, and if I did, how wonderful to be so lovingly remembered by those I left behind, in this simple classical style, in this quiet pastoral setting. Dying with so many others—the numbers comforted me. The cause comforted me.

But this man, this foreigner encoffined, lying before us in a tight grey suit with lipstick on, this man died alone, an American businessman in Manila, heart attack probably, we were too polite to ask how, during a business deal, making money, how crass his death seemed to me. No pilot he, braving enemy guns. Far from friends of his childhood, seated among brown men who looked at him and saw his white skin like a white canvas on which they painted their misconceptions of his character. Who knew him? Trapped now forever on foreign soil. Who will carve his memorial?

Finally, Esther turned and I followed. Still there were no tears, how well these Americans kept their grief private, but Gretchen occasionally looked at her father's coffin and her eyes would glaze over. Of course, she mourned, I chided myself for my insensitivity. There was always someone who would remember.

On the way home, Esther said it's pretty terrible, isn't it, I don't want to be buried, I'd rather be cremated.

That's against the teachings of the Church, I replied. You have to be buried on consecrated grounds so that on Judgement Day you can rise up with your fellow Catholics and God will know where you are.

That's silly, Esther scoffed. God knows where we are every minute.

"Anyway, it's a sin," I said, "to be cremated. You can't burn your holy body."

"They were burned sometimes in the middle ages."

"That's just because of the plague. There were extenuating circumstances—to protect the living."

"Well, I don't want to rot."

"You won't know the difference."

We fell silent for a few minutes. I was thinking of her grand entrance into the funeral parlour, how well she did that. She had been taking this course on how to finish herself, and one of the things to do was to arrive fashionably late, then pause at the entrance, look casually at the guests, eyes cool and somewhat distracted, forcing the others to look back at you and wonder who you are, and then direct one's eyes at the hostess and grandly float towards her while everyone whispers, my, how enchanting she looks. Esther had been practising this entrance at the parties recently; I didn't think she'd use it on this occasion as well.

"No on can die for you," she sighed heavily.

I agreed. "No, like the existentialists say, you're on your own on that one." So, she had not been praying as we stood over him. "Alone, the gunner in the sky, shot down."

"I'm going to die at home with everyone around me."

Alone, that was what made it frightening probably, because Mama, the servants, no one could accompany us, and I thought sleeping alone was frightening enough, what I didn't know . . . "If one had a home."

And then there's Pepys. 23 February 1669. He brought his wife and two girls to Westminster Abbey to show them the tombs. "And here we did see, by particular favour, the body of Queen Katherine of Valois . . . And I did kiss her mouth, reflecting upon it that I did kiss a Queen, and that this was my birthday, thirty-six years old, that I did first kiss a Queen."

Catherine, grandmother of the Tudor dynasty, Queen to Shakespeare's Patriot King, dead at thirty-six in 1437, lying open 232 years later when Pepys kissed her lips, and even in 1742 the skeleton still intact, the flesh like scrapings of tanned leather until her final rest in 1878. Was she a saint or was this a wonder of English embalming techniques? Was the kiss impertinence or a subject's adulation? *Reflecting upon it that I did kiss a Queen.* Joy of joys. Did they prefer their queens dead?

At one thirty-year period with 150 million diverse people under English rule, the English were going around the world destroying kingships while they venerated their own. What sense could be made of that? Why was their queen's civilization better than Tipu Sultan's? There were people back home who would kiss the lips of a dead queen. Ah, there within the white walls lie the bones, wise as runic stones.

The next day was entirely spent at Mama's friend's house. I had nothing to do but listen to them talk over coffee. Mrs Tolentino lived in Manila and Okinawa. In the latter she ran a business selling US Army surplus. When she was in Manila, she sold refrigerators from her house. The whole house, kitchen, living room, dining room, was stuffed full of shining refrigerators, vertical white empty coffins soon to be filled with dead meat in white sepulchral homes, with mirrorlike surfaces reflecting each other into material infinity, so packed closely together there was hardly any room to manoeuvre. It was a good thing she stayed in Manila only for a month or so. When she was divorced, after her husband left her and ran off with a younger woman, she had her flat nose altered in Okinawa, then found this job there. Mama said the nose surgery made her eyes come closer together. Okinawa also gave her a lot of money so she dressed differently now, more business suits, high heels. She looked quite stunning and confident. She used to be so poor Mama had to give her clothes. What a change this acquisition of money made. Mama liked her a lot. She said this woman deserved all the good things she now had because she had suffered deprivations. She had become so thin once Mama had to force-feed her; now she was still thin but fashionably so. It was hard work that paid off for her.

"Never be like Juan Tamad," she said to me as she handed me a glossy comics-size book on the folk hero and a bowlful of frizzy dark red mabolo.

I sat among the refrigerators reading and eating this apple-peach while they continued their animated conversation. They had that annoying Filipino habit of talking at the same time, followed by silence with their eyebrows raised to signify agreement or understanding. So Mrs Tolentino said, would you like a cup of coffee and I didn't hear Mama's reply but I heard the pouring. The only tête à tête habit Mama disdained was hitting the partner's shoulder to punctuate one's sentence—a body check akin to "do you follow what I'm saying?" or the tag "isn't it?"—as she would not touch the other unless it was politically useful. In any case, she presumed the other was listening properly to her every word.

Juan Tamad was so lazy he used to sit under the guava tree waiting for the fruit to rot and drop off. He couldn't even get up to pluck it off the branches. The illustration showed that the tree was quite low and all he had to do was extend an arm up. Juan, himself, was a burly, heavy-set Indio, healthy as a workhorse.

"Why was the native so lazy?" I asked Sis One.

"What do you mean? Filipinos are not lazy."

"I mean Juan Tamad, the legend."

"Oh that. That's just the picture the Spanish conjured up. They called us lazy because we wouldn't work for them. And I'm sure if one thought about this or did more research on it, one would find all kinds of explanation for it. Like the hot weather. Or that we had enough, we didn't feel we needed to accumulate."

"Mrs Tolentino's house is packed with refrigerators. She's a hard worker. She's no Juan Tamad."

"She's a capitalist."

I was looking for Sis Two but found out later that she had gone to the NCAA Basketball Championships at the Rizal Memorial Coliseum. The La Salle Archers were competing against our Ateneo Eagles, the Green against the Blue.

In the evening Rick phoned to invite me to their victory celebration but Papa and Mama wouldn't give their permission; too young to go out alone unless Sis Two would chaperone, but she had another party to go to.

On my way to isolate myself in my room, I saw Tina, the Redoubtable Laundress, coming down from her successful search-and-destroy mission of the bedrooms, a large round battered aluminum palanggana resting on her right hip, her right arm stretched to the tendon across the width of it. The satisfied smile on her face was for the dirty clothes up to her shoulders. On top of the pile I saw my yellow blouse with its slight stain, the one I casually draped over the dressing table because I thought it was still usable. In my room I discovered that the soiled jumper in my closet had disappeared. Servants not only anticipate our needs, they also think we're complete idiots incapable of caring for ourselves. The best servant is the one who thinks for us.

Chapter Ten

I have lost a day.
     —Augustus Caesar

Heavy tropical rains slowed our progress from Baclaran Church on our way back to Quezon City. We had to pass through Manila, on a direct route through Taft Avenue. Traffic was backed up for kilometres so Bienvenido decided to go via smaller streets. He cursed, inch by inch. The rain pummelled the hood and windows like a heavyweight, relentlessly boxing to knockout. Potholes, not as big or as deep as Tondo's Bienvenido assured me, made the drive even more hazardous because unseen under the rising flood. There was absolutely no drainage anywhere—water was contained within the streets. The city builders had covered up the natural esteros underneath Manila and so nature wreaked havoc on her defilement.

  Bienvenido's goal was to get to Quezon Boulevard, slightly better built and wider. We had now been in the car for two hours, just trying to cross at the Pasig River, a serpentine Thames that stretched from Laguna de Bay to Manila Bay through the heart of the city.

  His smoke filled the imprisoned air. Once in a while, he'd lower his window to freshen it and he'd curse as the rain hit his hair and shirt. Once in a while, I'd lower my window to defrost it and welcome the pelting rain. I'd see a glimpse of people huddled under awnings and umbrellas, people with newspapers or scarves on their heads, running to catch an overloaded jeepney or bus, people sloshing in undoubtedly thin shoes, soaked to levels of pneumonia. Each time I lowered the window the outside sounds impinged on our quietude: honking of horns, cursing, raised voices hailing any transportation passing by, surprised screams when tires whacked cold water onto frail bodies. "Oy!" They'd shout. "Ano ba!"

  The rain was torrential for about half an hour then there would be a respite for about twenty minutes, then it poured again for another half hour, but the flooding itself began within the first ten minutes of rain. Deep waist-length flood there, up-to-the-knees flood here, children frolicking, small cars fearing to pass, stream rising, jeepneys breaking down with wet brakes. The quick flashes of light across the wide gray sky were followed rapidly by the roll of artillery shells—thunder. Bombarded by the gods, petty abusive bosses who just this morning were hitting their wives and children, humiliating their secretaries, now stood about looking nervously at the earth's stronger weapons.

"Everytime it rains heavily, the streets fall apart," Bienvenido said. "It's those politicians and their cheap cement."

Then again before he could curse again, the car suddenly careened.

"Putang 'na," he muttered and I blushed to hear this obscenity. Somehow in Tagalog swear words sounded more sacrilegious. "Pothole."

"Deep enough to stop us," he assessed when he rushed back in, drenched. "There's a restaurant on this side of the street. You'll have to wait there."

My heart sank in fear. "Where will you be? What are you going to do?"

"There's a gas station near here. I'll get a mechanic, get some help."

I sidled out of the car in trepidation. He grabbed my arm and half-carried me across the way. My shoes got wet anyway. The café door banged shut like a leaden shield.

"I'll come back for you. Order something." He handed me a few pesos because I never carried money.

"Where? How?" I was near tears.

"Oy," he yelled. "Coke, nga. At yung biko." He pointed to a slab of brown square where a fly had just been. Then he set me at a counter stool and rushed back to the car he'd forgotten to lock. "Baka ninakaw na," he cursed, worried it'd be gone.

I sat frozen. My heart was thumping louder than the rain. To get there we had pushed though a crowd milled in front of the restaurant like shivering monkeys on tree branches. They looked like office workers at rush hour, going home. No one had expected the rain; it had just burst upon us.

Inside the small café were a handful of customers. Wet though it may have been, people were pressed to stay outside and try their luck at getting rides home. There were, aside from the proprietor and me, only six others, one of whom was a child, possibly my age. She had lain, full-length, on a wooden board behind the counter, near a curtained-off room which must have been their living quarters, but when she caught my eye she sat at the other end of the six-places counter, directly opposite me. She had the same blue-black hair, except where mine was long and braided across my head, hers floated around her cadaverous face in gossamer wings. She was skeletal thin whereas I was merely slender, over her frame hung a short shapeless brown dress. This in contrast to my jade Thai silk suit, but my eyes went back to her eyes because there I saw such languor, it was as if they had just emerged from a deep sleep and awakening had not yet surfaced. About her also was an unnerving sadness that pressed her down, down to her hunched shoulders. We stared at each other.

The room was oppressive. The stale odour commingling with the damp atmosphere made me nauseous. Folded white napkins tucked in a grimy glass looked like wilted feathers of a soaked dove. There were six square tables with two to four chairs each, covered with cracked plastic geometrically-designed cloths.

I ignored the girl and stared at the proprietor. He was wearing a once-white kamiseta, just this undershirt probably because he wanted to be comfortable on this long, dull, dark, soundless working day. Matted hair grew under his armpits. He smiled.

The five clients, all men, were drinking coffee or beer; two were together and the other three by themselves. The two men were talking earnestly over a column, Teodoro Valencia's "Over a Cup of Coffee," which I had read yesterday, about a political scandal yet again. They were arguing now heatedly. It was amazing how the whole country could discuss politics, it was all they discussed, they lived, breathed, and drank political news.

I looked at my biko. The fork, of course, was dirty.

Don't you like it? the proprietor said in Tagalog. I was taken aback by his rapid and harsh intonation, natural to the sound of the language. At home our Tagalog was softened by Mama's southern accent, very sweet and slow. I stared at him. He shrugged and walked away. I touched nothing. My heart had settled and now I was just numb. What took Bienvenido so long? Why couldn't this by M Y San in Escolta? Or even Botica Boie.

"Madalena." I heard a hoarse voice call feebly from behind the curtain.

The girl twitched as though cataleptic. She fixed me a last vacant gaze and in a tremulous, agitated quaver she replied, "Po!" and passed slowly out of the room. I stared astonished at her vanishing form. She was like a phantasmagoric figure that sailed past gothic tunnels and windless halls, a mad girl buried alive.

I was glad to quit this twin when Bienvenido burst in. "It's impossible," he half-shouted. "I got you a taxi." He was so wet his clothes melted into his muscles. "Hurry. We might lose him."

Everyone stared at us silently. The proprietor foolishly smiled goodbye. That perpetual Filipino smile, through sun or storm. Papa said you just can't take them seriously, they're perpetually smiling.

I scrambled off the stool and rushed out. Once again, the door shut behind us like a massive iron grating on its hinges. The rain had abated.

"A typhoon," Bienvenido announced. "This is the lull before it breaks all hell loose."

The car was in the garage, he said. He would take me home first, then come back for it later. Luckily the taxi had waited. Once we got to Quezon Boulevard, it was smooth sailing. My heart was heavy, though; it could not shake off that experience of the awful café. I was sure to have nightmares tonight.

The taxi driver's gearbox grated churlishly. The rain had stopped as Bienvenido had predicted, a lull indeed. Just before we reached the house the engine throttled and choked and the driver asked us to walk the rest of the way. I ran on ahead as Bienvenido paid him and yelled after me, "You should take a warm shower, now that you're all wet, so you won't catch a cold."

An iciness, doubtless from the cool breeze now infecting its way into my wet skin, gripped me. Home, sanctuary, looked like bleak walls, damp hedges, gloomy trees. Why did I suddenly feel depression emanating from this house?

In front of the gate, water had collected like a black and lurid tarn from which I saw the house again, ghastly and melancholy. I half expected the thunderbolt, rending the roof fissure wide, to strike it to fragments, and with that sound of a thousand waters, the house would collapse in one Fall, because I had intimations of the horrors, but I *dared not speak!*

Chapter Eleven

Bahay kubo, kahit munti
Ang halaman doon ay sari sari

—Children's song.

The Justice, reading his Isak Dinesen, had joined me in his library while I waited for Sis One, who was swimming in his pool in the back yard with her gang, the TRALDIGETS. The name of the gang was coined from the initials of their boyfriends of the month. The pool was a modest rectangle, just slightly bigger than a fish pond. It suited his modest house, all wood, rotting at parts, to be renovated in the future.

He had just been outside to cut another rose from his wife's rose garden which he placed underneath her picture in the dining room. Feeling insomniac tonight, I suspected from his wandering around the house in his pyjamas, he had espied me and was now filling some waking hours with small talk.

I mentioned the plastic-flower woman. He suggested that Papa should not have bought such a large house. Why bother to acquire wealth, I said, if you can't enjoy it?

"Oh, you can enjoy it, just don't display it. Enjoyment is a private affair."

"People do buy houses for enjoyment, for their friends, for parties—"

"For others to gawk over, for showing off, look, eight bedrooms, five bathrooms. True friends don't care how many bathrooms you have."

I thought about this.

"How long do those parties last? If you should lose that big house, will those party friends follow you to the smaller house?"

"No, I guess not. Mama didn't want him to buy that house."

"Sensible woman, Miriam."

His maid poked her head in and out.

"The nature of people, as well, remember, is that it will envy those who have too much. You set yourself up for robberies. People who do not have will take from people who do."

"Do you mean as Sun Tzu says, an army advances if it thinks it will gain something?"

"Hmm, yes. There's that too."

The maid returned with cool pineapple juice in tall tumblers.

We drank quietly as we sat on his simply designed cloth furniture, surrounded by his glassed-in books, bookcases which lined the walls all the way to the ceiling. Books lay on the coffee table and the side tables, some partly read with bookmarks. Fresh flowers in glass vases sent off a mild pungency in the enclosed air.

"Enjoyment, pleasure, is private. You can be alone and be very pleased with life." He smiled briefly, enjoying his solitude. I had ceased to exist in the room.

"My sister thinks," I broke into his privacy, "that having wealth is immoral. We shouldn't have it in the first place. We should give it all away, walk out of the palace like Siddhartha, take only the tunic on our back, like Christ."

"Does she," he murmured, coming out of his depths.

"And be like the poor, be one with the poor."

"Be poor."

"Yes."

"That solves nothing. Poverty is immoral, too. It's wretched, unhealthy, disgusting. Why not strive for balance—just enough to live decently, and rationally, do not lord over your neighbour, share what you have, give the excess but keep grain in your stores for the famine, have enough so you don't have to think all the time about having, leave yourself time to think of more creative things, free to have culture once you have freed yourself from nature."

My eyes alighted on his Voltaire behind the glass. "Tend my little garden," I said.

"Yes, *do* have a garden when you build your house, Jazz. A rose garden. Tending it keeps you civilized." He was falling asleep, finally. It had come around again to his dead wife. Sanctuary.

He made to go. "To bed," he murmured to himself.

"Did you say that conflict is inherent to human nature?"

He stopped at the door and turned slowly. "No, I believe you made that assumption based on your reading of Sun Tzu."

I watched his leaving, in very slow and cautious minimal movements. I tried to go back to my reading but I was stuck with the image of the dog that had taken hold of its tail and was going around and around. This was a rabid dog, a pariah, gone berserk. What was the difference between this dog and the other, with its Burma teak house and daily steak?

I picked up Mencius. "Is there any difference between killing a man with a stick and with a sword?"

"There is no difference."

"Is there any difference between doing it with a sword and with governmental measures?"

"There is not."

" . . . What shall be thought of him who causes his people to die of hunger?"

And those who abet in the death?

The next morning we woke up to the racket of soldering, iron on iron. Grilles were being put up on the back kitchen windows.

"What's going on?" I asked the cook.

"A robbery last night."

"What was stolen?" Sis Two asked.

We went around the house noting what was missing. Things looked in order. Mama was supervising the workers. Papa was still in Bangkok.

"Bienvenido and Pepito foiled the robbers. Nothing to worry about," Sis One said.

"Nothing to worry about?" Sis Two contradicted. "You mean someone was creeping around here last night and we didn't hear a thing?"

"Must have been our first sleep," I said.

"It's creepy. What if he had come upstairs to our rooms?" She felt defiled.

"How did they know Papa wasn't here?"

"They case the joint first."

"Don't be silly," Sis One silenced us. "Nothing was taken. We're OK and we're putting up preventative measures now."

Defences, I thought. We'd lost the battle if we had to put up defences. Why couldn't Papa have been deceptive?

"Do you mean they'll try again?" Sis Two shuddered.

"What's with this 'they'? It might have been just one person," Sis One dismissed her.

"One person wouldn't dare."

"All right, maybe two. We can handle two, can't we?"

"But we didn't even hear them!" Sis Two protested.

"Bienvenido did."

"What if Bienvenido hadn't been there?"

"But he was there and we're OK."

"And next time? If he's not there next time?" Sis Two persisted.

"There won't be a next time because we've now got grilles in our windows. They can't get in anymore."

"How do you know? Desperate men find desperate means."

"Are you intent on being scared?" Sis One attacked her personally.
"That's cheating," I said, in defence of Sis Two.
"Well, are you?" She ignored me.
"Yeah, I'm scared. Wouldn't you be, if some men were creeping around downstairs while you were asleep?"
"Then guard yourself if you're scared."
"Buy a gun," I said.
"Or else be brave and don't worry about it."
"Now that would be foolish," I countered. "Simply being brave and not doing anything about it."
"We are doing something, you nitwit," Sis One turned on me next.
"But I mean, upstairs," Sis Two continued. "What are we doing upstairs if they should get in and go upstairs?"
Sis One sighed.
"Remember Letty's family," I said. "Wiped out by one person while they slept."
They both looked at me and we three fell silent.
I mentioned the robbery attempt to the gang in school. We had ventured to our favourite bamboo clump at the edge of the field, near the fence to the boys' school, off-limits according to the nuns, but we went anyway, whenever we had private things to say.
"That's nothing," Esther said. "We get that all the time. We're used to it now. You should get a guard dog."
"Don't you think people never change?" Fina asked. "They're always doing bad things, breaking in and stealing and all that."
"People are like root verbs with modals," Nilda said, thinking perhaps of the grammar lessons we just finished. "You can put any modal you want before them but they still remain the same."
"You're using the wrong language," I said, being the foreigner once again. "Filipinos are like superlatives. Extremes. Ang taas taas. Mabait na mabait. Kaibigang kaibigang. Tuwid na tuwid. Just double the word."
"Triple. You could go tuwid na tuwid na tuwid," Fina corrected. "That's the tuwidest."
"People are like gerunds," Lita added, returning to the abstract. She had no interest in the Filipino identity. "Crying. Laughing."
"Whining," Esther said.
"Those are poor people," Fina corrected yet again.
"I don't know," Esther defended herself. "Rich people are beginning to whine, too. My mother is constantly complaining about the quality of service today. She says you can't get good servants anymore."

"You can still find good men," Lyn's eyes sparkled, looking like Liz Taylor's.

Distracted, we looked over the barbed wire and watched the Ateneans playing in their field. The topic changed to boys.

Chapter Twelve

My God, my God, why have you forsaken me?

I was in the library oblivious to the household routine. Our Father, who art in Heaven. First we name him. Then we praise: Hallowed be Thy name.

Thy kingdom come, Thy will be done on earth as it is in Heaven. These are stated truths, the verities. For certain his location, his space, will enter mine, for certain his will, his dominance will prevail over the world. God fills Heaven now, He will fill earth in the future.

Meanwhile (and Jesus should really have used transitions) give us this day our daily bread. This request should have been prefaced by please or some polite form, since it sounds so demanding, self-indulgent, arrogant. Or it could be a given—a right we all have for being, a socialist's viewpoint, a necessity for survival. The daily bread—the right to work, to be fed. If you are going to be the leader, we expect you to feed us. God's responsibility to see to our comfort and well-being. And that takes care of our physical needs. No mention of gold, savings; just the daily requirement of vitamins, the daily allotment of grain. No refrigeration.

Then suddenly, the shift of focus: and forgive us our trespasses, as though there were more things listed that God could have given us in terms of physical comfort, but these were edited out, in a condensed *Reader's Digest* version, because we are now talking about our social behaviour. Forgive us our trespasses—had there been a mention of stealing our neighbour's daily bread just before this "conclusion?" As we forgive those who trespass against us—those who stole our bread. Forgiveness is a significant concept in Christ's mind. God must forgive us only if we forgive others or as we normally also forgive others.

And lead us not into temptation: does this still refer to the bread which we are tempted to steal, or has he gone on to deeper moral truths—sin, for example. Perhaps so, since we have next: but deliver us from evil. Thus: And lead us not into temptation but deliver us from evil. This sentence structure points to heavy moral abstracts—good and evil. Forgiveness might have been an example of the Good. Or perhaps the bread was. Or the bread was the

Good. The Good is not named. But the evil is. Temptation might be an example of the Evil since it is closely connected in that sentence. But the Evil is not defined. And in any case, it is a very bad sentence—and lead us not into temptation but deliver us from evil. Might not this be corrected to: From *its* evil? Or should this compound sentence which does not have a logical connection be separated into two simple sentences: Lead us not into temptation. Deliver us from evil. Surely, to be tempted is a natural human failing and not an evil. Unless—are "temptation" and "evil" synonymous with "Satan?" If so, lead us not to Satan and deliver us from Satan, in case we are imprisoned by him. Which would make sense since Christ was tempted by Temptation Itself and was saved by Christ's nature, the God-half which prevailed over his Man-half. Since we know we are only human, we would need extra protection on this matter. The sentence should have read: And lead us not to, but deliver us from evil (or temptation).

So let us look at the givens, the responsibilities of God as leader.

1. Give us this day our daily bread.
2. Forgive us our trespasses.
3. Lead us not into temptation.
4. Deliver us from evil.

These sound like a worker's demands. On strike action. Christ was forming a union. If God should fulfil these, we will be good.

Perhaps, these are the Good: daily bread, forgiveness, no temptation, no evil. Perhaps Christ had simplified his thoughts into these four points as his life's experiences to that stage had given him. He liked to simplify things. Later on (or was it earlier on) he broke down his demands of us to two:

1. Love God.
2. Love thy neighbour as you would yourself.

Which was rather nice. No way could it be 2. Love yourself, and then 3. Love your neighbour, in case the third point was forgotten or edited out. And in any case, all humans are brought together in point 2. It was very kind of him to give us only two points while he expected God to remember four.

These are very reasonable demands. First of all: survival. We do the same with our children. When we have a child, we feed it. After the physical state, the social; forgiveness. Being only human, i.e., imperfect, we will blunder into your privacy, hurt you, make the usual social discourtesies, show bad manners, impertinence. We forgive among ourselves because we are civilized; do be the same. Now the moral state: virtue. A blameless life, clean slate, virginal, good habits. We want this of our children—why bring children into the world only to lead them to dishonour and vice? We expect you to guide us to virtuous thoughts and acts like good spirits in Buddhism guide the dead, who are focused on the Light at the end, through the narrow bridge. Then the spiritual state: good. Not evil. Not Satan. God. It is God's responsibility to make certain that we are released from Satan's hand. Having fallen into his hand (Temptation) we must be delivered. (Although we shouldn't have fallen, since God was supposed to prevent our way towards it: Lead us not. That sentence structure truly bothers me.)

Perhaps he meant bondage from life, from earth, from this kingdom. Deliver us to your kingdom which you said (and we believe) would come, as stated in the opening paragraph: Thy kingdom come. God must bring us to Him. And why not. We expect the same of ourselves with our children. We would release them from harm, from evil, if they were so captured. We would deliver them to a good condition; we would not wish them to suffer damnation. We would save their souls.

Take care of us, God. Love us. Why was it necessary to spell love out to God? Christ didn't spell love out for us because we already knew it, as the four points grew out of our interaction on earth. Might these have been meant for a father Christ didn't know? You, father, who are somewhere out there, in a heaven (not on earth, not here), who has not loved me because you didn't take care of me, you who neglected me, seeded my mother then left, let me greet you with a blessing, hallowed be your name, for I am a courteous man, and why not, I praise you as my father though I don't know you personally.

Were these the cries of an abandoned child? Psychologically wounded, he seeks his healing by making these demands of the perpetrator of his pain. Simon Peter, do you love me? If you love me, follow me. Love was all-consuming to him. Love me, father. Why don't you love me? Did I do something wrong?

Let me show you how, maybe you were a young man then who didn't know how to love a child. I have suffered. I know. I have observed people. I've seen good behaviour, parent-child relationships. Let me tell you what I've seen. Let me outline these points for you. Let me simplify things for you. All you have to remember—feed me, forgive me, guide me, save me.

Come. Let this be your will. Will it. Make it so. Now. And forever.

Everything depends on clear directions.

Chapter Thirteen

> Ay, ay kalisud
> Kalisud san binayaan,
> Adlaw, gab-i . . .
> How sad the sadness
> of the abandoned,
> day and night . . .
>
> —Visayan ballad

Someone disappeared almost every half year now. Oh, I don't mean the houseguests who came and went. The servants were disappearing. One day I woke up and one was gone. Today it was the old woman with the seven-year-old daughter. Along with them went Mama's bright metal safety pins, each one was linked to the other, several feet long, a Calder mobile, a snake sculpture. No explanation why she was let go. Just a shrug—she didn't come from Samar—what do you expect of these people?

Very disturbing. I didn't like waking up to an emptying house. It was very important to have a full house against the enemy out there.

"Jaspal!" Mama bellowed my name. When she was angry, I was a full-blooded Indian. I dropped *All Quiet on the Western Front*. Normally, I was left alone to do as I pleased—called only to eat and left to wander afterwards. Something was afoot.

The whole house was in an uproar. Mama was having a nervous breakdown and so everyone had to be miserable. Papa had learned to be quiet. In the past the more he had answered her back, the more she had screamed, so nothing was gained. She was a frustrated defence lawyer who got up to pre-law and then Papa made her stay home with the babies, so she practiced her failed art on him every so often—"She digs my grave," he said—as punishment. Because she was so good at verbal attack (I shunned the fights, hid in my bedroom or the library), I was not. I was so frightened of a blustering shrew, a wailing banshee, a woman whose skills aimed at demoralizing and insulting the opponent were so honed—yes, I think this was why I tried not to quarrel with anyone.

Papa, his face set, was sitting at the dinner table while the tirade spent itself out. We exchanged glances. Yes, I was more like Papa than Mama. I, too, wanted to live with someone who was quiet and pacific. A peace lover.

What the anger was about was inconsequential. These bouts were becoming more frequent. She had always been angry—ever since I'd known MOTHER, I'd known her to be an angry woman. I think it was because she thought she had married the wrong man. Papa was so domineering that she had been unable to strike out on her own, to release her creativity. He stopped her education. Once, when he was away for almost a year on his business trips, she opened up a restaurant which became very successful. He returned and closed it. She negotiated a tremendously big business deal, onions, I think; all he had to do was supply the goods from India and she would have made a huge amount of money. He didn't. She wanted to work in insurance because she had nothing to do at home once the kids were all in school all day. He wouldn't allow it.

What she had to do was to be at his side during business dealings, host the endless cocktail parties, look very attractive. She did all these extremely well. She had perfected three facial and body communication tactics: one, for the rich and necessary friends, an all-embracing wide smile, twinkling all-interested eyes, actively lunged body posture ready to take you in; two, for unimportant middle-class clerks, semi-raised eyebrows, drooping eyelids, non smile, a right hand that dismissed the other with a slight sweeping wave, like the flickering of dust off one's dress, a finger extended as though she were drinking tea; and three, for the servants, complete blank, body tucked in and retired, ignoring all humanity.

She got her way with Papa only when she was sick (or made herself sick) and when she harangued him so long that he gave up. They were a most unhappy couple. "When your mother is good, she's very good; when she's bad, she's hell," he would remark. "How Filipina, so unpredictable in her sudden change."

In any case, she wanted something so she was building up to getting it. I wondered if it was a thing, a thing, like another brass object, or a gown—"rags," Papa called her closets and closets of clothes—or a trip, since she hardly got to go anywhere while he traipsed around the world. We children always felt guilty that we must have chained her down by our existence. When we summered in Hongkong or Tokyo, everybody went, including Papa. She never travelled alone; we couldn't be "left behind." When she got married and had children, she lost her freedom.

The whole week had that tension in the air: Mama wants something. The servants made themselves scarce, Sis Two managed to sleep over at her friend's house, Sis One went on a retreat. I, of course, being the youngest, had no recourse but to stay around the house and observe. Papa left for Bangkok.

When I was twelve, four years before, and needed a haven, I would sit in Beauty's house. It was a real one-room house, made of Burma teak, kept scrupulously clean by the houseboys. We could stand in it, our heads just touching the ceiling. Her house was far more agreeable than ours with its too many rooms and too many things. All Beauty had was a bench I built on which I sat whenever I visited her.

When I was younger, about eight or nine, I had another haven. Inside Mama's clothes closet was a tiny door I discovered one day which led to a crawl space where the slanted roof met the ceiling beams in a triangle shaped much like a ship's mast. It had the musty odour of old wood, like a ship's hulk, but I could breathe well in it because here and there were cracks through which, also, the light from outside entered. I devised and survived many journeys in my hiding place. No one knew I sat in there for hours. It occurs to me now that anything could have happened to me—I could have slipped on a beam and hit my head—and no one would have found me. My body would have rotted away, bricked up like a Poe character. In spite of all the people in the house, all taking care of us, a child could be neglected.

Now with Beauty gone, this empty house was no longer a haven for me. I walked around the gardens, my circle of solitude a little larger, my solitude less hidden.

Near the unscalable western wall, where the gardener had allowed the weeds to overgrow, where the bamboo had fallen, cleaved and rotting onto the ground, where no one bothered to come, I whacked my way as to a savannah, and made a clearing in the grass. I saw that my old clay pots were still here, just as I had left them when I was a child, when I used to play cook the raw meat I had hunted down, the tough hind of a jungle cat made civilized by my fire. The jungle was not a fearsome place. Animals could be subdued and cooked.

I looked around me at the scattered poles. This was probably the last of my havens. Here, too, was a mound, an incomplete grotto, once intended to be a pedestal for Our Lady of Lourdes, but somehow forgotten in the way of things. Instead, it became my stone box from which I charged with the Light Brigade, cannons to the right and left of us.

I gathered some pebbles now and made a circle. Intrigued by this shape and activity, I ran around gathering more, making circles. I was going to build a Zen garden. It would come from a thousand stones, a millennia of stones, the ages of man. It would be life going round and round, beads of prayers, kalpas and mahakalpas, whirling dervish, pariah's head-tail, curled cat sleeping with its tail tucked in, pebbles of eternal peace.

The pebble stayed on that spot on the map for days. No one bothered to move it. They had been doing geography for weeks now and everyone was tired of it, so they moved on to another subject. The world map lay on a side table, gathering dust. Only Papa went back to it now and again, checking his pebble, picking it up to look at Manila, then putting it back down at the exact place. When his teacher had gone all around the world, instructing the village children of the riches in store for them once they had ventured forth, a spirit moved Papa's hand, gave him a black pebble and spoke through him: "There, that's where I'll go to live." And he put the pebble down decisively on the strange and foreign word.

"Why Manila?" His brother in Malaya said. "Stay here with me and help me in my business."

"Why Manila?" His best friend in Manila said. "Let's go to Oxford and finish our education there."

But he met Mama at university, then the war came. His life was engraved on that stone, pinioned for twenty-five years.

The pebbles on the beach glowed in the moonlight, as the water washed over them. The waves made a lapping sound, their rhythm broken only by the high chirping of the birds. Everyone was asleep. Only Mama, seven years old, sitting in her nightgown on the front wooden steps, kept vigil. It was cool. Her eyes traced the outline of the horizon, of the river bank at the other side, watching for her father's banca. He had gone courting across the river, a woman on another island, a second mother for her and her six sisters and one brother, a woman fifteen years younger than him, a woman to replace her dead mother who died at childbirth birthing her. The courting had taken months, and so she had sat for months waiting for his boat to get back every evening.

It was so cold she sometimes ran in to get a blanket. But still she sat, waiting. To while away the time, to see the water come alive, she would throw a pebble onto the river, her life engraved on that stone, on its black surface.

Our family disease was Melancholia.

Chapter Fourteen

Go to battle armed.
—Mama

The TRALDIGETS were in the lanai talking about Rock and Roll, *Archie* comics, and flat-chestedness. Sis Two was larger than Sis One, which didn't seem fair since she was younger. Sis One compensated by getting all A's in college. Sis Two didn't have to. All very silly talk, I thought, since both had loads of suitors. It may not be important to men, in spite of all those endowed Hollywood stars. Sis One made Grace Kelly her model.

I was budding. Mama pointed this out to Papa one day when they were going over my photographs in the magazine that featured Esther, Lyn our Liz Taylor, and me as cool teenagers. There we were on the cover, budding; I was so embarrassed I went around all day with my arms crossed and my shoulders humped so my chest would look caved in. To put it all into perspective, Sis One reminded me that merchants in the fish market used magazines to wrap fish.

While they talked nonsense, I sat in the library thinking philosophical thoughts. I was being an intellectual. I was being a poet. It was not as easy as it looked. Here I was sitting cross-legged, looking very intellectual to an outsider peeping in through the window. My face had a studied look, my eyes were glazed as though looking through the edge of the earth and beyond. If I hadn't combed my hair that morning, an unkempt style might have enhanced my intellectual look. A beard would have helped, too. In America, they were wearing all-black clothes, smoking and beating bongos. They had long hair. They smelled horrible.

It didn't matter. I liked the intellectual look. Once I was abroad, I would wear black, boots, and I would recite, not the Tennysons and Byrons, but my own poems, and people would say, "Look, an intellectual."

Now I thought, what do intellectuals think about? I had been reading all of Sis One's books and the thoughts were so deep, the language so obscure, I was most excited. If only I could think like that. So I opened my tract on Christ and wrote a little bit, throwing in being and nothingness types of words. But thinking like an intellectual was very hard. Soon I was falling asleep. Maybe all I needed were large breasts. And as for Christ, I thought He should be left alone. He had been mishandled enough.

"Intellectuals are driven," Sis One said while I interrupted her reading in her bedroom, "by their thoughts. Poets are driven by their words."

"They smell."

"Only because they have no time for hygiene. They are too busy intellectualizing, poeticizing."

"They're hairy."

I watched the progress of the lizard on the wall. It had a quick tail.

"They can't be bothered by how they look. They have visions. They're driven by their visions. You'd have to be somewhat insane." Her eyes flashed with vision.

"Who wants to be insane?"

"It's not a question of wanting. They are—they simply are what they are and that being must be expressed."

The lizard went quickly into a crack. Gone.

"Writing is a passion."

Mama was all emotion and passion. Her religiousness was emotional. Her anger, her socializing, her Spanishness—all passion.

"It's an addiction, a disease. You write until your arm drops off, your leg falls asleep, your back breaks, your mind numbs."

"Oh great."

In the evening I decided to shave my legs. I borrowed Papa's razor, a metal instrument of torture that came in two parts: the heavy stem that one had to push against a square that opened into two when the stem made contact with its ring, and then one slipped in a razor blade, twisted the square back close. I propped myself up on the camphor chest in the front kitchen. I was very hairy, very Indian, unlike Mama who prided herself on her naturally smooth legs, the Filipina in her blood that came out right. She sympathized whenever my two sisters come out nicked from their showers, but secretly smiled that she had been blessed. She spent inordinate hours creaming her legs.

At first the curls fell on the chest designs nonchalantly. Easy as cutting the top off dandelions with a stick. Then the rigid rows of leftover hair stood defiantly against the Wilkinson sword. When I was done, my legs looked lighter, like new-mown grass. After a few minutes, I saw the slits of blood. They hurt.

More importantly, I suddenly realized that now the die was cast. I must shave from this night forward because the new hair would no longer lie gently to its side. I washed my legs in the bathroom and dried them carefully, hurting and smarting in the meantime. The whole experience was pointless, and I didn't see why my sisters did it twice a week. But of course all the pretty girls were clean-shaven and so I had to be too. I wanted to be normal. No insanity here. Every inch of my legs was screaming, "help." It might have helped if I had done it with soap and water like my sisters did, or with some cream like Papa did with his face.

I spent an excruciating night, not knowing where to rest my legs. The touch of the sheets sent shivers all the way up. In the morning no one noticed I had mutilated myself. No one commented on it. It was as though no one had looked at me all day. This confirmed my suspicion that nobody at home cared about what I did. I went about silently, gliding by, like my cats. They went about noisily, attending to themselves.

This was good. I had finally achieved blending, disguise, concealment. No Nirvana for me. No holy Heaven. Just the Chameleon state. I'd never be attacked because I wouldn't be found. Yet, I'd be right there, observing the battle. The unknown knowing, the unseen seeing.

A week later and the hair was re-growing. The legs looked like porcupines with clipped quills. I scratched constantly, itchy to the bone. I would never be a visionary now, because I had to shave my legs.

Musashi went around hairy and unbathed, fearing he would be attacked while his weapons were laid aside. My family was certain to be attacked because we were too clean. We bathed twice a day, we shaved, we brushed our teeth the required three times, our hair the one hundred strokes, the manicurist came weekly to do our nails, our laundry woman was paramount even to the cook, the rooms girls scrubbed and waxed the floors daily, dusted every surface in the whole house, the chauffeur washed and waxed the car, the gardener mowed, clipped, watered the gardens, we were all entirely maintained, constantly with our guard down, pruning and preening ourselves, fluffing the fur in self-indulgence and satisfaction.

We were open on all eight sides.

Except for Papa who could flatten a man with one blow, none of us women could defend ourselves. No one was trained. I trained myself with dried papaya stems for my long sword, and later with bamboo sticks in my hideaway in the west garden. I knew how to parry, slash and cut. Broad strokes. Close clings.

There were more women than men in our household. Aside from us sisters, there was the procession of aunts and the gaggle of servants. The houseguests, the chauffeur, the gardener, the four houseboys, were male. None of us were warriors. We were too soft, ready for the plucking. I was constantly wary, watching for danger. I practiced my peripheral vision by gazing straight ahead and without moving my eyeballs, seeing to the right and left of me. I sensed the footfalls, knew whose they were. I knew all the exits of each room, all the secret nooks. I would survive.

This being the Christmas holidays, we would not be attacked. Filipinos fought seasonally, before or after Christmas, because they liked to pack up their arms and go home to celebrate. The Pasyon took a long time to enact, preparations in the provinces lasting many weeks. It was an all to-do.

Our Christmas tree was natural, of course, Papa being the way he was. He would not allow anything dead inside the house. Some of our friends, however, were now buying artificial trees they could pull out every Christmas from the closet. Mama thought it was much wiser and cheaper. But I liked the smell of pine. Our tree was bussed down from Baguio.

We had been decorating it now for the past week, adding on and adding on until it seemed overburdened. Snow was cottonballs layered here and there on the branches. This tree would stand until after January 6th, the Epiphany. Gifts were dutifully placed underneath. Blinking strips of lights were turned on.

We were so Westernized, it made me wonder. I sometimes forgot that Christ was a Middle Eastern Jew possibly with brown hair. In my mind he was blonde with blue eyes, cherubic as Raphael could make him, a Renaissance idol. Our house was littered with his image and that was all-Western. I've seen his back in Hollywood movies and if he were to turn around, I would see an American.

We went to Midnight Mass much like Americans do. The only difference perhaps, but this was Spanish, was the Noche Buena afterwards. There were times I felt alienated from this colonial religion. But my sisters were so devoted, I had to be also, or else I would not be with them in Heaven. At Christmas, I felt very lonely because of this.

I preferred New Year's Eve because we were allowed to stay up beyond midnight, jump up and down to make us grow taller, and rattle our piggy banks to give us a more profitable year. Parents had a loud drinking party in the lanai where everyone smoked and laughed and the brave supervised the firecrackers in the lawn.

The onion bomb cracked the loudest, so dangerous only the servants were allowed to set it off. Fingers had been known to blow off, blindness a routine end among the peasants who were too stupid to take precautions. Every year some congressman said these should be banned but every year we had them anyway. Like the potholes in the street after every flood, someone made corrupt money somewhere and the people suffered on.

Tonight one of the foolish was Jesse, eighteen years old and a rising film star. His father had just died and left him his film production company to run. A difficult feat for a child but his mother, who was half-American, was tough as nails and would see him through.

They were our closest family friend. Our lives were intertwined. Jesse and Sis Two were teased together but they were really like brother and sister.

"Spectacular," one of the guests said of the brief explosion in the sky. He was a radio announcer, so he probably felt inclined to give a running commentary. "Marvellous," to another outburst of noise. Of course he was so drunk every sound was loud.

We found out that Jesse was up to something even more spectacular at the far lawn. He had gathered bamboo and what-nots. We ran over to watch. It looked like liquid petroleum, naphtha, burning pitch, sulphur, pitch, resin, quicklime, bitumen and a homemade brew of olive oil, a Greek fire to surpass all Greek fires. He intended it to eject from the bamboo tube sideways and upwards like an incendiary dragon. The devils would flee in confusion, routed from their perch on our rooftops, manananggals shattered to the core.

Jesse's eyes blazed like his match. Cunning to the quick, he set the match to. We all pulled back. Let Jesse be the hero. Eleemon against the Pisans. And he was! And the noise! It cracked open God's sky and down rained on us all the blessings it had hoarded.

Chapter Fifteen

> Thus all, sweet fair, in time must have an end,
> Except thy beauty, virtues, and thy friend.
> —Giles Fletcher

These days Sis One was very moody so we kept out of her way. She didn't even tease me at the dinner table as was her wont. She would say, "There now, Jazz is going to cry, she's going to cry," and of course, there I went, I cried. She didn't correct me when I made mistakes. She didn't call me in to tell me I'd been self-conscious in front of her friends, as I passed by in my shorts, worrying about the hair on my thighs. I felt exposed, now they could see that the shaving ended at the knees.

Sis Two and I sat on the front steps playing gin rummy until the mosquitoes drove us in. The house was very quiet. Mama was not on a rampage—she'd even contained herself, in respect for Sis One's moodiness.

She listened to "Soon" over and over. *Soon the lonely nights would be ended.* Each time I passed by her room I heard it and it was driving me crazy. I didn't understand this all-consuming loneliness.

Sis One was in love. With whom of all those suitors, only God knew. Where he was at the moment and for how long he was to be away, who cared. Gone to Baguio, Sis Two told me. Big deal. Baguio was just a zigzag road away up the mountains. We used to summer there, with cousins or friends, but in the past two years, we'd stayed home. She awaited his letters, his phone calls like they were manna. Remembering Baguio, with its golf courses on lands taken from Datus, Camp John Hay, *the* R and R in Asia, she could well have wailed.

Meanwhile, we all had to behave and wait this loneliness out with her. She played Rachmaninoff when she was not listening to "Soon." She wore her favourite spaghetti-strappped chemise all around the house and no one dared tell her she should get dressed. Of course, she wouldn't eat. Papa said to us she was getting too thin. She cut Mama down with an insult or a dismissive word when she beat Mama at chess. Mama felt foolish but didn't rebuke her for her insolence. She was getting away with murder, I told Sis Two, who shrugged. You don't cross her path, she warned.

Her other suitors pressed on regardless. She told the maid to turn them away at the gate. She was not in to anyone. Phone calls were screened. Life went on for us, but outside. Since she wouldn't go, Mama took me instead with Sis Two to the nightclub where we were entertained by flamenco dancing. At first we were enthralled by the finger speed of the guitarist doing "Malagueña." But nothing could compare to the flamenco that followed.

The woman in her elaborate and gaudy red and white outfit was undoubtedly superb. It was the man I fell in love with. His hair was slicked back, taut on his head. His form was lean, without fat. It was his back that got me. Perfectly curved, it propelled the rest of him from the waist down forward, his buttocks tightly tensed, his legs sharp enough to cut. The excitement that flamed within him, all reined in like a horse at the tether, shot with alacrity to us, his gawking audience. We were driven onward with his gypsy energy, rhythmically, passionately. I think we were all sweating along with him by the time he was done.

I guess I understood Sis One's loneliness a little bit that night. When the band picked up again its bland Glenn Miller tunes, I felt lonely for something I couldn't define. So in the ensuing days, I did leave her alone to nurture her loneliness in peace.

It didn't last for much longer, anyway. The ending was so abrupt. She had fond feelings for a pianist who was married and so she had given up trying to seduce him. For a while there, however, she thought about and wanted him a lot.

One Monday, since she was unaccustomed to holding money, she lost a few hundred pesos while she was shopping. She came home somewhat depressed because she was then unable to buy what she had intended to; but in the end she consoled herself that it was just money she lost, not a life. It had been a bad few weeks, anyway; this was just the culmination of that. The pianist kept coming back to her mind in spite of herself. It was nearing his birthday, she thought. He must be celebrating with his friends. She could see them gathering. Five days later, she discovered he had died that Monday. Then she realized she had been wrong about that birth date; for the first time since she'd known him, she had forgotten his birth date. She had "seen" his friends gathering for the service, not for a party. He had died of leukaemia. Although everyone knew it was terminal, she had never really accepted the fact that he would die. His death mobilized her. She stopped moaning, got dressed, lived again.

The household went back to normal. Well, almost normal.

If it were not for Mama's mystery books, we wouldn't have been prepared for the haunting. As it was, we were all bred in concealed documents, secret doors, the chains in the night, the howling dog, the spectre in Old Balete Drive, a young woman in white who flagged down a car then disappeared after she entered the car. It was said that this woman had been raped and murdered so her ghost came again and again to haunt men. It got so bad that young men went all around, out of their way, just to avoid driving though Old Balete.

Luckily, Papa was at home. From the second floor, we heard a crash one evening. It originated outside, as though a giant mango tree had fallen on its side. We didn't investigate until the next morning but there was no sign of disturbance inside or outside. And we had no giant mango tree.

The next night, we heard the refrigerator door open and close while we sat talking about this phenomenon in the living room. The servants were all in the back kitchen. Papa checked to see if everything was in order. All appliances gleamed as for show.

The next day, while the family was away and the servants outside, I was left alone at home. I heard someone walking on the second floor. There were distinct footsteps, as if someone was patrolling, making the rounds. Of course, I didn't go upstairs, even if Nancy Drew might have. I waited and listened. After about half an hour, this walking stopped. I waited for this visitor to come down the stairs. Nothing. When Emiliana came in, I asked her to go up and get my pink shirt. When she came down I asked her if everything looked okay and she said there was nothing wrong.

Then Emiliana and I heard the piano play. We looked at each other. Made courageous by our togetherness, we went to the music room. The music stopped. There was no one.

That's when Papa asked Fr Mark, our family priest, to come and bless the house. The Sacred Heart enthroned was prominently displayed at the entrance. The priest covered every cranny in the house with his holy water. Incense filled the air for days afterwards. Choking and gagging, I followed this medieval man room by room as he exorcised or appeased the poor spirit.

"Laid to rest," he exclaimed triumphantly in the end.

Mama was much relieved. Papa would have liked to confront it, he loved the occult so. Sis One loved the Gothic romance or terror of it. Sis Two was convinced it was an angel.

We had a splendid dinner afterwards, the Irish Fr Mark managing his share of wine. Dinner talk consisted of psychic research and death tunnels and such. That night while everyone else slept soundly, I had bad dreams. The ghost *did* go away or was lulled into a deep sleep by the breath-taking incense.

Good continued to come. My eyes were skipping the flowery prose, the long descriptive passages about the landscape and twittering birds, since I preferred to use my imagination, when I saw Gracing running below the starapple tree branch I was perched on. She seemed all excited.

"What is it?" I yelled. I marked my page with an estampita.

"Celso is here, visiting."

Another visitor from Vietnam. It must be their R and R week. I climbed down, eager to meet this man. Celso was our first servant. An orphan, he was brought to Mama's sister's house when he was twelve. Her brother-in-law, who had a temper, used to beat him up, so Mama's sister gave Celso to Mama to save him. Mama was pregnant with her first child and needed a helper, anyway, because she and Papa were both at university, he taking his MA in political science, she in pre-law. When Sis One was born, Celso took care of her exclusively, while another servant was brought to do the house chores. Mama said he was so good he even changed Sis One's diapers. They sent him to school, taught him English, and cared for him. When the Americans were recruiting ostensibly for labourers in Vietnam, he asked if he could go, and they gave him their blessing. He blended well and he was trustworthy—the Americans could rely on him to give them the right information.

He was in the sitting room surrounded by the family and household. On the coffee table were basketfuls of lychees, white, round and pitted, imported from Hong Kong. Mama was holding his gun in her hand, trying it out, feeling its weight. Papa was saying, watch where you point that, and Celso was laughing, it's OK, it's not loaded.

"Are you a soldier?" I asked him.

"No, no, the Americans just gave me a gun for protection."

He had his arm around Sis One, both of them very happy and contented, he looking like a proud second father. He told stories and Mama told reminscences. He had left when Sis One was thirteen and her memory was sketchy. I didn't remember him; I was only seven then, but I had often heard from everyone at home about him, a legend among servants.

He had to return to Vietnam in a few days and he was in Manila only for the day as he had to go to the province to see his relatives. So we made the best of our time with him. We were sad to see him leave and once again Sis One decried the fact that our best men were being taken from us, the country's loss. Mama was concerned about his safety. I placed the gold bracelet he gave me on my wrist and wore it for a long time to remember him by.

Chapter Sixteen

Do not attack an opponent on his own ground.
—Papa

Sis One had broken ground in the August 1958 issue of *The Knoll* as editor by publishing students' work in Tagalog as well as English. The book reviews were on Nick Joaquin's *A Portrait of an Artist as a Filipino*, a play; NVM Gonzalez's *A Season of Grace*, a novel; and Francisco Balagtas's *Florante at Laura*, a narrative poem. Her editorial ran:

> One Step Forward
>
> We have only to look at ourselves, to listen to the way we talk, to note how we feel or write, to realize that in spite of the many cultures we have assimilated, we are still one people with our own unique ways, customs and traditions. The editors, fully conscious of this richness of the Filipino culture, endeavour to express their appreciation by devoting the first issue of the KNOLL to it—expressing not the gradual development of the culture, but rather the various interpretations of local colour, theme and characterization.
>
> It is only now, more than ever, that we are starting to be truly conscious of the value of our native surroundings. And because we are excited in the realization of this awakening, we can't help but share it with you. Thus, this issue.
>
> The writers are taking their first faltering steps, groping through the dim guideposts of their yet untrained minds. Each one is attempting to express what is truly Filipino in the best possible way she can; and if she doesn't fully succeed, it is because she is still learning to avoid the pitfalls of over-emphasis on form, substance and style. Yet the fact is, she dares to write. And for us that is more than enough.
>
> We climb the KNOLL with this load on our shoulders. It is a painful,

but worthwhile ascent. Several times, we slipped; many times, we dropped it. But we take it up again and again—leaving some things behind and carrying what we can carry. For we know that someone else in the future will continue where we leave off.

Meanwhile, we are aware of these above all: that out of the first cries of babies newly born and the lullabies that mothers sing; out of the songs of the farmers at sunrise when they go to work in the field; out of the crunch of the ploughs upturning the earth; out of the silent endurance of the converts of Mt. Province; out of all these was born a yearning for love and recognition of "one people under one roof."

The cover, black, was a line drawing in yellow of a child walking towards a nipa hut; the writing, THE KNOLL, was accompanied by a Chinese script of the name.

The student body loved the issue. Some nuns gave my sisters and me cautious looks. They seemed to wait to see what this upstart would do next.

Her second issue had no Tagalog writing, after the faculty advisors had a talk with her, but it was entirely about Asia—"My Man Chan," "My Native Land," "A Saigon Holiday," "Siam," "Land of Contrast" (meaning the Orient), "Dream Behind the Iron Curtain"—she even got a Jesuit to write "The Eastern Face of Christ" as the centrefold. The book reviews were: John Hersey's *A Single Pebble*, about an American engineer in China; Junichiró Tanizaki's *The Makioka Sisters*; and Rumer Godden's *Mooltiki*, stories and poems from India.

Our high school contributions followed suit: "Impressions from Chinese Poetry," "What Being a Christian Oriental Means To Me," "The Pasig: Peace," "Malayan Kaleidoscope," "Hong Kong."

Since she said she hated doing copy work, I helped her proofread the articles. The whole process was fascinating. I saw my teacher's essay on Tagore. We went over the editorial carefully, corrected the galleys from the printers. For the cover she chose a light blue and white background, the blue silhouette of a schoolgirl, in young adulthood, her back to the viewer, standing at the edge or brink of a mountain at a road which led to a white light, a sun, enlightenment, possibly God's revelation, or just a bright future. Overhanging leaves of trees framed her, while the suggestion of an old majestic tree in the bottom left corner with its deep, massive roots brought the eye back to the central figure. The drawing opened up to the right side suggesting the world was open for her.

When this October issue came out it was well received again by the student body. But Sis One was called into the principal's office. She was given a severe reprimand. It was her birthday that day and although she felt bad about this scolding, she and her gangmates went to a movie to cheer her up. I was incensed by this nun's treatment of my sister. All week I burned with this.

Four days later, the nun took Sis One out of the graduation issue. She and her gangmates arrived home all crying, Susan, her closest friend and my chessmate, who was given the editorship, crying as much. We all sat at home stunned, angry, and sad. Sis One was heartbroken. Mama and Papa were distressed. Papa phoned Fr Mark, who immediately came to console Sis One. He advised us to lay low. I was further incensed by that thought. How typical.

The next day Sis One didn't go to school but had controlled herself sufficiently to function. The editorial that had caused the nun to break her was this:

Thoughts at Random

We look to the east and we witness the hope that enkindles the salvation of humanity. We gaze at the sun rising from the eastern horizon and we visualize the gradual fulfillment of this hope. A hope that once rose to great heights, but because we were blinded by the superficial beauty of our "outer garments" it was not properly nourished. And it fell. Yet for the first time, a new and different Orient is rising up before the rest of the world who had almost forgotten its existence, or attached little importance to it. It is a disturbing sight but an encouraging one, no less, not only because of the magnitude of its problems, but more so because of its rising influence. Egypt, Lebanon, Quemoy. Nehru, Chiang Kai-Shek, Nasser. Christianity. Communism. Reactions are varied—producing both understanding and conflict within us.

No people, no race continues unchanged. Continually, it is mixing with others and slowly changing; it may appear to die almost and then rise again as a new people . . . or just a variation of the old. Often, that old retains an external form only, as a kind of symbol. It is the inner content that changes. Something vital and living continues—driving a people in a direction whereby the desire for happiness, for peace, for contentment, is satisfied.

Christ came from the Orient. But like "the prophet who was not accepted in his own country" we drove Him away. And only when He was gone, did we realize how much we needed Him.

"The world is so big and we are so small . . . " We must not forget, however, that we are the very foundation from which the rest of the world was built. So that if the world crumbles, we have only ourselves to blame.

In the heart of every man, there is conflict. True. In the heart of every Oriental, this is more than just a conflict. It is a struggle—a search. A constant seeking for the Truth, the Good, and the Beautiful. Some have found it; others have not. Yet, the Lord said: "seek and ye shall find; knock and it shall be opened unto you . . . " We must persevere. We must wear out our knuckles. For only then, will the Door of Truth be opened and the light shine forth. It is difficult. It is tiring. But the reward is great.

Sis One carried on with life. She was the Turk in their annual play, "Puppet Prince," which we all went to see. Behind Esther and me sat the *Heights* editor whom I admired, sitting with one of the extraordinary college seniors, and I wished I were older. He was one of the three Edmund Campions in *Who Ride on White Horses* but I had missed his performance which he played effectively, according to the reviews, his voice making the "lines all fire and music." He walked with a limp, having been wounded as a child in the battle of Manila, 1945; it made me like him more, like Byron, like my chess Rook. But Esther said, forget it, they never look twice at us.

The other Edmund Campion whom we did see perform was fabulous. The play ran for three and a half hours yet this man maintained his vigour and vitality all throughout. His grace, agility, and charisma filled the stage. I swooned over him for days and days. Esther investigated his background and came up with five feet and nine inches, dark hair, good singer, shy, didn't dance, didn't care for girls, didn't appeal to her, didn't look handsome off-stage, and forget it, they never looked twice at us. But she played "Splish Splash" three times at her party for me, with a mean twinkle in her eye, because he'd sung that with his band, the Alleycats, when Sis Two, her friends and I went to watch them one evening. Bits of information about him came to me from everyone because once one said one liked so-and-so, everyone participated. The school spirit. We were well trained. Even Sis Two said he was a track star, grandson of a senator, and our neighbour.

The Sodalists continued to bring Christian education to the barrios, rising at 5 a.m. to take a train by 6, so that they could be home by 7:30 p.m. They went to the Mandaluyong Welfareville Institute and saw the nursery, the orphans, the juvenile delinquents imprisoned there. Each time, my sisters grew in holiness, with their corporal acts of mercy. The Torquemada nun should have gone with them.

If she had, the second blow might not have fallen. It came four months later on Friday, the 13th of March, ghoulishly appropriate. Sis One's friends, Susan among them, brought her home because she had almost fainted in school. She had not been given the cum laude everyone thought she would get and deserved. Instead she was given the "Journalism Award of St Francis de Sales." They couldn't deny her that publicly. I could just see the good nun battling the bad nun, both standing in judgement of her academic fate, their arms folded inside their robes: should we give her what she deserves or *give her what she deserves?* All tone and register. I could hear Diderot's Monsieur Manouri yelling from the gallery: "Where is the dwelling place of hatred, disgust and hysteria? Where is the place of servitude and despotism? Where are undying hatreds and passions nurtured in silence? Where is the home of cruelty and morbid curiosity?" I could answer these questions now. The despair spilled over from the convent into the girls' school, staining their lives. It was all so grotesque, it was almost comic. No one phoned Fr Mark this time.

I sank down into a chair and listened to my sister's mute cry. Effectively silenced. Outside the window a dragon rain pelted the panes: large, violent drops that tried mercilessly to break the glass behind which we cowered.

Chapter Seventeen

> While Austerity and Sputniks are favourite topics in coffee shops, picnics and parties make headlines in Maryknoll.
> —*Chi Rho* (school newspaper)

Everything, it seemed, was a passion. Pasyon. From the extremes of whipping oneself publicly in the Pasyon of Christ at Lent to the wild surrender of hot secular nights. Or so I was told, never having seen or experienced either.

Sis One glowed in the room, her radiant eyes like candles in the dark. Passion. Agony. Suffering transmuted into joy. She didn't have to speak. We knew she had been at her charitable work, among the slums, and she had done much good. When she did speak, a light emanated from her mouth, from within her depths and struck at the listener's heart, at the very core. Sympathetic and compassionate, Sis Two promised she would assist at the next outing, she was so driven with our eldest sister's passion. They were competing for sainthood.

Meanwhile, I, too young to join the army of God, could only watch bedeviled and baffled at such profusion of joy like myriad leis of sweet-smelling sampaguita hanging from one's neck, assailing one's nostrils. Religion here, nay, worship here, was an overwhelming experience. It engulfed all of one's senses and would not let go unless it was for martyrdom.

The sunstroke of passion hit us at pledge time, as well. First we sang the national anthem, in Tagalog now, then we had to recite the pledge in words the meaning of which was lost to us. They were long convoluted words, much syllabication, strings of sausages on a running dog's neck, word derivations borrowed from Indian, Chinese, Arabic, Polynesian, in this mongrel language. The stress required that they be spat out, harshly and barkingly. Esther took everything seriously now that she was a rabid nationalist, having dug into her proud roots and discovered there all the security and stability one needed to maintain the generations. I envied her place in the sun. I envied my sisters their cause. Everyone, in their passion, fitted. I alone, was just hot. I dreamed of a cold land, a northern frozen waste, fjords, tundras, the Rockies. I was the Snow Queen.

But my word order, my world order, was wrong. My life was written in small index cards, three by fives, dropped by Hermes in his flight, fallen from the sky onto a field of dry cogon, where each solitary word was picked up off the scratchy grass and the whole lot laid out on a clearing, baked by the fierce sun, all in disarray, verbs without their linking companions, prepositions without their phrases, adjectives modifying lost nouns, full stops in the middle of clauses. Gone awry. Nothing fit. I was not a sentence. I had no logic, no sequence, no time modulation.

"I am the Snow Queen," I said to Esther over at the bamboo grove.

"Yeah, you're the darkest Snow Queen I've ever seen."

"I live in the Rockies."

"Where's that?"

"Canada. 'The linchpin of the Alliances.' "

"Where's that?"

"Jazz finds the most exotic places," Fina said.

"It's in America," Nilda said, pulling at her light brown ponytail, looking very white.

"My ice-cave has crystal stalagmite pillars."

"Stalactite."

"Whichever. I can never remember which is which."

"I'm going to Australia," Nilda said.

"Why there? They hate Filipinos."

"Mommy got a job there." Her mother was a young widow. There were just the two of them. We didn't pursue the subject.

"Good luck. Maybe you can pass for white."

"I'm going to live in Paris," Esther said. She had gone with the nuns on a pilgrimage last December along with nine other girls at school. "In Paris, you can walk on the streets. Promenade. Look at shops, sit in a café and look at people go by. For hours!"

We all envisioned it. Total freedom. We were silent for a long time, walking the streets of all the countries of the world. The buzzer sounded. We saw Sr Rose in her heavy penguin outfit supervising the picking up of volleyballs.

"She must have seen us," Fina said.

Esther shrugged. "They know we're breaking the rules. What can they do? Kick us out?" Ha, ha, she laughed heartily, her sinister laugh reminding one that she was the queen of pranks, having reduced the senator's daughter to tears when she couldn't reach the first-ever hula hoop in the country she brought to school to show off, which Esther promptly hid on top of a locker only Esther could reach. It took Fina to mediate all day to get Esther to give in.

Assured, we lingered longer before heeding the bell. This was the only space in which we breathed real air—unbounded, clean, clear air. Outside. Stretches of mown grass on our side, football field on the Soldier's of Christ side. Since everyone else adhered to the rules, we were deliciously alone, surrounded only by cultivated nature and a light cooling breeze. It was our sanctuary. We called it that. "See you at the sanctuary at noon. I have something to say," we'd say. It was reserved only for private musings, when we felt the need to be cordoned off from the rabble, although this rabble was our equal.

"This arrogance will not do," Sis Two said to me after dinner. I had behaved badly at a party she had brought me to.

"What did she do?" Sis One asked without interest.

"It's a general thing, an attitude."

"But the fellow smelled of sweat," I mumbled. "His shirt was sticky."

"So you wouldn't dance with him?" Sis One concluded.

Sis Two threw up her arms in the air and left the room.

"Don't be so fussy," Sis One said. "Sometimes you have to get your hands dirty. Remember that to set the souls free, Jesus had to descend into hell." I followed my second sister out. Not another Jesus story, I thought. I wish he'd be left alone.

"Carelessness wastes time and energy," Sr Judy said as she prodded grammar into our throats with her metal tongs. "Do this again."

Being careful, I reduced my adverbials. I looked forward to the summer vacation. "My sister says I'm arrogant."

Esther looked up, surprised. "You're a product of your class."

"My education?" My mind still on this interminable class time.

"Stop that chatter," Sr Judy rasped over some unfortunate's head. "Pay attention to your lesson now or you will have to do it over next time." She had served in a leper colony; she was revered.

Horrors. I didn't want to see these reductions again. I applied myself.

Esther observed, "You're too obsessive. Look at you—you look like you're actually enjoying these drills. Repetitions." She didn't care where Sr Judy had been, she talked on. I filled in the blanks, diagrammed my sentences, produced new ones, fleshed in details, stroking, stroking.

Drills. This morning in religion, first class of the day, Sr St Anthony was lecturing, yet again on communism. My fingers flew for note-taking.

Communist Party—soul is an epiphenomenon generated by physical processes social and economic determinism only good lies in work for

the rev. and for the proletarian community impersonal group—no individuality—
Communication Theory—soul represented in terms of a vastly intricate thinking machine, a root unconscious of its own nature, in which the will has little if any part to play, its being is essentially passive
Cybernetics—Keynote — separation—Theme—that either the body or the soul is significant, but not both.

Then I got tired and my notes faltered.
"Esther," I whispered. "Do you sometimes have this song that's stuck in your mind and it just sings and sings?"
"Yeah."
"Just the one line, over and over?"
"Yeah. Which one are you singing in your head?"
"Hold me in your loving arms and never let me go."
Sr St Anthony was the incarnation of Mrs Gargery except she didn't need a stick to bring us up; she herself was the stick. She gave us a sharp defaulters look and stopped talking. Esther shuffled her notebooks. I reread my notes. Soul is an epiphenomenon.
Hinduism is a thrifty religion; in it, souls are used over and over, parcelled out to different bodies at different times, like streams to the one Ocean which sends the water back out to the streams. A natural balance.
"What about a reused soul?" I asked the gang at recess.
"Heresy. You'll burn at the stake," Fina said.
"Transmigration. Reincarnation."
"Each soul is unique. You only live once. That's why you have to make the best of it."
"I get only one chance?"
"One chance in the gamble of life," Esther said.
"I worry about you," Fina added. "You have heretical tendencies."
"I don't like this black or white way of thinking. I want grey."
"She's a Confederate soldier," Esther mocked. "I wish I were in Dixie," she faltered. "Umm—hooray, hooray—"
"Today, today . . . " from Fina.
They both broke into "Dixie," as we marched back into class at the bell.
"I wish I was in the land of cotton, old times there are not forgotten. Look away! Look away! Look away! Dixie Land." How like them to think American. I would have thought Scots Greys of the flashing sabres, Sir Colin Campbell at the lead.
Hold me in your loving arms and never let me go, went the line, thin and

red, red hot, round and round my head. All through physics class while I watched through the window the horses nibbling at the grass in the far corner of the field—free, no chains on them, contented.

It was July, 1958, the Middle East crisis was raging with the US troops in Lebanon. Two years before, it was the Hungarian revolt against the Russians, superpowers clashing, crushing the puppets underneath. It went on and on. *Hold me in your loving arms.*

We distracted our minds with Ateneans. We waited for the ones we wanted while we sat at the foyer before morning bell, waving as their cars dropped off their sisters before they made the circle down the road to their college. A subtle wave, lest we should look forward, a nod really, a smile of the eye. This segregation made us more passionate, like longing for the forbidden fruit, but as useless as Donna Inez bowdlerizing the classics. Don Juan and Donna Julia found a way.

As soon as we got home, the phone calls started from 6:30 until 10:30, until we said the last goodnight to our loved one of the month. Teenagers, we were little fires, mirrored only the seductions that gripped our elders playing out *Der Rosenkavalier* in daily lives. The violent seductions, the Toscas were done by the peasants. With us, give us only the light waltzes. Bienvenido liked to sing "La Donna è mobile" in the car but let us remember that Rigoletto's daughter was murdered in that opera. Changeable we may be, ha ha, but we were also vulnerable. Men were irresistible.

And didn't the besieged mothers know it. So irresistible was Rick that Doña Inez devised a means of keeping him pure. He called her the MP He cut our phone call short with, "Oh, oh, I have to go, the MP is here."

At a party I sacrificed two dances and rejected six boys to talk to his best friend, Ben, about him. A stag line had formed behind me, scarlet coats frightening in the distance, the thin red advancing, each one poised to give me a line. Ben asked permission from all the boys who were rejected and danced with me.

"His father's great. It's his mother. Do you know about the necklace?"

"Yes."

"Did he tell you about the ring?"

"No."

"Well, when he lost the white gold necklace his mom gave him so he wouldn't be caught by a girl, his mom gave him her diamond ring and took his class ring to keep, so that when he would give it to a girl, it would be for keeps. The diamond ring was to remind him that his mother loves him very much."

"That's sick."

"Yes ... well ... he's the eldest."

"She's possessive."

"But there's something I'll tell you. Rick isn't the responsible type. He's got a younger brother in high school who's more mature than him."

"That's understandable since he can't move with his mom at his heels."

While we danced, Norman ran by followed by a group of boys. Trouble outside the gate. They came back later, successful.

On the way home, we passed by his house directly in front of Pinaglabanan Church called Villa Lilli—after his grandmother who died two weeks ago.

"They have sheep and geese in there," Ben said.

"It looks haunted." A few years back when I first saw this house I wondered who would live in such a place, a decrepit Spanish villa.

At school the next day, Lita said some groups were saying that he and I were already going steady. I was furious. Amelia said, "Don't let him pick you up alone or people will talk." Thus we did go round and round. *Hold me in your loving arms and never let me go.* I had a showdown with him on Saturday.

Monday morning, on the way to school, we saw Rick standing at Cubao waiting for the school bus. He was in an all-white outfit; it was either a Chinese funeral garb or he had wiped his slate clean. Meanwhile, Dave's sister Lola gave me a love note from Dave and followed me all around the school all day.

On Valentine's Day, Dave asked to come to the house. At around half past six I was surprised to see Rick carrying a box of three roses from Dave.

He said, "There's a letter underneath from me. Don't raise it because Dave might see it." Just like Teodoro Patiño in 1896, betraying his fellow Katipuneros.

"Why is he sending this box through you?"

"Why not through me? He can't come in because he's not dressed."

This childishness went on for months and months.

Dave's sister gave me a copy of the *Heights* graduation issue, March 1959. Reading this Atenean magazine was a far cry from the day-by-day blow of living with the Ateneans. The writing was brilliant, idealistic, philosophical. There was even an essay on Kierkegaard.

The editorial ran:

As he gives his future field an initial look-over, the perplexed Ateneo graduate, 1959, wonders whether his education has not been a mistake .... Ateneans may be well-steeped in the proper ideals and ideas, but they are shaken by the onslaught of practical unromantic problems that they, in their idealism, never expected. Hence, it falls on the Atenean to demolish the snobbish intellectual ivory tower in which he locks himself in his school days . . . He must dispel the self-deceiving myth that the life of the Catholic intellectual is up among the clouds, or he's in for a resounding thud. . . . No, the Ateneo has no lost causes. There are only lost Ateneans. They are the ones who march out to the world unprepared. Let us keep their number at a minimum.

Where were all the writers of such pieces? All I met were these Ateneans, lost even as they were still in the hallowed halls of Loyola Heights, failing in their Latin, chasing after Grade 7s. Maybe they transformed into that editor, the grand metamorphosis after three more years with the Jesuits. The problem was, meanwhile the extraordinary college seniors went out with Sis One's extraordinary college gangmates while patting us high school seniors on the head.

Life went on. Dave went to Mindoro with his uncle and twenty bullets, and bagged two tamaraws. We continued to go to all the parties, beach resorts, movies and plays, restaurants, and everyone cracked jokes and Dave was very loving and so on. Because I had invited Tony as my escort to the grad ball, Dave phoned every day in any way he could, sometimes two or three times a night. He said, "A boy has to be a little jealous so that he will be a good husband." Uh-huh. Tony said he was teasing Dave; he sang him "I know a secret." I asked Sis Two what song this was. She replied, the line went, "My best friend's stealing my girl." Tony said this was the first time Dave had gone after only one girl at one time. Uh-huh.

So this is how it went: the boys chased several girls, all at the same time, or one at a time, but all the time. They interchanged girlfriends among themselves, and in this my introduction to the line-up I was with two of the notorious artists of seduction. Trade commodities in the bull exchange.

I spoke to Papa about all these things. After a long philosophical digression, he said it was up to me. My decision. However, since I was leaving the country in a few months, what was the point of going steady with any of them?

And so I said no to Dave, and I saw Rick at the Araneta Coliseum rotunda waiting for the school bus, resplendent in his red jacket, if he was wounded no one would have distinguished the blood from his cover, brave infantryman, it was the last time I wanted to look at him, the line finally spread out against the sky, I etherised, the line of my heartbeat. While we were dancing, Dave asked me if I had ever been kissed, I said never, and he said he had and

I felt dejected. He drove home madly, kicking up dust.
Hold me in your loving arms and never let me go.
Rick was from the Tagalog region—Bulacan, Rizal, Laguna, Batangas. He came from Laguna. Men from there were jealous and temperamental. Batangueños were fighters. Batangas coffee was renowned for being raw, strong and bitter.

Dave was from the Visayas—Samar, Leyte, Cebu. Men from there were easy-going, fun-loving, large tracts of land gave them largesse.

Tony was Ilocano. He was thrifty and industrious.

So and so was from Pampanga. Pampangueños were "dugong aso." What did that mean, I asked, "A dog's blood?" They ate dogmeat there, a delicacy.

They came from a variety of regions but they were all young, talented, wealthy señoritos. They had one thing in common: infidelity. Don Juan to whom each day was the 6th of June, each hour half past six—perhaps still nearer seven—and a Donna Julia sat within the bower whispering "I will ne'er consent" and consented. Teen Don Juans who grew up to be the señor Don Juans who carried on the fine tradition: queridas in the haciendas. The fun was the predictable dialogue, the turn of phrase, of ankle, how did that compare with the other, honing the skills, the spirit of school competition gone berserk, better yet next time, Dave dropping his head, closing his eyes at my rejection, saying later, does this mean I'm free again?—free yet again for the next conquest, each one of them betraying the other.

I was sick of the whole lot.

At home, Sis Two was practising a song—"Dahil sa Iyo"—and I could hear that she thought it was now her own voice, her true self expressed: *Because of you, I want to live until death.* Suddenly the radio was full of love songs—if I had a heart, it would ache. We were inundated with songs written from the 1920s to the 1940s, songs of longing, unrequited love, *I'll be seeing you in all the old familiar places,* women were women all left behind, it was you, it was *you must go and I must bide,* pining for their Danny Boy gone to war, and these tremendous surges of longing filled me, would I had a heart so I could ache, and I was envious of the lovers at the graduation ball, I was so empty, *I hunger for your love.*

At her grad party, Esther had invited all the hot young men from the University of the Philippines, that den of radicalism where to look at the campus alone, or to glance at the nude "Oblation" guarding the campus, was as sinful as stepping into a Protestant church or seeing a B movie. Commies, Sr Rose said, UP students are communists. I was shocked to discover Esther knew so many of them. She wore a strapless, backless, and all that blue dress, finally flinging Mary-like fashion to the wind in one glorious rebellion. I wished I had her daring, her acceptance of this way of life, this reckless abandon; instead, I thought politely, no, this won't do, enough of this.

I got 96 in religion. Just before letting us go, they enrolled us in the Confraternity of Angelic Warfare. We graduated Tuesday, 17 March 1959. Godmother gave me a gift—a rosary.

Chapter Eighteen

They made him drunk and he gave away his business secrets.

—Mama

I followed Mama around the room, my eyes leaden with shyness, my arms locked to my sides. She wanted me to "show my face" at this party; I thought it was a ruse to expose me to proper social behaviour. My neck was heavy with jewels. I dragged myself, weighted down by the code of ages, socializing. Mama was perfect. Her body moved like a leopard's, slowly and stately at some points, pouncingly and swiftly at others. She knew whom to embrace and kiss, whom to hold by hand and arm, whom to wave at, and whom to nod to with a peremptory smile. Each of her guests had a place in the cocktail circus.

After a while, she got tired of me following her around. She sent me off to a kind group with a laugh, one eye to the clutch around her who laughed in return, "Ay, this child. Always following me around. Go and talk to the Ramoses over there. There's your Godfather Pamfilo, go entertain him."

Other guests were posing for pictures. It was a country of posers. Poseurs. One invited friends to an exclusive restaurant for one's birthday in order to pose. Document of one's existence. Legal evidence. Name-dropping time.

Cameras forever clicking. Click. Click. A transparent blue flashbulb popped into someone's cocktail. Laughter. Ha ha ha. Very funny. Click on. Did you catch that candid pose? Natural lang. I swore they spent hundreds of pesos on new ternos just so they could pose for the camera. Or was it because they spent so much on gowns they had to have a picture of it, pictures lasting longer than clothes? Drama. Theatre. It was a country of actors. Artista. Ay, napaka artista. Sis One told me, stop being an artista. Be straightforward, straighten up, pull your body up and speak plainly.

The guests moved as one, their bodies slightly bent to a side, the women giving in, the men taking. They swayed as in a dance, thrusting out when laughing, concaving when smiling, A bow, a flicker, a glance, a flirtation. Legs sidled, buttocks rolled, arms soared to the hair. It was a regular ballet, all arms and legs.

Very tiring to watch. I got away from my congenial, soft-spoken godfather and went off to the library.

"Mr Lanjit," Papa's Chinese businessman friend was saying, "No one will know the diffelence."

Papa was already drunk but his burly build soaked alcohol well. Even though he was sitting down, he still had a commanding presence. He was tall, heavy-set and charismatic. He filled a room standing in one spot whereas Mama flitted everywhere. I sat on his lap for a while. He tapped my arm.

"Just a few bags. We have a man at Customs," his friend continued.

"Diamonds," he mumbled to me. "No," he said out loud. "If I were caught how would this look on my children? I have three girls. Their reputation would be stained."

Mr Go shook his head. I got up and went to the garden through the French doors.

"People would look at them and say their father was a smuggler. I'd rather be bankrupt."

"No loom for molals in business, Mr Lanjit. You'll be poor," Mr Go lamented. He might have said, seize the opportunity, but he said, "take bull by its—"

I looked back and saw that Papa was a rion who didn't know how to be a fox. How could there be children "to the manor born" if the manor were not established first? Those lovely country houses—were they not built and kept up by clever men whose abilities to keep their land throughout the generations, the changes in Edward Edward Edward Richard Henry Henry allowed their children's children to maintain their private gardens, their privacy? How was one to keep off the wilderness, to keep out the wildlife that would, like weeds, engulf one? How marvellous it would be to leave behind the Ming vase from one's Oriental campaign to that great-child of the future. (How was it that none of these things ever got broken by one of those lively children?) Then it became tradition. Property. What was an Englishman without it? Only cared-for things survived. I glanced at the life-size oil paintings over Papa's head: would these three gaze down at my children to evoke for them their grandfather's chimeric world, where the serpent/goat/lion breathe out the fire of his existence?

I sat under the low kalamansi bush. It was a cool night. A clump of male guests in their crisp jusi Barong Tagalog were smoking near the grapevines. They were a circle of white light in their translucent white shirts designed by the Spanish administrators so weapons could not be concealed. One saw right into the undershirts. Now worn for formal parties, very expensive, these thin, straight, pocketless shirts were fitted carefully and painstakingly onto the wearer. Woe to the man with a paunch. I thought they looked uncomfortable and hot. Very silly. Duped. The drivers in their loose Hawaiian shirts looked far more sensible. Papa refused to wear either one. He always wore light suits. "It's the pockets," he'd say. "You've got to have pockets."

What a round of parties. All we did was party. School and party. Tonight both sisters had to attend two other parties, so they couldn't stay for ours. Of course, one didn't attend all the parties one had to accept. It was a ritual, in fact, not to show up. It was called "Indyan"—"Inindyan ko siya" was the phrase: I stood her/him up. I'm not sure whether the word was racist, as in people from India, or native, as in Indio, the irresponsible, unreliable Indio of Spanish times. This person never calls back the next day to apologize or on the same day to let you know if he's delayed, if you can still expect him. Worse than doing an Indyan for a party was doing it on an ordinary day. I'll call you later or right back, this person said. You waited, you wasted your day, he didn't call back. When he did show up, he made no mention of the long delay as if it hadn't crossed his mind, and if you told him you didn't like his action or that you waited and couldn't do anything else that day (not to mention the anxiety the waiting caused you) when you had planned other things to do, he would be quite surprised, I don't know over what—whether over your forthrightness in speaking your mind or over his sudden consciousness: *Me? What did I do?* Inindyan. Verb. What irony. They never followed through, from the mañana habit, maybe.

Tina found me under the bush. "Your mother is looking for you."

I moaned. I thought she had forgotten about me.

"She wants you to play the piano."

I was second best to Sis One whose chore this would have been. I slid closer to the bush, as though it would hide me.

"I could say that I didn't see you."

"But you did."

Tina shrugged and wandered off. If I waited for half an hour, this whim of hers might pass. Delay, delay. Gracing came by with a piece of cake and juice for me.

"Tina said to give you these," she mumbled.

I ate very slowly. A welcome excuse.

In the morning, while she was doing her exercises, Mama scolded me. I hadn't lived up to her expectations. She wanted to show me off, naturally. Children were to be seen and as I was the only one around that night, I was morally bound to mingle.

I felt like an utter failure. Why was I so shy? Why couldn't I be as open and cordial as her? I sat gloomily at the edge of her enormous bed. She was flinging a leg as if she were at the barre. She was very proud of her good figure and she maintained it with these daily exercises. She also swam and played golf at Wack Wack. A sports enthusiast since her childhood, she went to all the basketball games to cheer her head off. Unlike her compadres and women of her age, she trained her body, not simply oiled it. Although this morning she seemed to ache a little. She was gobbing off Tiger Balm onto her joints like it felt they needed all the gob they could get. Nevertheless, the scolding didn't stop. I endured it all. Finally, when the words subsided, I was made to apologize and was dismissed.

Feeling very small, feeling I would never succeed in life, I sat beside the marigolds and zinnias. My eyes trailed the vines along the west wall to the passive face of the northern wall that separated us from the convent, to the eastern wall which the servants' quarters guarded and by my mind's eye, I drew the line at the massive front wall and its closed gate. Then I looked up at the square sky above me, heavy with typhoon clouds.

There was no knight to rescue me. Tres Marias, Mama called us when she was kind; her lucky three girls in a row, three years of space between each of us. When she was unkind, she would begin with "If I had had a son . . . " and leave us to imagine the wonders which would have been wrought, and the Tres Marias would squirm at their seats, feeling guilty about their existence.

If we had had a brother, he would have rescued us. It was a man's world, the Old Boy system, men at the back room drinking San Miguel and dividing the world among them. We could only get married, albeit to these powerful leaders, and nothing else. Sis Two wanted to be a full-time singer. It was vetoed because the entertainment field was too low-class. Sis One didn't even bother to have ambitions. She was a poet, and poets don't have to earn a living. If she couldn't be a nun, she was going to be a good wife and mother. I had no discernible talent, and being youngest, didn't count anyway. But this brother, this noumenous nebulous brother who could have rescued us was never going to exist.

Mama had had a tubal ligation because she nearly died after delivering me. Her doctor suggested it, Papa consented; all the while, Mama was unconscious. She woke up to this blocked passage, tied at the entrance, strangled at the exit, to this emptiness, this death of possibilities. We were doomed forever, damsels without the knight. Thus, meanwhile, men on earth were looking for a ruler who could bear such a burden of responsibility, and succeed so great a king. No Numa to be found anywhere.

On the radio, Jo San Diego's voice, low, smooth and Americanized, was lulling me to sleep. From her voice I imagined her to look like a long tall Sally with Marlene Dietrich's heavily-lidded eyes. What she probably really looked like was some short dumpy woman with large hips from sitting down too long in front of the mike. Who knew? She must have studied in the States, her stress and intonation were so perfect, not like the Filipino accent with its Spanish overtones.

Miss Gutierrez, one of the lay faculty in the college section, had that same beautiful pattern. She had just been with us this past year and rumour was she'd be a nun. Pity. She was stunning. Thinking of nuns, we had a new American teacher for religion—Sr Alix, whom we all adored. Sr St Anthony was sent off at the end of the year to Yap Island, which seemed to be the elephant's burial ground. Sr Alix was great fun. She didn't humiliate the timid questioner and she could be approached after class. There was someone out there orchestrating these changes, someone who knew whom to take out and whom to put in, probably by some form of intelligence activity, as all things go in these organizations, clandestine observations, discreet eavesdropping, mental notes, report to headquarters.

Someone ran noiselessly by my door. I leapt up. Was that Sis One? I ran down after her.

"What's going on?"

She looked distraught. "Mama asked me to get Papa. Go back to bed."

Sis Two came down the stairs. We were all in our nightgowns.

"What do you mean, get Papa?"

The house was dark. The servants were in their quarters. We followed her outside. A large full moon, fever-yellow, hung low, lighting up the front lawn like an absurd Beckett set. The cool breeze hit us and I felt chilled. We were barefoot. In our haste, we forgot robes and slippers.

On the driveway cement, near the gates, we saw a bulky figure sprawled. There was Papa, dead drunk. He was gazing upwards at the moon. Sis One knelt down beside him and coaxed him to come in.

"It's too cold out here, you'll catch a cold."

He mumbled something about Mama and that he would sleep where he lay.

"You can't do that," Sis One fought back tears.

We tried moving him but he was too heavy. His legs wouldn't budge.

"What will the servants say?" Sis One urged. "And Mama is waiting for you."

She continued to reason with him, as patiently as she could, though I could see her heart was about to burst with sorrow. How difficult it must be, I thought, to be the eldest. On her shoulders lay all the responsibilities of the name that Mama and Papa bore and couldn't bear. It was her actions that guided us and she knew it. She chose her words carefully, she modelled

Christian virtues for us. Her marriage would be right and dynastic. She couldn't do anything wrong. She wasn't allowed to.

We sat a long time on the cold pavement, trying to think of how to make him get up. He was incoherent but he probably thought he was lucid because he kept on talking. What a headache he was going to have the next day. I looked at him plaintively. This was the man who at the age of fourteen had to flee India for Persia while his companions were being rounded up and hanged by the British, who led the exiled Indians to continue to fight for independence, who turned down Nehru's rewards because he said his love for his country was its own reward, this rich poor man, this uncommon common man. I was marked by ambivalences.

Sis One stood up to, what it seemed to be, bay at the moon, call down the gods, mark the spot. She stood over him like the Italian baron's sculpture.

The Marochetti angel stood grimly with its arms clasped against its breast, long white wings decidedly stern. Remember Cawnpore. You could say those two words and chills would run down a proper British spine. Not to worry. Sixty-two years later, General Dyer managed to double the score, not just to settle it, and throw in some hefty injuries besides. Same victims: women and children. Cawnpore, Amritsar, what did it matter. Hatred runs deep and long like the nourishing sea. Not until swaraj was achieved did the common Indian see the angel because no one was allowed to enter the compound. Incapable of despotism, or so the claim went, the British in leaving India hurriedly, left these stunning works of art anyway for the despised masses to enjoy, and who remembered Cawnpore now? Art endures but memory wanes and waxes only when politically expedient. Sixteen hundred and fifty rounds of ammunition, with the superior officer's and the Lt Governor of the Punjab's approval. The noble men felt vindicated.

And so the need for vindication grew—the Memorial was immemorial. Soon the entire earth would be covered by white crosses and white angels— the grass pushing against the stone. The stone over bones.

And he lay there, dead drunk, the impractical philosopher-soldier, the retired freedom fighter, as though freedom didn't have to be won again and again. Like Rizal the hero in his stone topcoat at the park, he had done his orations and had simply let the new generation rediscover the fight in its own way. Well, thanks a lot, Papa. What you secured you must maintain until we are strong enough to maintain it. Revenge, like flotsam waxing in with memory, was stronger than universal love. It came, it came again, it would come, even the British were still reeling from losing the Raj, they would never recover. In spite of you. A sentimental fool driven drunk.

"What shall we do? Shall I call Bienvenido?" Sis Two asked.

This was the last resort.

"We could get a blanket and just cover him up here," I suggested.

"And in the morning, when everyone wakes up and sees him? No, we must get him up. Lying here is bad for his health." Sis One insisted.

Not to mention ours in our flimsy cotton. There was not a cloud in the sky; just this one-eyed Cyclops staring down at us, three thin girls for the gobbling.

"I think he's falling asleep." We would never be able to move him now.

Sis One rubbed his hands. "Papa, Papa," she tried to shake him awake.

"I'll get a blanket," I said again.

"Go ask Mama what we should do," Sis Two said.

I got up quickly, my legs numb from sitting on the ground at an awkward position. Down the driveway came Bienvenido. He said he was going to check if the gates were locked. He did so and came back to us. We felt foolish but relieved. He seemed to know what was going on. He said he'd call Peping and another houseboy. It took half an hour to get Papa up to his bed, after much heaving, pushing and dragging of the heavy body. I went back to bed, very cold and very sad.

No one woke me up. I woke myself up with a sensation of falling, at 4 p.m. My throat was parched and I had waves of dizziness and hunger. The house was like Mausoleum, Halicarnassus revisited, Mausolos dead drunk upstairs. Romy the bodyguard was at his usual post, waiting. I sat with him. He spoke about his passion for cooking. He described how to cook adobo which reminded me that I was hungry so I called a passing zombie to bring me something to eat. Mona was sitting by the phone monitoring all the calls like a radio operator on the field after the battle, wearily, wounded. I found out everyone was out, including me. Romy continued to entertain me with visions of guinatan, escabeche, and something about crabs with eggs, or was that legs. Such long and involved preparations for a few moments of chewing. We were now both eating young green mango slices with salt which were giving me a stomach ache. I think I'm going to be sick, I told Romy.

"You have to be strong, Jazz," he said. "Like a rock."

Like a stone. I tried this for a few minutes, but I threw up, anyway, all over the cerulean Persian carpet with its two thousand knots per square inch.

Chapter Nineteen

A man in the Philippines is only an individual. He is not a member of a nation.
—Jose Rizal, *The Indolence of Filipinos*

Normally, Papa checked his post office box at noon hour, but today he couldn't, so he went back downtown to Plaza Lawton late in the afternoon to do that. I went with him.

The European architecture was formidable. The cream-coloured exterior was impressive with its columns and imposing steps. I was thrilled to be out there. We walked into the cool interior (the afternoon sun outside was smoldering) and to the sides where the boxes were. A whiff of rancid smell from what could only be the latrines in the basement hit me as I walked past the stairs going down.

"Ugh," I said to Papa, walking on ahead. "Do you have to smell that everyday?"

He was going 1675, 1676, 1677. "Ah, here we are."

The box was loaded with mail even though he had checked it yesterday. He had had his box ever since the year he arrived in the country. He never lost any mail even after moving to different addresses in twenty-five years.

On the way back I held my breath. Why couldn't public places be kept clean? Why couldn't people keep themselves clean? I was so disgusted I never went to the post office ever again.

Since we were near the Sta Cruz Church over Jones Bridge, at the end of Escolta, at the gates of Chinatown, we stopped by to visit. Papa had just been converted to Catholicism from his Sikh religion, so was still following his confessor's suggestions. After that, we went to his favourite European bakery and bought Vienna bread. At home, I tunnelled through the hard crust and ate only the white fluff.

"I see you've been through this," Sis Two said when she came home for her late merienda. "Do you want to come with me to Josie's house?"

Josie, the expelled, had a sister who used to be Sis Two's classmate but had a bad accident one day and was confined to a wheelchair. For the past year she couldn't attend school, so her friends visited her at home instead.

Josie lived in Horseshoe Drive, where two of Sis One's gangmates also lived, a new hilly subdivision. As the name implied, it was shaped like a horseshoe. It was a steep climb. Our cars were all parked perilously on an incline. Their house was very new, very modern, a bungalow with sliding doors and interlocking terraces. A proper merienda cena was laid out in the front terrace, stacks of pancit malabon, finger snacks of small fried lumpiang Shanghai, bowls of steaming hot guinatan, of cold sweet soft papaya cut in squares, dishes of cassava cakes, of small fried sweet bananas sprinkled with brown sugar—nothing was spared in generosity. The girls were already there when we arrived.

They were members of Sis Two's gang, the Rockers, after "Rock around the Clock." Unlike Sis One's gang, they were more cheerful, in a delirious kind of way, and better dancers. At school, they were also leaders but it was after school where they differed. Somehow, they partied more and harder, had more fun. They also did risqué things. One of their gangmates had a father who owned disreputable nightclubs in Manila and Hongkong. Another drove her own sports car at high speeds, and would pick up Sis Two by honking her horn at the gate, a behaviour Mama hated intensely. Another wore a beehive hairdo so tall it was half the length of her tiny height. Papa used to poke fun at how she looked. Another was a fanatic, so pious one suspected she wore hair shirts and slept directly on metal slats. Then, of course, there was Dave's uncle's girlfriend on the rebound from another affair, the "fast one" whose expulsion we all awaited. Yes, the Rockers were a strange and motley crew.

Josie's sister was in her wheelchair talking to everyone, full of humour, hysterically so, I thought, laughing right along with everybody. She must be putting up a brave front, she had to be the little soldier. It was the first time I had ever met her because I hadn't noticed her at school. She had very short hair and a luminous face, the eyes too bright.

After a while, she got tired. Josie wheeled her back to the bedroom which opened through French doors to an adjoining terrace. As I was talking to Josie at that moment, I had to follow them.

We got her onto her bed and she lay there for long seconds, after the exertion, quite still. Worried, Josie said, I'll get you a glass of water. She told me to stay for a minute.

I stood by her bed uneasily. I didn't know what to do. Her eyes were closed and she didn't move. Her face was grey. I thought, oh my God, she's dying, I'm actually watching a woman dying. What if she dies while I'm here, all alone with her? Where was her wound? If I touched her where her wound was, would it heal? Her wound was nowhere and everywhere, her agony only she could disclose.

I sat at her dressing table. It was one of those tables that had a lift-up mirror so I lifted it up to see her behind me. The squeaking hinge may have alerted her, because as I looked into the mirror I saw her staring. I was taken aback.

"Are you nervous?" She asked me in a dry tone and a bitter smile.

I didn't reply.

Josie came back in. I stood to go, her sister's gaze following me out.

Back in the front terrace, the girls were telling stories. I stood in a corner and looked down at the valley of new, shining concrete houses below, each a Monsalvat castle to last a thousand years. When it was time to go, some of the girls went to her room to say goodbye.

At the gate, we met two men who were their neighbours, brothers of a famous movie actor. Josie signed to them. "They're deaf," Sis Two explained. One was extremely handsome. I had never met deaf people before. Sis Two and her friends were quite adept at the sign language; I didn't know they had this skill. They never ceased to amaze me. Later on, I asked Sis Two to teach me the alphabet.

Soon after this visit, a few weeks later, Josie's sister died.

When we got home I locked myself in my room and listened to *Parsifal* for two hours and twenty-five minutes, reclining on my chair in the balcony, the wind in my face. I would breathe in "dienen, dienen" in the last act and Parsifal's head would float by being anointed at the sacred spring, and I would breathe out "dienen, dienen" and Kundry's head would float by as she dried his feet with her flowing hair. Flowing in "dienen, dienen" *Gesegnet sei, du Reiner, durch das Reine!* blessings and blessings upon you, flowing out "dienen, dienen" and Parsifal's hands over Kundry's head, sinner redeemed and all of Nature blossoming. Blossoming in "dienen, dienen" the earth in joy at the duty done and guilt gone, blossoming out "dienen, dienen" while Parsifal's arm stretches out to Amfortas, *Gesegnet sei dein Leiden . . .* and all, the whole world, my room, my self reclining on my chair in the balcony, all were swept up in the sphere of the symphony, all tone and no more words, pure music, pure fool, the oneness achieved, *Die Wunde seh' ich bluten, nun blutet sie in mir! Hier!—hier!*

At half past eight Sis One knocked on my door, yelling "If I hear anymore of that Nazi, I'll throw up." I forced myself to get dressed. We had to go to Manila Hotel for dinner with our good friends, the family of Jesse, actor and onion bomber. In the Candle Room there were so many American sailors who all looked alike. Jesse's sister said that was because they were in uniform.

We came home late, too full. Dave phoned to say that the nipa hut burned down that night. A cigarette, carelessly thrown. I felt very bad about it.

Outside, on a side lawn of their house in Parañaque, was a full-size nipa hut, the quintessential home found in the provinces, made of wood and a straw roof. It was a one-room house with one window, set open by a bar of wood propped in the middle of the window, and three front steps leading to the one entrance. "Bahay kubo, kahit munti" we used to sing as children: a value of the race. "Straw house, even though it's small, the plants around it are various." Then it listed the names of the plants one could grow in one's tiny garden: singkamas, talong . . . These were all sufficient for living—a simple way of life. Just a small house and a garden.

That wasn't why Dave's family had a bahay kubo in their lawn. It was a showpiece, an interesting Filipiniana, a rather largish coffee table artifact, a Philippine gazebo. I loved it. I made Dave let me sit inside for a little while. It felt like Beauty's home. It felt like a doll house. Dave felt silly in it.

"People in the provinces actually live in this kind of house?" I asked him.

"Yes, it's too small, don't you think?"

"If you have lots of children. It's so quaint."

"Quaint? I guess so. It's a real house."

"With real people living in them."

"What's your point?" He lost interest. He was fingering a cigarette which he couldn't light in there.

"How did your mom get this?" I wanted one badly.

"I don't know. She just had it sent down, maybe."

"I could live in this."

He laughed.

"Seriously. I could be like a Desert Father living in a cave except here it would be a bahay kubo."

"This is crazy. You're just playing. Come on, let's get out of here. I want to smoke."

I took away his lighter. He sighed.

"Give that back." He put his hand on my thigh where my arm rested with his lighter. His hand felt very heavy. I wondered if he would become violent. While I wondered, he withdrew his hand and gazed with puppy-eyes at me.

"Smoke then," I returned it. "I do really love this."

"It's nothing. It's just a nipa hut. It doesn't even have a bathroom. You prefer this to that?" He waved his hand to his pleasure dome villa-by-the-sea.

"Maybe I might make a back door, make some alterations."

"You would."

I wondered if it was Dave's cigarette that consumed it. It would have gone up in one red tongue of flame, a pentecostal conflagration.

After Jesse's family left, we prayed our rosary, then talked all early morning in our parents' bedroom while the lights were out.

Chapter Twenty

> I have seen a shell from our artillery strike a bunch of Filipinos, and then they would go scattering through the air, legs, arms, heads, all disconnected, And such sights actually made our boys laugh and yell, "That shot was a peach!"
> —Charles R Wyland, Company C, Washington Volunteers

Olongapo. When Mama said the word, you could see her convulse. It was synonymous with sin, VD, American sailors. I had no idea where it was; all we knew was that it was outside a base, a hell in our midst. Ever since I could remember, this outcry of "Get the American bases out" was a perpetual drone.

Today, Tita Nita was arriving from Olongapo. She owned a restaurant there. Very wealthy from her lucrative post, she loved Olongapo; she loved Americans. Every so often we'd read about terrible things from that city—almost always something sordid of the male-female mis-relations variety; a Filipina killed or abused, an American killed or robbed. Never anything pleasant. I had never heard anything good that came out of Olongapo.

Except money. Tita Nita had been a poor relation from the province—now, she was very, very rich.

"If the Americans pull out," she said over a cup of coffee, from china which Mama would never use again, "the communists will take over the Philippines. It's the Americans who are protecting us."

"Are we not targets instead? The communists will hit us because the bases are here."

Tita Celia, a pediatrician, added, "And all those children left behind, the souvenirs..."

"The communists are already here. They've infiltrated the remote areas. Look at the Huks..." Tita Nita needed so much to complete her thoughts that she didn't listen to what her companions were saying in response to what she had just uttered, because she then continued her sentence which had nothing to do with what her companions said. This put off Mama for a moment, who was embarrassed to have spoken up too rapidly, as though she had interrupted Tita Nita's speech, a terrible breach of formal dissension etiquette. Undaunted, Tita Nita spoke on, her eyes on the solid brass bull dominating the coffee table, her stretched sentences punctuated by ruminating pauses. Mama wanted to see if she was indeed done, having now lost the build-up to the main point that had yet to come or perhaps had come earlier, in which case Mama didn't seem to care anymore what the hell Tita Nita was talking about. Tita Celia, who wasn't particularly listening anymore because she was forming her own line of defence, was a sheepish voice in the witness box, muttering and discordant, whispering ominously in the background, as if anyone cared to stretch one's hearing to pick up her inaudible bits of wisdom.

"I mean," Mama's voice stayed low but turned firm, "the bases are here to protect American interests in Asia—they're using us for their own operations."

"So? We're profiting from them now."

Tita Celia said, "We have their money, diseases, crime, and children."

"And," Mama pursued her line of thought, "when they go to war with Russia so would we because we are allies. There go our sons again, dying for other people."

And there went Mama's eyes, all misty, thinking of the son she couldn't send off to war.

"Plus they're having a good time at our expense," Tita Celia added. "They couldn't get all these from any other Asian country. We're strategically located, we're English-speaking, we're Christians—"

"The only Christian country in Asia."

"And they've been here since 1947. In the past ten years they've entrenched themselves; it would take thousands of dollars to set up elsewhere."

Tita Nita put her fork down decisively. "Nonsense. Americans are our friends. They're here for our mutual benefit."

Unable to pursue this argument logically, in clear syllogisms, Mama finally blew up in a ferocious personal attack. "How can you take that filthy money?"

Tita Nita's eyes flared. "Money is money. When you're hungry, you'll take anything. You wouldn't know." Mama inspired jealousy from anyone who knew her. They coveted her looks, her smooth legs, her American accent, her solid brass bull.

"You have enough now," Tita Celia said calmly, in a conciliatory tone. "Why not go back to Samar, get married, settle down, have children."

I watched Tita Nita's drop-dead face. She had seen Paree. Tita Celia was too naive, too conciliatory, an Aguinaldo taking an oath of allegiance to the US in 1901, taking the easy way out.

Mama, on the other hand, was wishing an *Ovide Moralisé* flood on Olongapo. "Stop selling yourself to the devil, Nita."

I sensed bad feelings looming, so I left the room. Tita Nita was close to tears but still defiant. I sought out Sis One who was reading a magazine in her bedroom.

"Look at this," she pointed to an advertisement of Alpine Milk. "A white baby. 'Where's my Alpine Milk? Alpine Milk carries the Nestlé guarantee of purity and quality, and strict control during manufacture ensures the highest of standards necessary for infants. So nothing but the best is good enough for baby, and the best is there in Alpine Milk—' " She flipped pages. "Now here, a white man drinking coffee with KLIM. 'To add delicious flavour, you need KLIM . . . the best milk!' Borden Company." She went flip, flip, flip. "Do you realize that when they haven't got a white face, they just draw a caricature?"

I looked over her shoulder. "No, there's Camay bath soap with a photograph."

"That's Lolita Rodriguez, star of Sampaguita Pictures, looking more white than the whites." She returned to counting how many Americans per Filipinos in ads.

"Tita Nita is here," I said. "They're fighting."

She shrugged. Nothing new. Discussions always descended to arguments. The Filipinos were a quarrelsome race. I gave her a synopsis.

"It's all based on the Mutual Defense Act, 1951. After the Japanese left us in ruins, we thought we needed help to strengthen our defences. The Americans are our special friends."

"Are they?"

"Yes. We're inextricably bound with them."

"Inextricably?"

"Historically, through blood, in death, in consanguinity, in marriage, etcetera. There's no escape."

"Will the communists attack us because of the bases?"

"No. The communists do not attack. They infiltrate and turn people into commies. They don't have to make dramatic attacks."

"I mean, should we fear the Russians?"

"No. We should fear the Chinese. Except it's too late; they're already here. Just as they took over Formosa."

"You make it sound like a bad science fiction movie."

"They have to expand. They're too overcrowded. We have a natural historical tie with the Chinese, too, remember. They've been with us since the beginning of recorded time."

"But it sounds like everybody's had a claim on the Philippines. Everbody's been here and still here. Are we so mongrelized? What's a Filipino?"

"Hmmm, that's what I'm working on."

"So, what are you saying? Should the Americans leave?"

"The bases are irrelevant."

"Well, they seem to be causing a lot of damage right now. That seems to be very relevant."

"You need to develop a sense of perspective. What Beckett calls 'distancing.' They are irrelevant in the long run. When the Americans realize that, they will pick up and go away. Now you, too, can go away. I have no interest in this conversation. Go bother Julie."

I got off her bed. "Can I bother you later?"

"Yes, much later."

Much later, I came back. She was now lying in bed, asleep, with her eyeballs half covered by her eyelids. How could she sleep like that? Sis Two was listening to Filipino artists, consummate imitators. It never failed to amaze me how they could copy American singers so well, complete to the Southern accent, while they were singing, but as soon as they talked, back to Filipino accents, the f's confused with the p's, the e's the sound of i's, the pronouns all mixed up.

Sis One was lying flat on her back, without a blanket. It was strange watching her half-eyeballs making her look awake as she slept. I sat at her desk and waited for her to wake up.

"Time to eat," Emiliana poked her head in and out of the room.

Startled, Sis One looked to her left. As I was to her right, it took her a few seconds to turn to her right to see me. I could have shot her plane down by now. She had poor defence instincts.

"What are you doing?" She stammered.

"Nothing. I was waiting for you to wake up."

"Hmm," she mumbled, then turned over and went back to sleep.

Hmm, I thought. I'll have to train my sisters how to survive the enemy attack. In spite of their intelligence, they were too complacent, trusting and naive.

"Land."

"Land?"

"Yup."

Papa had just finished talking about a sugar baron and his political connivances. He had visited the plantation once and was sickened by what he saw there—the feudal system, the wretched conditions of the workers. Sis

One then said, "land."
"Service."
"Service?"
"Yup."
He had seen tenants who were forever in debt and still had utang na loob to their master, still had to fulfill their oath of loyalty.
"Control."
I gave up repeating her grunts.
He had seen women there as chattel, and he had shuddered, having three daughters, to think this may be our fate. He had decided that we would leave the Philippines.
"This is no country for you children. I will send you abroad."
The problem was, where? Other countries were not attractive, either. Everyone went to America, despite the rhetoric. England was anathema to Papa, who had fought for Indian independence, yet he prized it over the US. I wanted to go to Germany.
"Liberté, fraternité, egalité," Sis One said.
"To France?" Sis Two asked.
"We need a revolution," I interpreted.
Mama ordered Emiliana to bring in desserts. Papa began to sing a song by the Platters often heard in the airwaves. Oh, oh, oh, oh, I—I—I'm just, a great pretender. Oooh, oooh, oooh, oooh, oooh, ahhh. One may have sung Bengal into a nation, but in Manila the note was false.
We were like coconuts—brown on the outside, white inside. Who said that? Some critic of lackeys? E M Forster, maybe? Originality and my reading blurred—sometimes I didn't know if I was using another person's imagery. I was just a collage of other people's work, cut and pasted symbols and signs that purported to be words. Mine? Theirs? This education we underwent, this lobotomy of crammed studies, repeated throughout the ages, institutionalized knowledge passed down the generations as though newly discovered—look, let me interpret that hack anew, let me add to the addendum—this fraudulent education brought us up to be like each other, to give us the same referents and references so that we could say, is this a dagger—and the other would finish the line or wittily offer a rejoinder from another bard, and we'd go ha ha ha, don't we know our allusions, we who belong to the same class.
And there I was, shocked to see Eton at the end of a narrow road and the bottom of the hill, hallowed ground in my imagination—grim Eton that made me feel walled-in as we stood in the quad. Outside, a series of low doors that would have frightened Alice made me wonder, my stomach turning, what

horrors they hid—particularly one that said CONDUCT. I thought if I were a nine-year-old boy I'd feel abandoned by my parents. Why would fathers send their sons to experience the horrors they had experienced? Was this rite of passage for the leaders of society necessary? Was this suffering part of the system that liked to gobble up the finest minds? Were not the whole graduating classes sent off to die in the wars, so fine were these young men that they were the best sacrifices for the country?

Was that love? Was Conduct, the perpetuity of correct conduct, more important than a life? Was the point Humanity, not a human?

Through adversity to the stars.

The pretense, the shrug of the shoulder, the carry on with daily life somehow affected all of us.

Sis One was looking out the balcony and saw a guest alighting from her car. She said, "Watch this. As soon as she comes in, her voice will rise two octaves, her arms will go up over her head, her words will be, 'Aaay, it's *so* good to see you.' "

I looked at the woman's face; in spite of the thick makeup, it looked tired and bored, and the party hadn't even begun yet.

"Hurry," Sis One urged. "Run down and see how I'm right."

I rushed down the stairs. She was coming in when I got there, her stride confident and gracious, towards Mama, who was equally smiling.

"Aaay, it's *so* good to see you," her high voice rose.

I laughed out loud. She turned and saw my bright face which mirrored hers. She didn't lose a beat; the show was on. Her slender body composed into an imitation of an exquisite noblewoman in a Japanese silkscreen.

I ran back to Sis One, laughing all the way up.

"Well?"

I mimicked the woman.

Sis One shook her head. "Artificial. Everyone's artificial."

In the early morning, I turned on the light and read "Tales from the Crypt" and other horror stories. One was about a Martian posing as an Earthman and as he was about to be extinguished by another Earthman, he pulled off his face to lay the other to waste, but the attacker turned out to be Venusian. So, two aliens in one swoop—one wonders how many real Earthmen there are left on earth. In fact, another story was about an Earthman who'd been taken over by an alien form—a grotesque figure that had changed his right arm and hand. So he kept his hand gloved. He went to a bar and as he was drinking, the other customers teased him about it. In the scuffle, the glove came off and he was devastated because he didn't want people to know that he had been captured. But everyone laughed and suddenly the last strip exposed right hands—all heads of this alien form. What metamorphoses, even Ovid, even Kafka would have applauded. If their right hands could. All these hiding and revealing. The whole world was obsessed with transformations, magical or horrible.

At noon I was half-awake when Mama and I went to see the movie, *The Journey*. The Hungarian prisoners floated past my consciousness like alien forms. When they began singing their national anthem as the bells tolled, I cried. We repeated the movie then bought Merton's *Seeds of Contemplation* and ate at D & E.

In the late afternoon, Sis One read an article in the *Reader's Digest* about communism that she said was meant to make her hate it. I spent my time being a Desert Father cum Buddhist while reading Merton. Sis Two was on the phone all day.

In the evening, Sis One lent me her pencil-cut skirt for a dinner at Casa Marcos before the ballet. I was so excited to wear this—instead of the usual trapeze, semi-trapeze, and balloons. She wore a copper sheath; Sis Two, a velvet cocktail dress. Mama was stunning, as always, in a black lace with gold threads. It never mattered what the three of them wore. They carried clothes, even their housedresses, with elegance and flair. That they had the fine Gujarati silks and bolts of Bengali cloth which Papa faithfully brought home made them feel confident that in the toss of their accessory there were more where that came from. We were like the families of the Ottoman Empire in the seventeenth century.

Papa was in his light grey Italian silk suit. He never wore anything Asian. Dressing up was such a ritual. Putting on makeup alone took forever. At the end we would look like we had just stepped out of a hatbox, the white tissue just draped so, exposing our bright new crispness. We were the ad-maker's ideal. It occurred to me that we spent an inordinate time layering ourselves and what we did echoed in all the families' homes we knew. We were like the Manila Cathedral, the Post Office, the National Museum—all solid sixteenth Century magnificent stone architectural wonders while the rest of the populace huddled under rusted corrugated iron roofs.

While my splendid family continued to dress, I went to the library and sat under the gaze of the three Marx-like brothers and skimmed over a comic. In this comics, the poor didn't spend so much time in front of the mirror. There was one story of a woman whose husband loved her because of her beautiful long hair. It was the one thing she prized most. Then one day she went to a beauty parlour and had it cut off. She had sold her long hair so that she could buy food for the family.

I sighed. Here was another one. A twelve-year-old boy, hungry, peering through the windows of a restaurant. He had only enough money to buy medicine for his sick grandfather at home. Dizzy and weak, he got to the pharmacist, bought the medicine, and ran home. When he got there, his grandfather was dead.

What had I to write about? Nobel Prizes were given to writers of anguish and pain, not of the decadent rich. All these comic stories, born of true struggles—these were all true winners—I would award them all. But I knew nothing except for immature boys and empty dialogues. No suffering or loss. We were all whole with complete minds and bodies—no shattering disabilities or terminal illnesses. We had no dead to visit on All Souls' Day. There were no madwomen in the attic, no dramatic conflicts to peak to a fictional climax for our family history. The boss on our shield was omphalos. We were untested, poised at the edge of the mountain ready for flight or fall. We were still to be wrenched apart, to be devoured by the Furies. Till then, I had nothing to write about. I could only live each dissipated day until the gods saw us.

Yet for all that I saw of our vanities, I was not immune to vanity. I didn't want to go up to the communion rail because my slip kept falling. I mumbled this to Sis One. She helped me tuck it up but I insisted it would surely be seen past the hem of my skirt. She was infuriated. She whispered hoarsely: Do you think God cares how you look?

"It's not God, it's the people," I whispered back, glancing quickly at all the acquaintances who happened to be there this Sunday. Before communion, anyway, I fainted yet again, not having eaten since eight p.m. and that, my sparrow portion. I regained consciousness on the hard wooden seat while people were walking up to the rail. Sis One allowed me to stay behind them but brought me to the Stations of the Cross later that night.

"This no food after midnight and before receiving rule should change," I said to her at home.

"You should go to earlier Mass," she answered.

"What's earlier than 6:30? I'd have to live in the Rectory."

Since I felt weak, I lay around the house. I had officially read all the books at home, even Mama's *Lady Chatterley's Lover* and *The Fountainhead* which I found hidden in her closet and over which I wondered why they had been banned reading, and Sis One's Emily Loring romances, with its tall men with lapis lazuli eyes, which she hid in her armoire along with magazine photographs of Marlon Brando, I think more in shame than in rebellion, and so I had nothing to read. I had finished the books Susan had lent me and the trash Jerry left behind. I missed the Justice's library where the best books rested. I had re-read Graham Greene. I had worried over the fact that our generation grew up under Teilhard de Chardin. I had solaced myself with Camus, with the sharp edge of his clarity.

I had played the piano, cards, chess, checkers, record player, radio; watched Tina iron; talked to an aunt in one of the rooms, and to Mr Choith, the Indian jeweller who was our current houseguest. The phone rang. Sis One said, "She's not in." She put the receiver down. "It was Al Aguinaldo." Too bad, I thought. That might have been a diversion, at least. She then went to see *Asintado* with Jesse's older sister whose husband had the leading role. Asintado: sharpshooter. Right on target. No bluffs, fogs, lies. They asked me if I wanted to join them but it would have been useless, with my one thousand functional Tagalog words. One time we passed by a movie house marquee and I read out loud "Mga daing sa libingan." I said, "Must be a comedy. Why would there be fish in the cemetery?" Jesse's sister laughed. "Wrong accent. Stress on the second syllable. Moans. Moans from the grave."

How could anyone know? What did one make of this "bababa ka ba?" Looking at all those repeated syllables, it was all gibberish. "Are you going down?" had distinctive individual words joined together to make sense. But its counterpart: "Bababa ka ba?" Are you kidding?

Dave said he was visiting Rene who had a fever. Esther said she just got her white lace for a party. Nilda said Lyn's discovered she has a tumor in her breast. We felt sorry for her. I got tired of talking to people on the phone in between Sis Two who hung on longer than I did. She had a new boyfriend who was taking up law in Ateneo. In the afternoon, friends came and went, probably bored as I was, making the rounds to spend the day. What an interesting idiom that was—"to spend the day." It had the ring of money to it, like so many pesos per minute, but in fact we didn't spend any money all day. Why not "to unfold the day" as in the scroll of life, or "to weave the day" as in the fabric of life. What was a day? Did we unravel from birth or accumulate to death? Why was I accounting for the days of 1955 to 1959? What did it matter if today Dave was kind and yesterday Sr St Anthony was not? Why am I filling the day with our actions? Is it "to act the day?" And if these actions have meaning—"to mean the day?" To be: the first verb in any language. "To be the day." To create it. I must rise earlier to greet the dawn, like Rimbaud and Van Gogh, who wanted to be present in the creation of a new day.

And then it was night. Papa had gone to the airport to watch planes land and take-off, a pastime he indulged more often on days when business deals troubled him. He should have been an aviator; he certainly wasn't a businessman, even though his first deal was to buy airplanes for this country. When he was not actually flying, he watched them fly—he loved planes so. Or maybe it was the actual movement, the graceful and astonishing flight into the air, the primitive desire to be a bird, to take wing, to be an angel, to reach God. Papa's original wish was to become a guru. He sat at the foot of one who told him to go experience the world first then come back. He did so reluctantly, and the experience trapped him so that he never got back. Maybe watching the plane's departure simulated that going back for him.

Mama was in her room pasting tiny black triangles onto the scrapbook, then filling in the squares they made with family photographs. Sis One was playing a manic Mephisto waltz No. 1 with no Gretchen in sight. I listened to her pounding and thought up rock and roll lyrics to go with the rhythm, this music a precursor I think. Liszt got back—he fulfilled his desire to become a priest—and a Franciscan, at that! Faust was fulfilled and redeemed as well. How fortunate. Knowledge. How can I serve you if I don't know you? I don't know you—go from me. Who are you?

Sis Two was in her locked room and I didn't know what she was doing. She was a mystery sometimes; I didn't know what went on in her mind. She was all music, tonality, orchestral phrase, harmony. Some maids were in the back kitchen separating husk from the grain. They were telling stories, very relaxed, very happy. Bienvenido was smoking with Tina near the grapevines.

God's blessing on solitude. I was alone in the library reading Carl von Clausewitz's *Vom Kriege*, having difficulties comprehending it since my eyes darted from word to dictionary, all meaning suspended until I could find the verb at the end of the sentence. It was slow going because I was self-taught in German and without Coleridge's patience. Why I bothered to study this ponderous opus, I didn't know. Was he not proven wrong, anyway, this book removed from the required reading list after the resounding defeat in the First World War showed the Germans that following his ideas was ineffective, if not fatal? Ah, political silence. Politics a science, the science of war. And approximately every twenty years the Americans have been at war: the Revolutionary War, War of 1812, Mexican War, Spanish-American War, World War I, World War II, Korean War, and now since 1957, Vietnam. My generation's parents suffered through one war, we suffered through another, and our children, by scientific predictability, will suffer their own. Is peace just fluting between the edges of the column, the rest period between the wars?

Perhaps I was echoing Papa's ideas and sentiments kicked around as we sat in the living room after supper because even as I mouthed them, my eyes watered at the sound of "And rockets' red glare, the bombs bursting in air, / Gave proof through the night that our flag was still there." And they misted as the bombardment over Fort McHenry began. Papa laughed at my sentimentality, telling me that the tune came from an old British drinking song. Sis One reminded me that no country had had a monopoly on warmongering. All humans were accountable. What separated the civilized from the barbarians was the quality of their mercy. Mama nodded. She recalled the POW camp at the University of Santo Tomas grounds and the concentration camp in Capas, Cavite, where her uncle, the congressman and resistance leader, ate the sour heart-shaped leaves of the alibangbang tree overhanging the barbed wires just to survive.

Chapter Twenty-one

Patriotism is not enough. I must have no hatred or bitterness towards anyone.
—Nurse Cavell

Papa said I was scatter-brained. I talked about one thing and then I quickly talked about another, changing topics as if my thoughts eluded me. Sis One agreed. She said she had to fill in the blanks between my leaps of thought. But I got bored with one idea and another was fired in my brain so I had to run after it. In any case, I left something for the listener to do, rather than just passively listen to my rambling. At least there was response, participation in my thinking process, a multiple-choice test. Sis Two disagreed with my analysis. She said it was because my thoughts were unclear, like indistinguishable objects in a fog.

The fog. She and I were playing gin rummy in Beauty's house near the gates when we suddenly heard a heavy rumbling sound. We looked out and saw a thick white pall drifting over the fence. I thought it was war, the smoke coming from guns.

But Sis Two said it looked like fog, the kind that England gets. We opened the gate a little and peeked out. It was a government truck spraying the street with some chemicals against mosquitoes. We closed the gate quickly, coughing and choking as with tear gas in the movies, but we were enveloped anyway in this fog.

That night I couldn't sleep. I had so many thoughts running in my head. I would think of the Theatre Guild and acting, and then suddenly Dave would come into the picture. I thought of England and what my life would be like if I lived there. I was sleeping in Sis Two's bed and she suddenly pushed me, so I woke up. She said I was dreaming aloud but I couldn't remember the dream.

We got up to go to mass but Sis Two was suddenly taken ill on our way there, so we hailed a passing taxi, brought her home, and Tina and I walked back, just in time for communion. She was well enough in the afternoon for the whole family to eat lunch at Rainbow Luncheonette and then see *Objective Germany*. We sat there for four hours, ate at Rainbow again and when we got home, all the three of us sisters were dead over Dirk Bogarde.

Sis Two and I were sick off and on for a week. I did a lot of sleeping during the day. I slept past eleven, and then ate lunch, and slept until around past four. I was terribly tired. Had no energy to stay up too long. Spent the time reading a comic. It was about Plastic Man—his elongated, rubbery arms could slide longer and longer past and around the corner of buildings until they encircled the bad guy several blocks away. He didn't even have to leave his house. Sis Two read about Mandrake the magician, and Phantom who never seemed to die but actually did and someone else donned the silly purple costume. Such deceit. She also read Prince Valiant who had a silly hairdo. Sis One's gang, who kept us company, read *Archie* comics, bound in handsome leather bindings so they looked like real books, which could be read during silent-reading time in class.

We played cards at home—gin rummy, bluff, the game Colonel Richards taught us. At the end of the week, Jesse's sister came by to bring us to the studio. We were going to preview Jesse's latest film tonight at their house, but first we watched a film being made. The actor kept pushing the actress against a wardrobe, the contents would fall out and a straw basket full of clothes would fall on her head. Then studio men would put everything back as they were, and the actor would push the actress again against the wardrobe and the contents would fall out again. I wondered what the story was. By the tenth time she didn't look like she was acting—the pained expression on her face looked real—and I wondered if she was really aching because the actor was really slamming her. All this punishment for a few bucks? I hoped for her sake that she was a famous actress. Most of them came from very poor families and when they became famous the first thing they did was to buy a house for their parents.

I wandered off to another set because I felt sorry for her. It looked as though she were trapped in this tiny square of life, this Sisyphean role. Here they were shooting an audience scene. Someone told me to sit down and put my hands up over my head and clap along with the others—all that was required were hands clapping in the air. I did this for a few minutes but as I noticed they were going to shoot this again I got up and left because my palms were aching.

I looked for Jesse's sister and hung around with her until it was time to go. At their house, Jesse's mother had the film ready to roll, so we sat and snacked while we watched. She prefaced it by saying it was more of the same action film—that's what people wanted to see. In other words, it was Jesse again on a horse, rescuing the distressed damsel. And that's what it turned out to be. Jesse went, "Tayo na mga kasama!" and his companions leapt to their horses and off they rode. Jesse could never do wrong. He was one of the elect, the hero, the good. I should ask him what that felt like.

If the original battle was between God and Lucifer, why use us in their struggle for power? What if I wasn't one of the elect? What if I was one of the damned? Why allow me to damn myself?

"You have free will," Sr. Alix answered.

Why did God risk my soul by giving me free will? Why give me free will if I were just going to use it against me? If I am damned, even if I have free will, can I choose God? No, because by definition, I am damned.

"There is Grace," Sr Alix said.

Susan had to pick up something and I went along for the ride, so while I was waiting for her, Sr Alix entertained me with small talk that led to the above exchange. When Susan returned, Sr Alix said, "That was a lovely graduation ceremony, don't you think? All those forty-four girls, lovely in their robes."

Susan agreed.

"And your class," she told me, "eighty-two innocent souls. Everything went so well."

The school was very quiet, not one of those souls around. It felt strange to be in this quiet—no laughter, no gossiping, no active participation. It was dead. We left quickly.

It was Sis Two's birthday. We had gone to 6:30 Mass at Cubao and stayed in Susan's place in the morning, listening to Buddy Holly and reading *Catcher in the Rye*. When we got home, Sis Two's friends started pouring in. We served cake, Coke, etc. They became so many, exceeding the number we anticipated (I guess we didn't realize how popular Sis Two was!) that we ran out of food. The maids had to make sandwiches. After a frenetic while, everything was fine again. We slept around eleven p.m.—it had been a whole day and night party. We were so tired. Sis Two gave me the golden heart necklace she once cherished, now no longer of value.

While we were undergoing this celebration, Sis One arrived from Maryknoll with my report card. For the first time in my life I got a D. In algebra. I slept in my bed that night. I was so ashamed.

Chapter Twenty-two

> Jane Lister, deare child
> Hannah Lister, deare wife
> —Epitaphs, Westminster Abbey

This was the only country in the world where one could find a Davao, Davao Oriental, Davao del Sur, and no Davao Occidental; where Lanao del Norte and Lanao del Sur lay side by side on a west-east direction; where Agusan del Sur could be found north of North Cotabato, and where Ilocos Norte and Ilocos Sur lay on the west side of Luzon island; as both Negros Occidental and Negros Oriental lay on the west side of the Visayas. Needless to add, there were a Northern Samar, an Eastern Samar and a Samar, but no Western Samar. Dare to find Misamis Occidental and Misamis Oriental where their names purport to be. Either the Spanish map makers were drunk or this deception was designed to confuse the Chinese pirates. Not only were people misdirected but, now ingrained into their bones for centuries, they were also misplaced.

Those who have found us have been invaders: Spanish, American, Japanese; or refugees who had nowhere else to go. Here they got, after the land-hopping through the Sulu Sea, the Celebes, the Bohol, the Philippine Sea, and here they constructed their houses on stilts, planted shakily on those waters, and here they stayed, their roots gone with the eddy of those tides. Some of us were trapped here by the unfolding of life, the marriage, the children, the business, the War, trapped before we knew it, in a confused country, 7,107 islands, most uninhabited and uninhabitable, the rest populated to the teeth with such a variety of cultures that to extract their origins is a daunting task.

Islas de San Lazarus: that was its original Spanish name. What it was called before the Spanish destroyed everything is unrecorded. What it is called now is a misnomer, a subservience to a king who didn't rise from the dead. Call it Lazarus. Call it forth from the dead.

As Grandfather Apolonio did. He was pronounced dead and laid out on the dining table. This was during the time when the dead were not embalmed and were buried after a day's wake. The candles were lit all around him, his children, Mama a baby, and friends wailing beside him, when he suddenly sat up and said "St. Anthony," calling after a departing figure, the robed back turned towards the front door. Some people fainted. He had a devotion to St Anthony and he believed that the saint woke him up, called him from the dead. He lived a long full life and finally died over ninety.

Which apocryphal story made me fear burial. Suppose one were still alive—buried alive. How Usher. And your whole being would focus on this one thought: escape. Push against the heavy door. Push out. Nails bleeding.

So there we were in the heart of the necropolis, among the dead, among the immortals, the angels, saints, poets, philosophers, scientists, statesmen, priests, nobles, military heroes, kings and queens, with their attendant rosy cherubs, kneeling weepers, faithful dogs and nubile servants. One could almost hear the Benedictines chanting down the ages, hear them down the five hundred feet of immortality from the west door to the Chapel of the Knights.

Of course we would begin at the north transept with the naval heroes, for what was England without them, flanked by Sir Charles Wager and Edward Vernon. Then we came upon the East India Company's Sir Eyre Coote with his mourning Indians. And could the colonies forget Charles Buller? Not to be outdone, Scheemakers's Admiral Watson of the Black Hole of Calcutta. All under palm trees.

And in the Sanctuary, 50,000 pieces of marble plundered from Rome by Abbot de Ware, bright colours arranged in circles, a mosaic to delight and to honour his bones buried underneath. At the back of the Sanctuary under the sedilia, King Sebert's tomb, the oldest grave, this entire giant memorial building a shrine to him built by his uncle Ethelbert, King of Kent. Behind the Sanctuary, Edward the Confessor's chapel, beside it was set the Stone of Scone, twenty-six inches long, sixteen wide, brought by a Scottish king to the Abbey of Scone where it was used to crown kings of Scotland for four hundred years before being brought here by Edward I. Carved with a penknife on its Coronation Chair: "Peter Abbott slept in this chair July 5, 1800."

So there was Peter Abbott, Westminster schoolboy, a commoner who acted on his desire for royal entrapments, scratching in his name for fame. And the Benedictine's Gregorian chant is drowned by the boys' song, "Let us now praise famous men" in the service of the Commemoration of Benefactors.

Square inch upon square inch of immortals, Henry VII's Chapel with its over seventy royals, the Warrior's chapel with the flags of the Empire, Died for the Empire (Great War): 1,069,825. This place was the Taj Mahal 10,000 times over, full concentrated energies of memory, sacred and beloved. But where the one has delicate poignancy in its uniqueness, this one hammers the grief down, over and over, in overwhelming dabs of paint, like an obsession, an artist gone berserk over the one spot, daubing it to perfection, articulating the fire in his mind, this passion for the Memorial, this civilization memorialized, this memory civilized into style. In this long day of the night, all is permanence.

And here it was again, another commoner who would be king: "William Miles of 30 Tufton Street, Westminster, repaired this window February 1797, bloed out by the wind" scratched on the window pane near the roof (but you must climb out to see it from outside) of Henry VIII's chapel. The little man asserting his sovereignty, commemorating his benefaction, celebrating his life among the dead, repairing the window against the wind, pushing against the lid.

Out. Getting out.

People we hadn't talked to in years had been phoning since our pictures came out in the newspapers with the caption: England Bound. It was like a vicarious escape for them, as if talking to us, touching us, gave them the illusion or hope that they, too, would leave. This wasn't just the euphoria of summer holidays abroad because then one came back for the school year. This was the great flight across the Pacific, the great adventure, beginnings of life. Everyone dreamed of getting away permanently from Manila. No nation in the world was more obsessed with leaving. It was the UN Year of the Refugee, and we all had that sense of going elsewhere for a better life.

It was around nine and the whole family was sitting in the sala enjoying the last hours before bedtime, when suddenly we heard my name called by many girls. At the door were my classmates (not the gang) and my English teacher, come to fetch me for Ana's hen party. While the family entertained them, I got dressed. At the party they kidded me about the London trip. This escape gave me a new credibility, a new glow, in their eyes.

The one that got away.

What was it about the country that made us want to leave it? We had everything—we had each other—and still we thought what we had was not enough, was inferior, that there was something better yet ordained for us. Our country was insufficient; it did not satisfy. Worse, it was a place to run away from. The islands imprisoned us, the waters surrounded us, the slippery barnacle-encrusted walls we could not climb. We had no footholds. Why was life better in America? In England?

We were like POWs digging tunnels, crossing minefields, dodging bullets. Run, run, run. Get up, and run.

PART THREE

THE THIRD ORDER

Cavalry to advance and take advantage of any opportunity to recover the Heights. They will be supported by infantry, which have been ordered to advance on two fronts.

OR was it:

They will be supported by infantry which have been ordered. Advance on two fronts.

Chapter Twenty-three

But everything is over. If I were really a writer, I would have to be able to prevent the war.   —Anonymous, August 23, 1939

Waiting. We were waiting for orders while someone deliberated.

A self-styled prophet had informed the radio stations and the newspapers that on a certain date and time, the world would come to an end. He urged people to come to a certain place, to bring candles with them. There would be a prayer rally. On that day, a Saturday night, people began to mass to this chosen spot. The candle parade was impressive. Thousands of people thronged, all praying in unison, waiting for the world to end. We listened to the radio broadcasts all night. Then it began to rain. They hadn't prepared for that. Without umbrellas, they stood in the rain, still praying, waiting for the particular second of destruction. The prophet led them from his sheltered stage, his voice booming through the microphones. More and more people arrived, some now with umbrellas, as the moment neared. When the appointed hour passed and still the world lay intact, they waited a little longer, just in case God was operating on a different time zone. Finally, at midnight, candles having been extinguished five hours before, the gathered people muttered among themselves. Where was the promised miracle? The prophet said, our prayers forestalled the doom. God heard us and so the world had been saved. That appeased them somewhat. Some left feeling good that they had been instruments of conciliation against nature's forces, some left feeling satisfied that because their prayers were answered this meant God was on their side, some left feeling forgiven for their sins, some left feeling foolish. Everyone left soaked to the bone.

While the maids could not be stopped from going to this rally, they could be picked up after the time had passed. Mama sent Bienvenido, and I waited in the car for an hour while he searched among the thousands. Finally, he gave up and Emiliana came down with a fever next day. It seemed like it *was* the end of the world for her.

Like a falling cadence, the rain dropped hard on the driveway, soft on the lawn. It was always the beginning of an end, this falling, this ending. I saw the thin slivers through the French windows coming down and then I heard the staccato sounds on the balcony cement, pthak, pthak, pthak. A melancholy sound.

While I was waiting I read *Horror* comics. This story was about some Egyptian worshipping an ancient Egyptian god, and the marble statue came to life, pursued the neophyte and created havoc on the streets; an uncontrolled god. As I was alone upstairs, I was thoroughly frightened, so I threw the comic out of my room and ran down to seek out an aunt or whoever. I did find one, trying on bolo ties and listening to "Sh-boom Sh-boom." Past the music room I stopped and studied a reproduction of Velasquez's *The Maids of Honour*. The artist stared back at me. Did he become a Knight of Order of Santiago after all? I must ask Fina, who was an art aficionada. I asked Velasquez. Only verdad, he answered, no pintura. Sure, I said, you hypocrite.

I picked up a long white curtain rod in the ironing room. I was Jean Peters of the Indies, swashbuckling on the Spanish *Main*. Or was that Tyrone Power?

Tina came in with a loaded basket and told me to go away. I told her I was bored. As she set up her heavy ironing board and heavier iron, she recounted, "You know your mother's cousin, Mana Iday, was forced to get married. Arranged marriage."

Oh no, I thought, another relationship story.

"On the wedding day, while she and her groom were crossing the river in a banca, she jumped in."

"In her white gown and all?"

"Yes, of course. The groom plunged right in and tried to pull her out but she swam underneath the boat. Finally, after quite a struggle, he got her. Throughout the marriage, she never called him by his name. 'Oy!' she'd say. 'Oy! Kunin mo yan.' 'Oy! alisin mo ito.' "

Oy!, an exclamation, a primal scream. Tina recounted how if someone asked where the husband was, Mana Iday would say, "Wala *siya*" or "*he*'s out" referring to him in the pronoun; if someone asked about what he was doing, she'd say "may ginagawa si *ano*" referring to him in the relative pronoun or subordinating conjunction *what* or *who*. Never a noun. They had seven children.

Tina let me sprinkle the clothes with water and then fold them into a tight knot, preparatory to ironing them. I asked her if I could iron and she grunted, just one. As I was pushing away on the recalcitrant iron, she checked my work and barked, Oh, go away. You make my work longer. I'll just have to re-iron this and doing something over is harder than doing it right the first time. Rejected, I shuffled away.

I saw Mama in the living room entertaining her friend, the wife of the Central Bank director, whose fifteen-year-old son, Alex, was sprawled on a sofa, his head on his mother's rotund stomach.

She said when she saw me, "There's Jazz. Why don't you get up and talk to her?"

Alex curled up and jabbed his head further into his mother. She laughed, half embarrassed, half joyful. "He is so shy. He clings so."

Mama laughed generously. "Oh he has lots of time to grow up."

Could you beat that, I thought.

They were waiting for Papa who had gone to Mary Johnston Hospital to donate blood for his lawyer's wife, dying of cancer. Two nights before, when the lawyer came to the house to tell him of his wife's condition, he had gone to the hospital right then and there, but his alcohol blood level count was so high they sent him home.

I was going insane. There was nothing to do. Leila phoned and pleaded for me to come visit her. She was lonely and bored. Much as I liked her, I felt too self-centred to amuse her. I said, we would see. Now that she and I were attending the college senior journalism class, plucked out of algebra by Sr Judy who thought we should be given this chance to sit in on the distinguished visiting lecturer from the University of Durham, Leila thought we should become real friends. We were chosen because our sisters were writers—the nuns thought it was genetic, ha ha.

I phoned Esther. She said she was going insane, too. She said she was the writer, why didn't she get chosen for that class? I said I didn't care, she could go in my stead; I should probably stay for algebra anyway, I thought I was going to fail it. The distinguished professor also kept on throwing French phrases onto us, and it was Esther who had French pretensions.

Then she came up with a great idea. "Come over to my grandmother's house. Let's write a Philippine play."

I was so bored, I'd have done anything.

Her grandmother came to pick me up in her car, because it was not safe to ride alone with a driver. Doña Gerarda, Vda de Ruiz, was my favourite grandmother in the world; I had not known my own. She was probably sixty years old, wore only one colour—brown—and prayed the rosary nonstop in the car. She talked to me even as her fingers rubbed the beads. As she was doing now, smiling and chatting and praying all at the same time. I really loved this old woman. I said to myself that when I grew old, I would be just like her, pleasantly plump, no wrinkles on her contented face, and no jewellery. "Let me grow lovely, growing old." She dropped me off at her house, told me to wait inside for Esther who was coming presently, and then went off to church.

I sat around in the living room with nothing to do. She was a widow so there was no one else at home except for the servants. I wandered all around the house, touching nothing.

When I got to an empty ante-room leading to her bedroom, which lay to my left side as I stopped at the threshold, my eyes were pulled towards the right by the compelling vision of a life-size crucified Christ hanging suspended from the low ceiling, touching the shining hardwood floor. There was absolutely no other furniture in this small, square, windowless room—just this giant crucifix dominating this "stage," this foreshortened altar. Should I dare enter? It would be like stepping on to the altar itself, the whole floor slab a surrealistic table.

I entered. The Christ was dead because his eyes had that dead look, his head had slumped forward. He was not at the three-hour dreadful dying stage; he was assuredly dreadfully dead. It was a muscular Christ, all tension and ready to spring up. What paradox. A strange feeling crept up on me. What did the artist intend? Why were the muscles articulated so, why were they not relaxed? Was he indeed the tiger and the lamb all in one? All over his face and body there were blood stains in different globs of hideous pigments. Everywhere the signs of torture the man had endured. The dark wood on which he hung must have weighed a dangerous 500 pounds. It had been rubbed and polished to a disturbing sheen. Were it to come down on me, I would be crushed to death. It was a Spanish carving, meant to shock one into penitence. I sat underneath this burdened Christ, thinking about all the sins I had committed and would yet commit before I died. It was in this position that Esther saw me.

"What are you doing?" she said.

"Scaring myself."

"I know. It *is* scary, isn't it?"

"How can your grandmother wake up to this day after day?"

She shrugged, "Let's write that play."

Esther had library books, paper, pens and paraphernalia ready. She sat on the floor across from me and laid everything out, as in a picnic.

"It has to be Lapu-Lapu."

Of course.

I skimmed through some books. "You write about Lapu-Lapu, I'll do Magellan. What's this?"

"Antonio Pigafetta's account of the voyage."

An hour later, after reading here and there, we came up with a cast of characters;

Villains:
King Charles I (later V) of Spain
Dom Manual, King of Portugal
Bishop Fonseca
Cristobal de Haro
Juan de Cartagena—Bishop's son
Estevan Gomes
Dom Sebastian Alvarez—Portuguese Consul
John Lopes Carvalho
Gaspar Quesada
Luis de Mendoza
Sebastian del Cano
Fr Pedro Sanchez de Reina
Minor Villains:
Antonio de Coco—Fonseca's nephew
Geronimo Guerra
Whatnots:
Master Andrew
Master Hans Vargue
Surgeon Morales
1 or 2 more chaplains
Crew (270 men), mostly young, boys
Major Characters:
Beatriz Magellan—his wife
Rodrigo—his son, 2 years old
Ferdinand Magellan
Diego Barbosa
Duarte Barbosa
John Serrano
Alvaro de Mesquita
Cristobal Rabelo
George the Moor
Enrique
Antonio Pigafetta
Padre Pedro Valderrama
Andres de Sam Martem
Francisco Serrano
Rajah Humabon
Queen

Lapu Lapu
Natives

"There are too many characters," Esther said. " How many Acts are we going to have?"
"Three Acts? OK, Let me see if I can put them into scenes."

"But that's just as long," Esther complained.
"I can't help it. It was an epic voyage."
"Cut it down. We have to focus on main characters."
"I give up. You cut it down. I'll list the events."

"What's with the Bishop's son?"
"This is all before the Council of Nicene."

After three hours of this wandering in and out of books, we got tired. We ate a snack with her grandmother then went back to our writing.

Act I, Scene 1:
Francisco Serrano on beach in Ternate. Looking out to sea with a letter in his hand. 1512.
"Dear Ferdinand: I have discovered a new world larger and richer than that found by Vasco de Gama."
—Serrano goes on about his hedonistic rich life, the spices he has hoarded, his expectation of rescue and remonstrates Magellan for not coming to him instead of going to Luzon where there was gold. Here we have the first indication that Magellan saw the Philippines in 1512. Also that he abandoned Serrano. This would be symbolic and foreshadows the abandonment of John Serrano, his brother, in Cebu.

"What's this? You've got 10 scenes for one Act. I thought it was going to be three Acts?"

Islas de San Lazarus
Prologue: Pope Alexander VI dividing the world
Act I, Sc. 1: One side of stage: FS reads letter to M
　Sc. 2: Lights on centre stage. Stricken crew
　Sc. 3: Samar 1521
　Sc. 4: Lights on FS, reads M's letter
Act II, Sc. 1: 10 days at Homonhon

Sc. 2: at Limassawa
Sc. 3: at Cebu
ActIII, Sc. 1: at Mactan M's death
Sc. 2. Flashbacks 1, 2, 3
Sc. 3: at Cebu
Sc. 4: JS abandoned at beach

"This isn't working. Why can't we really start," I said.
"Looking at these scribblings, I say we're too focused on Magellan."
"Well, it's Pigafetta's book. We're looking at these events from his point of view." I seized a piece of paper and wrote furiously. I was writing so fast that Esther had to ink all the fountain pens in readiness, like loaded rifles in vertical rows, squeezing the inner tube with such vigor she almost knocked down the inkwell. In panic, she grabbed at it as though the life would run out.

Finally, I threw the paper away in anguish, literally in anguish since my back was hurting from our position underneath the bleeding cross.
"What's with this disorientation? Why can't we write about Lapu Lapu's bravery—his repulsion of the invaders? Why am I seeing Magellan, falling gallantly onto the water, assailed on all sides by these natives who thrust their spears on to his sides, a Christ dying for humanity?"
"I don't know," Esther muttered, exhausted.
"You're supposed to do Lapu Lapu. Let's see what you wrote."
"I couldn't."
We lay on the floor, papers and books strewn all around us.
"What's wrong with us Jazz?"
"I don't know. Maybe we should wait for inspiration, or for gestation of materials."
"Or talent," Esther laughed.
We stared at the dead Christ's eyes staring blankly at us.
"Hey, did you know that Magellan was wounded and lamed for life at Morocco around 1513-1514?" I suddenly remembered.
"Oh yeah? You'd never guess that from the paintings."
"Did you know that the last twenty years of the sixteenth century were years of melancholy and soul-searching? St Theresa, St John of the Cross, El Greco 1586, burial of the count of Orgaz."
"Hmmm. You've been talking to Fina."
"Are we stupid?"
"So what if we are. We're free." She spread-eagled on the floor.
"Ignorance isn't freedom."

157

" 'Ignorance is bliss.' " She quoted a favourite motto around the school.

"I could never understand that one."

"Better not to know. Blind faith, blind justice, only the blind who see."

"I see you've also been talking with Fina. We're all beginning to sound alike. Inbreeding."

We contemplated the ceiling, which seemed to close down on us, once more.

"What was Magellan's tactical error?"

"Not enough men?" Esther offered.

"No air support? No Churchill?"

"Churchill?"

"No tanks."

"No, thanks."

"What was Lapu Lapu's advantage?" I asked.

"It was his beach."

"But what were spears to their muskets and swords? What was a loin cloth to armour?"

"Maybe you can't move as fast in those steel outfits. Maybe it was hot in them," Esther said.

"Cumbersome and hot."

"Yeah."

"So you think Magellan's men were defeated because of what they thought were far more superior weaponry? Hubris. Arrogance."

"Yeah."

"They ganged up on him when they saw him go down," I said.

"Ignorant natives, you see. No chivalry. Lapu Lapu was no Il Cortegiano."

"Listen to you," I chided Esther.

"I mean according to Pigafetta."

"Yeah. How do we know if Pigafetta's account was true?"

"Yeah, he was a Venetian. Didn't they invent spies, ambassadors?"

"Hmmm, on the other hand, he would have written everything down as accurately as he could."

"They burned all the records when they came around again and won." Esther was now on to her favourite subject, the desecration of the Archives. "A civilization destroyed, no trace except the word of the conqueror."

"How can we live by the words of others? Our lives are not authentic."

"Whom have you been reading now? That's a new word."

"What do you mean? Can't I have an original thought?"

"You?" Esther laughed aloud. "You live on books!"

"Do you think it was blind Faith? That Magellan thought God was on his side?" I had just seen a movie about God being this American flier's co-pilot, a war film.

"God *was* on his side."

"Only if your God likes wars, a God of War. What about a God who was a peace lover?"

"Peace comes later. You have to put the enemy to flight first."

"Why is Lapu Lapu the enemy? I thought you said you would write about his heroism. What about his God?"

"He wasn't Catholic."

"Esther, you're full of contradictions!"

"Oh yeah? You're not exactly Miss Clarity, dear señorita. In spite of all your Aquinas, you're no Thomas."

"So sor—ree. So I'm stupid."

"Maybe that's our problem. Maybe we are stupid."

"Like Lord Cardigan. Like Lord Raglan without the Duke's words."

"Who?"

"If we recognize that we're stupid, are we really stupid?"

"I don't know. I'm too stupid to know."

"What does the word *stupid* really mean? What's its etymological derivation?"

"I don't know. I'm too stupid to know."

"Hasn't it got some connection with stupendous?"

"If you say it to yourself enough times, you'll begin to believe it. That's communist propaganda."

"That's prayer."

"Oh, no. Prayer is an affirmation of belief. I think I've got you there. Checkmate," Esther concluded.

"Yeah, OK. I concede the point."

"That's you and your endless repetitions. I bet you'll end up a teacher someday—you're so repetitive."

"It's oral history. The next generation has to know. It's catechetics. Memorial Rites. The Holy Sacrifice of the Mass. Death and Resurrection. Look at him. He hangs forever like a pendulum endlessly swinging above us while we lie under his cutting edge in this pit, tied down by our ignorance."

"No I take that back. You're going to be a hack journalist, forever reusing other writers' words."

"But it has all been said before!" I wailed in lamentation.

"And better!"

"Oohhh!" Moaning, I spread my arms straight out, taut on the wood, my cry a passage to silence. Truth was not words, it was action, it was the Valley of Death.

A maid had come in and was picking up our papers. She worked around us while we stared at the ceiling. Her body bent up and down as though she were planting rice.

I sang, "Planting rice is never fun, bent from morn till the set of sun, cannot stand and cannot sit, cannot rest for a little bit."

Esther joined,

"Planting rice
is no fun
bent from morn
till the set of sun
cannot stand
cannot sit
cannot stop
for a little bit."

The maid smiled. She recognized the tune, if not the English words. It was the rhythmic song of the Magsasaka. She kept at her work until not one piece of paper remained.

"She's going to throw away all our efforts." I laughed insanely.

Esther laughed in unison. "Garbage. All our writing was garbage. What a way to spend the day."

"Clear up, simplify
Throw away, put away
dust dust dust
Clean up, stupefied
Fold up, fold in
must must must
Fix up —"

"—Shut up, clam up." Esther sat up suddenly and pushed her arms back and forth like the Itik-Itik dance. "I must, I must, do something about my bust."

"What? Why does it always come down to that?"

"Why not? C'est la vie. C'est la guerre."

Her Franciscan grandmother passed by, rosary in hand.

PART FOUR

THE FOURTH ORDER

Lord Raglan wishes the cavalry to advance rapidly to the front—follow the enemy and try to prevent the enemy carrying away the guns. Troop Horse Artillery may accompany. French cavalry is on your left. Immediate.

Chapter Twenty-four

"Attack, sir? Attack what? What guns, sir?"
—Lord Lucan

Dagdae, the Good God, wanted Boand, wife of Elcmar, so he sent Elcmar away on a mission, and slept with Boand. Out of this union came Öengus. The Dagdae, not wishing Elcmar to know of this event, brought Öengus to a foster home (the house of Midar) where he was raised for nine years. It happened that the young Öengus quarrelled with one of the boys, a son of Febal of the Fir Bolg, and discovered that he was a foundling. On questioning Midar about this (in the midst of many tears and much anguish) he found out his true parents' names. "Come with me then," said Öengus, "that my father may acknowledge me and that I may no longer be hidden away and be reviled by the Fir Bolg." And his father did acknowledge him. From this recognition, Öengus gained land and power, through a trick. His king-father told him to threaten to kill Elcmar during a day of peace and friendship, obtain the kingship of the land for a day and a night, and when Elcmar returned the next day to reclaim it, argue that they must put the question of claim to the Dagdae. Öengus did all these. He argued that the land was his because he spared Elcmar's life and that he had the kingship for a day and a night and that "it is in days and nights that the world passes." Elcmar conceded. The Dagdae agreed. "He hewed at you menacingly on a day of peace and friendship, and since your life was dearer to you than your land, you surrendered the land in return for being spared." Öengus, now known also as Macc Öc, then helped his foster father, Midar, obtain the fairest woman in Eriu, Etáin. What followed were all tricks. The wooing of Etáin was gained by two tricks, among many other tricks made by other characters. In all these the woman who seemed to be acquiescent, ready to sleep with the man of the hour, and had a special talent for serving wine to men, was sold by her father for lands, rivers, gold and silver, and was won from her husband in a fidchell game.

The ways of men made me dizzy.

"Boand" means white cow.
I didn't know comparable Philippine sagas.

Tina was resting, a fresh brown cigarillo in her mouth.

Sis One was playing the Hungarian Rhapsody on the piano as I passed by, completely absorbed in her music, bent over, as though she would devour the instrument. Sis Two and Mama were deciding over which jewels matched their Maria Claras best. Papa was in Colombo. I had just finished rereading Pearl S Buck and feeling despondent.

The putrefaction, the fetid decay, the stench of urine that permeated her novel depressed me, not because they were negative images, but because they were the odours of humanity and she had known them, revelled in them. I was depressed because I knew that Tondo existed but I had never been there. I didn't even know where it was. Bienvenido said men urinated against the side walls of Quiapo Church. I had never seen that though I believed it, judging from the one time I went to the post office building. I had never ridden in a jeepney or taken a public bus. I had never yelled "Para!" like the maids said they did, over a mass of heads, that the bus driver didn't hear and they missed their stop so they had to walk that kilometre, anyway. There was a joke in the comics: A woman boarding a jeepney took off her wooden clogs, her bakya, and then sat down. When she got to her destination, she came down fully expecting her bakya to be at the bottom of the steps, but they were gone. I couldn't understand the joke. I didn't know the bakya crowd. Did it mean she was stupid or that she was very correct? Humour was supposed to be a cultural enjoyment—you laughed at the familiar. But I was cut off from a large portion of my culture.

I didn't know the names of local flowers, trees, regional folk stories, the superstitions of the provinces. Once we went to Samar but I was six years old and I didn't remember much except Mama retching in a ferry, auntie nearly drowning. The carabao was all I knew and that from illustrations in books. I think I saw some Negritos in the hills towards Baguio—they were smaller, darker, and half-naked.

I had heard of T Pinpin, the Chinese section, but I had never seen it. I knew that people bought their food in Quiapo Market, their clothes in Divisoria. I had never seen the stalls inside these places. All I knew were Makati, Cubao, Katipunan Road, Diliman, Quezon City. I had been to Padre Faura and Ermita where the bookstores and tourist spots were, I had been to Dewey Boulevard for the nightclubs. I had driven to Escolta to get to the movie houses. I knew San Juan and Parañaque where my friends lived. This was my Philippines. This was my narrow circle of life, this footlight that gave my face an eerie glow. This was all I knew. This was all I knew!

It was like charging into battle hearing the shots falling all around you while enclosed in clouds of smoke, seeing flashes of fire emanating from guns but not certain where the battery stood, crashing against riderless horses crazed with fear but trained to gallop on with the closest squadron, tripping over the casualties of the first line of Lancers and Light Dragoons, some still alive and crawling on the slaughter field, and that cloud of smoke turned to dense pall darkening everything until only the sounds mattered: the zing of bullets, the agonizing cries, the shells, the thundering chargers, and as the ranks thinned out, the dreadful order: "Close in! Close in to the centre!" And all along you followed Nolan's finger—"There, my lord is your enemy, there are your guns."

And then there was despicable Jerry, nineteen years old, a student at La Salle, who came to visit in a taxi or just suddenly stood there at the gates, alone. I suspected he had no car. He said his father was in the United States; I didn't believe him. He was too desperate; he wanted me too much. He called up from Bulakeña at such odd hours, I think he worked there. Why would a student be working? He must have been poor. What did he think of us? If he thought so badly of us, why did he want us so badly?

No, if I remained in this country I would end up married to some Atenean and we would have children who would go to our schools, know only the parts of the city we knew. I must break this chain. I would never be a true Filipina. I didn't have the deep roots or wide base. I was damned to be without a country because in my childhood I had not known the country I was born in. This hidden half, this unrevealed mystery. To us, the uninitiated, we would romanticize our nebulous beginnings and we would only die in the end for them. Byron in Missolonghi on the thirty-sixth year, the poet seeking out a soldier's grave for glory and Greece, regretting his youth, *Why live?* We would hear Pericles above the tumult before the fall of the empire: *For the whole earth is a sepulchre of famous men; and their story is not graven only on stone over their native earth, but lives on far away, without visible symbol, woven into the stuff of other men's lives. For you now it remains to rival what they have done and, knowing the secret of happiness to be freedom and the secret of freedom a brave heart, not idly to stand aside from the enemy's onset.*

And so we lived by dead men's words and dead men's imaginations. But first we had to know where the enemy was or else the ending would be swift—there would be no time to write our rhythmic epitaph—and we would say, What was that? To what end?

As an exile, in some dreadful future, I would see films on the Philippines while I sat in front of some television in some other foreign country, and I would shed tears for this exotic land, a country I would not recognize, a country I could not acknowledge to be mine, a country where I was sired and abandoned.

Du bist der Gast,
der wieder weitergeht.
God, who can hold you?

Gracing peeled the skin off the red grapes and pitted them with her fingers. When she had a bowlful, she left the table. I ate the denuded fruit absent-mindedly, my mind on Maria.

"Maria?" Sis Two's nose crinkled. She was trying to remember 1955; four years was a long time. "Oh yeah. She got pregnant."

"Do you know how?"

"Senator Juarez's driver."

"Our neighbour's driver?"

"Yes, he used to sneak in to see her. When Mama found out about the pregnancy she consulted her uncle, what's his name, the congressman, about what legal thing she should do—Maria was a minor, remember? And the man was already married."

"Where was the wife?"

"In the province. So then Mama found out one night that he was with Maria in the basement so she confronted him and asked him what he was going to do about this. He said he wanted to marry Maria—"

"I thought he was already married?"

Sis Two shrugged "—that he really loved her and he would take care of Maria and the baby. He asked Mama for permission and she gave it. What else could she do?"

I nibbled at the grapes. "Does that sound right to you?"

She shrugged again. "That's life." She was in a bad state because Muneekneek, her pet cat, was seen a week ago going out the gate, left open by accident, and hadn't returned. He was a tomcat, black lord of my white cats, Sultana and Snowball. No other cat could replace Muneekneek; he was unique. I sympathized.

"Did we ever hear from them again? Do we know how she is now?"

"No. There's nothing one can do in these matters."

"Aren't you curious?"

"No." She left.

"Maria?" Sis One said. "She eloped before Mama could settle it."

In the late afternoon, sitting with Fina in her yacht, I recounted the story of Maria. It had turned cold so I pulled my cardigan on over my light voile dress. There was a flurry of activity in the galley as her cooks boiled lobsters and crabs for the night's party. We had gone horseback-riding earlier and Esther was saddle-sore, so she had her long legs up on a table, her bottom on a cushion.

"Ah, the vicissitudes of life," she moaned as she massaged her inner thighs.

"And we don't even know her last name."

"None of us know our servants' last names."

"I wonder if she had a girl or a boy. I wonder how they're doing."

"Do you care so much?" Fina drawled.

"No, she doesn't. Jazz is manic-compulsive. She just wants to tie up loose ends."

Fina changed the subject. She was never interested in maids. "Did you two remember that Lapu Lapu's people had a code of laws, a system of government, a form of writing, and crafts?"

Esther hit her head with her palm. "Of course, the sandugo!"

My eyes lighted up. There was a huge mosaic of the blood compact between Rajah Humabon and Magellan on the wall of Jesse's house that I often admired.

"Exactly." Fina was delighted. "Magellan landed on a real community of Malays who were already trading with their Asian neighbours. We were no Indians in New York who would give away land for coloured glass."

"So when the datus and rajahs realized that being baptized meant swearing fealty to the Spanish king, they thought, this isn't possible, we already have our civilizations," I inferred.

"Enter: Lapu Lapu, chief of Mactan," Esther said triumphantly.

"Right. But forty-four years later Legaspi came back to try it again, this time winning."

"Magellan's piety made him a poor soldier," I said.

"Will you forget about Magellan?" Esther screamed.

"How do you know so much about all this," I asked Fina suspiciously.

"I asked my sister. So the king gave Legaspi and his men encomiendas and they in turn made the datus tax collectors. I have to tell you quickly or I'll forget what she said."

"What was the tax?"

"They were called tribute, polo, and bandala. Tribute was the usual gold, silver, rice, one Indio who was later sold by the government. Polo meant labour in the mines or camps, and bandala was compelled selling of produce at government prices."

"Confiscation, you mean."

"How does your sister know so much? Do the nuns know your sister knows so much?" Her sister was Sis Two's gang mate. How come Sis Two never talked about this?

"Sure. They don't like the Spanish. She got all this from her Philippine history teacher."

"Will you stop interrupting? I have to do the writing on Lapu Lapu."

"She's gone past Lapu Lapu."

"Legaspi and his men formed the principalia, Indios who could have titles of lands if they served Spanish interests . . . "

"Ah yes, the colonial lackeys. This all sounds like the British Raj. I know all this already."

"OK. Do you know about Intramuros?"

"What about it? It's ruins."

"This fortress was built from the lands of Rajah Sulayman. Legaspi took them from him. Maynilad, it was called, at the banks of the Pasig River."

"Oh yeah, I know this one," Esther said. "It's like the Forbidden City in Peking. People lived inside the fortress while the outsiders, the rabble, starved outside. I've seen the Forbidden City."

"It's impossible to teach the two of you. You're such know-it-alls. Oh, I have to greet this one." Fina got up and went to an approaching guest.

"Hmmm. Cute."

Esther retorted: "He comes up to my navel."

I burst out laughing at the image. The young man glanced at us, blushed.

"Oh, gee. I'm sorry. I think he thinks we're laughing at him."

"And well he should."

After a few minutes, Fina returned.

"Well, I've settled him with another group. I was going to bring him over but he didn't seem to want to."

"We must look formidable," Esther laughed.

"Obviously not an Atenean."

"No, he's San Bedan."

Esther's eyebrow arched.

"Still cute," I shrugged. "And they do have Caloy Loyzaga." This appeased Esther, who was a basketball fan.

"The point I was trying to get to," Fina continued, "was that we were a peace-loving country before the Spanish came. Revolts periodically broke out against them starting with friar-owned estates bought through the abuse of obras pias. "She turned to me, "They owned a lot of haciendas in Laguna," referring to Rick.

I sighed. "That's finished business."

"You're better off with Dave," Esther said.

"That's finished, too. My parents were asking me about him the other day and when I said it was hopeless, they said I should treat him better. But really there's no point in dangling him. It's not fair to him."

"So—I've got several boys dangling," Esther shrugged.

"Are you two listening to me?"

"Yeah, we were peace-loving. We know this. Tell us something we don't know."

"Yeah. What else does your sister say?"

"OK. Do you know why we have such bitter regionalism?" Fina continued.

"No, why?"

"Because the Spanish made one province put down the revolts of another province. In other words, they used Visayan Indio against Ilocano Indio. And that's why to this day, we have factions."

"Dugong aso!" Esther shouted.

"What? Doesn't that just mean those people eat dogs, that's why it's in their blood?" I asked, surprised.

"Oh, no. It means they're taksil."

"What does taksil mean?"

"And your point about economics, Jazz—Europe wanted our gold but they couldn't get us to mine them fast enough. However, we were a good base for the trade routes to China and the East. The Galleon Trade."

"So the Islands were stepping stones." As Papa said.

"Yes. For profit. Later on, of course in, 1834, I think, we were opened to world trade, free trade, British and American banks were built here, we lost our copra, sugar, etc. to them."

"Who cares? You've gone way beyond Lapu Lapu."

"Just a minute, Es. I think Fina's making an important point here. She's talking about greed. Lapu Lapu foresaw it. We should have called these islands Lapu Lapu, instead of the fish. If Magellan hadn't come around, we would have lived a life of communal sharing, of using only what is enough, the Baranggay spirit—"

"That's nonsense. If Magellan hadn't seen us, some other explorer would have. In any case, there are 21 million Filipinos now. You can't live off the trees anymore. You have to go along with the times."

"You're being more than usually contrary tonight."

"I'm sick. I'm frustrated. I can't move. I can't do anything."

I sang, "How can you keep 'em after they've seen gay Paree—"

Fina smirked. "Woman of action. Woman of purpose."

I looked at the other boats bobbing in the water. We were docked as we waited for the other guests to arrive.

" 'I am half-sick of shadows.' "

I thought of the four gray walls and the four gray towers, overlooking the space of flowers. Did I not know what of imprisoned women spoke? Surrounded we were by water thick enough to cut with a butcher knife, and would that knife be turned against us? Wasn't Anne Frank betrayed, her hiding place ripped open?

" 'The curse is come upon me.' "

"Hmmm," Fina murmured. We had performed this to our English class. She declaimed:

" 'Down she came and found a boat,
Beneath a willow left afloat,
And round about the prow she wrote
The Lady of Shalott.' "

"For ere she reach'd upon the tide
The first house by the water-side,
singing in her song she died,
    The Lady of Shallot," I added.

"Lancelot, " Fina murmured.

"I'm sick of Tennyson," Esther cried out.

Fina and I, Victorian to the core, gasped. How could she say that?

She had betrayed her Romantic leanings. She had thrown decorum to the winds. Esther was being root Filipina again, lacking decorum at tragic moments.

Almost to a voice, Fina and I broke out, "Break, break, break."

Esther groaned, "Ohhh!" Her hands to her ears.

I persisted,

"Their's not to make reply,
Their's not to reason why,
Their's but to do and die;
Into the valley of Death
    Rode the six hundred."

Fina took it up and finished:

"'When can their glory fade?
O the wild charge they made!
    All the world wonder'd.
Honour the charge they made
Honour the Light Brigade
    Noble six hundred!'"

"Aaargh!" Esther screamed.
We sighed.
Someone had blundered.

At the other end of the world, Sir Benjamin Hall chimed, "So hour by hour, be Thou my Guide ... " as the guests began to arrive in streams, an hour or more late, Filipino time, arrived all night so we couldn't set sail, who looked at the clock, they just came and came, this party one of the stops in the round for this evening, these guests, these children of oligarchs, came and went like that water lapping against the yacht—"Steady as she goes"—one of them shouts to be heard above Elvis Presley's "Jailhouse Rock," acting like an admiral but of a moored ship, fastened securely. We were Captains of our Fate, the sea was ours.

Lyn arrived with her younger sister, fourteen, more fully blossomed and mistress to a well-known lawyer, an activity their mother encouraged, who disentangled herself from Lyn immediately and floated past us in her stiff petticoats and three-inch heels to a glut of men at the bar. We moaned over the whiff of overwhelming perfume as she sailed by— "From Rubens, the satyr," Fina recoiled. How was it she hadn't been expelled, I wondered. Surely, no one else in the entire school was as scandalous as she was. The nuns' preoccupations and priorities puzzled me.

I followed her with my eyes because she was smiling from ear to ear, so happy, it fascinated me. The eating, drinking, dancing, the effervescence fascinated me. The Filipinos must be the happiest people in the world because they know how to party: the jokes, witticisms, repartee that zing by, the artistry of decorations, the sumptuousness of food, the varieties of musical fare, the uninhibited attitude towards making an evening truly fun. If ever one missed anything from this country if one left it, it would be this, this joyful Filipino.

This happy race.
Lyn's face was flushed. "Have you heard?"
"What?"

"Do you remember Gina de la Luna, she was two years ahead of us, graduated last year?"

"Oh yeah, very pretty, very pink."

"Everyone was in love with her."

"She became a movie star, didn't she?"

"To Sr Rose's heartbreak."

"Heartbreak. You don't know heartbreak."

"What? Is she dead?"

"Worse. She was raped by three or more men last night. Basketball players."

We all fell silent after a gasp.

"How do you know?" Fina whispered.

Lyn nodded towards her sister. "From Jose. He's convincing Gina to press charges. It'll be in the papers tomorrow. Can you imagine it?"

Esther shook her head. We couldn't speak. Gina was so vulnerable, so fragile, so beautiful, we couldn't think of her so broken. Esther cursed and shook her head again. We didn't want to know the details, we could hardly deal with this one fact. Collectively, we felt defiled. Our entire convent school was defiled. *The mirror cracked from side to side.*

At the rail, my cardigan wrapped tightly around me against a rising wind, I stared at the diffused colours on Manila Bay. Out near the horizon, like a black cutout figure superimposed on the orange and red sea, stood the *Seahorse* in 1644, its imperial head rearing up ready for the attack, the land before it just so many piece goods to be devoured. Plundering and serving— all there was to life. Madras-Manila trade.

Nos Senhora de Boa Vista over there. There the *Sao Paulo*. There again the *Nos Senhora Rosario*, cloaked ships all British to the core. We were taught to hate the Spanish whose Reconquista mind had spread its net to our shores, but the true enemy had conquered its armada in 1588. The true enemy occupied us for two years, left no trace of its culture because this outpost of the empire wasn't even worth the trouble, it was merely a canal, a passage in the geopolitical emporia.

The true enemy was Diego Silang, precursor of a continuing leadership, "Sargento Mayor, Alcalde-Mayor Y Capitan a Guerra por SM Britanica," selling his people for a title and some Glasgow textiles. The true enemy was the tulisanes in our hearts.

Truth was overwhelming. One spent one's whole external life's energies defending oneself against the lies, fighting off the enemy, instead of getting on with the cultivation of one's inner life. All one did was react against the hated Other rather than act for the loved One.

Against the black backdrop of a set sun, I sighed. " 'Oh well, it is nothing to Chillianwallah.' "